David Cherrington was born and raise.   Wiltshire/Hampshire border. He survived a three-year tour studying at the agricultural faculty of the University of Newcastle-Upon-Tyne and then embarked on the obligatory post-graduation trip around the world. On his return, he built up a small woodland business, which included restoring the family farm's 100 acres of semi-ancient woodland, and even a spot of charcoal production. He is married with an 18-month-old daughter and another pending. *Red Sky in the Morning* is his first novel.

Red Sky
in the
Morning

David Cherrington

Glenmill

A Glenmill Publication

First published in 2000

Glenmill
Dumfries
Scotland
DG2 8PX

tel: 01387 730 655
http://www.glenmill.freeserve.co.uk

British Library Cataloguing in Publication Data.
A catalogue record of this book is available from the British Library.

ISBN 0 9535944 1 6

Design, Layout & Typesetting by Ψasmin
email: nomad@cableinet.co.uk

Printed and bound in Great Britain by
Redwood Books, Trowbridge, Wiltshire

To E.J.B.

CONTENTS

PREFACE

Self-defence (n) 3.Law:
The right to defend one's person, family,
or property against attack or threat of attack
by the use of no more force than is reasonable.

The motivation behind writing this novel arose following a burglary on our family farm. I wanted to write about the possible consequences of confronting the burglars, and the absurdity of the law that allows a person to go from being the victim to the accused in a blink of an eye, just for defending themselves or their property.

Having completed this work of fiction and whilst awaiting publication, a chillingly similar incident occurred which received widespread media attention. With rural crime on the increase and the police services stretched to the limit, I doubt it will be the last.

ACKNOWLEDGEMENTS

To my family, especially Emma, Rowan, Audrey and Susie
for their help, advice and encouragement.

To friends, Danny, Verity, Gary and Sal,
for their honest (I hope) opinions and criticisms.

To Mark, Yasmin and Tony,
for their guidance and counsel in the world of publishing.

CHAPTER ONE

DOWNLANDS FARM

When Harry Sinton awoke, a couple of minutes before his alarm was set to wake him anyway, he carefully reached out and turned it off so it would not disturb his wife. Betty Sinton was lying on her side, still deep in sleep, oblivious to the sounds Harry was making as he stumbled from the bed and scrabbled for his work clothes draped over the armchair that sat in the corner of the bedroom. He had left them there not five hours earlier. The light from the bathroom provided enough visibility through the pitch blackness of the early March morning for Harry to gather up his clothes and take them across the landing to the bathroom. He was careful not to step on any of the floorboards that creaked in case they woke Betty. After thirty-six years in the same old farmhouse he knew which boards to avoid.

In the bathroom he took off his pyjamas, leaving them where they fell. He replaced them with pants, brown corduroy trousers, vest, checked shirt, blue woollen jumper and two pairs of socks, all of which were bought from the local farm suppliers shop, all of which he had worn the day before, and all of which were in a various state of disrepair.

"You look like the typical farmer," Betty would tease him.

"Good," was Harry's usual blunt reply.

Still blurry eyed he padded down the staircase and felt his way in the half darkness towards the kitchen, only then did he turn on a light, shielding his eyes from the sudden brilliance as he did so. He allowed time for them to become accustomed to the glare, regretting that last scotch he'd had in the *Pig and Whistle* the night before.

In front of the Aga, Bracken, the Sintons' black Labrador of thirteen years, looked up from her basket expectantly, the grey hair

1

around her mouth and eyebrows betraying her age, but at the same time giving her an air of wisdom.

"Good morning girl," Harry whispered, peering towards Bracken through squinting eyes.

He made his way towards her, bent down and patted her on the head, she replied with swift wags of her tail but did not attempt to rise out of her basket. Harry then went to the sink, picking up the kettle on the way, and filled it with water for the morning cup of coffee, placing it on the Aga's hot plate.

Harry Sinton had learnt over his forty-five years of lambing that there was no point in racing out to the lambing barns in case two or three ewes had lambed simultaneously in close proximity, leaving him the puzzle of three ewes and five, six, or seven lambs, and trying to interpret which was whose, or some other type of problem such as a lamb's swollen head, protruding from the ewe, sticking its tongue out to the world, or a lamb left in its embryotic bag, suffocated. He realised that sheep were of the nature that if you were to rush out and check them, they would conspire to lamb half an hour earlier just to leave you with the same problem, and keep you busy for the rest of the morning so that you would miss out on the morning cup of coffee anyway.

To this end he made his coffee and leant back into the armchair to the side of the Aga, Bracken slowly climbed out of her basket and sat next to Harry's feet, her head on his knee; and under the adoring gaze of his dog, Harry Sinton started to consider the day's schedule whilst enjoying the warmth from the Aga. This had been the morning's ritual for the last ten days and was to continue until the lambing flock numbers had reduced from their initial five hundred and twenty to the last stragglers of twenty-five or thirty when they could be let out into a paddock and not need as much attention. They had already lambed three hundred ewes, hoping to catch the higher early market prices. This had also been the ritual for this time of year for the last thirty-six years Harry Sinton had lived in the Downlands Farm farmhouse. Thirty-six years of early morning wake-up alarms, thirty-six years of stumbling down the stairs, thirty-six years of warming himself by the kitchen stove before he ventured into the biting cold of the early March mornings – and long may it continue – he often thought to himself.

Harry Sinton had moved to the farmhouse three years after he had married Betty in 1957, and after his mother had decided the farmhouse was too big for her since the death of his father one year before. He was the eldest child and only son of George and Mary Sinton, the brother of two sisters, Mary and Caroline. He was, therefore, the natural successor to the family's seven hundred and sixty-three acres of permanent pasture, arable, and some seventy acres of semi-ancient woodland, set in the undulating countryside of the East Wiltshire, North West Hampshire border. He had worked on the farm since he was a child without any thought of changing for a different way of life, and he considered himself very lucky. So in his sixty-fifth year Harry Sinton sat in his kitchen in the early morning darkness, mulling over the coming day's schedule, as he had done in this house for thirty-six years, ready to venture out into the cold morning air, always before five o'clock.

William Stevens, Billy to all but his mother from the day he was born, had not had a good evening. He knew he had to be in his van heading up the M27 at around four in the morning to be able to get the jobs done, but the evening had gone from bad to worse. Now speeding up the motorway an hour later than planned, the atmosphere in the front of the van was far from happy. Stevens had decided to sit-in on the game of cards in the back room of the Kings Head to pass the time before picking up his two passengers for the morning's work. Three hours later and around three thousand pounds down he had been forced to leave the game in case his passengers would not wait in the raw March morning. The loss on the card game had wiped out any thought of a good profit from this morning's 'farm visits', as Stevens liked to call them.

He had picked up his two passengers half an hour late and instantly they realised this morning's work was not going to be easy. No words were exchanged as they climbed into the front of the transit van and now, halfway up the motorway, they still sat in silence. Billy Stevens was hunched over the steering wheel staring out of the windscreen, concentrating on the road, his two passengers sitting tentatively beside him on the bench seat, watching the windscreen wipers crossing the glass, intermittently clearing the snowflakes that were trying to settle.

Sean Robson and Paul Allen were the two silent passengers. Sean had known Stevens since his secondary school days and had been going out with him on these jobs for the last four years. He knew his moods and knew not to say anything. This was Paul's first time on a farm visit but he knew all about Stevens' reputation, especially his short temper. Paul was usually a cheeky lad, but a mixture of cold bones, tiredness, and trepidation for the morning's work, combined with the apprehension of Billy Stevens, made sure he kept the silence in the front of the van.

The two of them had been waiting on the street corner for three-quarters of an hour before the old, blue transit came into view. They would have stayed for another fifteen minutes, more out of fright than any loyalty to Stevens. Their baggy jeans and flimsy bomber jackets did little against the biting cold, so they had stamped their feet, hunched their shoulders, pulled their L.A. Raiders ski hats down over their ears and waited. Sean had persuaded Stevens to let Paul come along, reassuring him of his ability to keep quiet and work hard. Paul had wanted to go ever since Sean had bragged to him of his early morning adventures, and shown him the 'easy money' he got for going. This was on top of the street credibility it would give Paul over his other seventeen-year-old mates.

Struggling out of his armchair, Harry Sinton ambled to his office to fetch his shotgun and drop a handful of five-shot cartridges into his pockets. A fox had been taking some interest in the lambs lately so he had decided to take a walk around the closer paddocks with his shotgun, on the off-chance of seeing the culprit of the five dead lambs he had picked up in the last ten days. Gone were the days when he use to leave his shotgun on the table in the hall with the cartridges in the drawer, in case a wayward magpie, jay, or better still a grey squirrel, would find itself in the garden, although these moments of 'vermin control' had had to be restricted when his children had been growing up in the house. Now the gun had to be kept under lock and key, in a specially made cabinet with no outside hinges, secured to an inside wall and inspected by the local police . Harry didn't mind this, although it meant that no magpie or jay worth its salt would wait around whilst he found the keys to the cabinet, unlocked the steel doors, retrieve the gun, find the cartridges in another locked drawer and return to the hallway for the shot. He understood the need for legislation on firearms, especially after the local tragedy at Hungerford, and more recently at Dunblane. He would laugh as he told of how the cabinet had cost more than his guns put together, but the law was the law and he was happy to go along with it.

Harry knew that if he were to walk around the paddocks checking the ewes and lambs without his shotgun then he would not only see the fox but it would be in range for an easy shot, but if he carried his gun he would not see hide-nor-hair of it. He would always rather carry his gun and not see the fox than vice versa.

Crossing back through the kitchen, the gun under his left arm, towards the back door, Harry noticed Bracken suddenly perk up with interest; she had seen the shotgun and was hoping for an early morning walk around.

"Not this morning girl, I'll see you in a couple of hours and then you can come out." Hearing the tone of her master's voice, she sloped off back to her basket, stretched, and then coiled back up on her side, ready to chase rabbits and retrieve pheasants in her early morning dreams.

In the back kitchen Harry put on his wellington boots, an old waxed jacket and a flat cap. He unlocked the door, picked up the torch in his right hand, put the shotgun under his left arm and entered the bleak black morning. A hard frost covered the ground, reflecting silver in the moonlight. Wisps of snowflakes fluttered about on the chill wind, looking for any nook and cranny to shelter, stop and rest.

"And the forecast was for wintry showers," he thought to himself. "Lambing must have started."

The cold bit into his face as he walked the short distance to the farmyard. The light from the barns made the outline of the buildings detectable, they loomed large in the darkness of the morning. He could hear the muffled sounds of the ewes in the barns, the rustling of the bedding straw, the munching of hay from the hay racks and the bleating of a ewe that sounded in distress, coming from the main barn. He walked past the hay barn, skimming the torch light over the bales as he walked. The hay barn looked very depleted, a bad haymaking season the summer before and a cold winter had reduced the stocks, but with a little luck he had enough to see him through this lambing. It would then be all hands to the pump to fill up the barns for next year, and so the cycle continued.

Walking past the straw barns, the torch light revealed a different picture. There was now plenty of straw to go around since the laws banning the burning of straw in the fields had come into practice. Harry Sinton was even considering selling some to the stock farmers of the west country, adding to the growing number of straw-stacked lorries making their way down the A303.

Turning into the main yard, Harry noticed the reason for the bleating ewe's distress. A solitary lamb was trotting up and down the pens that housed the ewes which had lambed the day before. It had escaped the confines of its pen and was now exploring the wider world of the main barn. Each ewe and her lambs had a separate pen constructed from two, three foot high, six foot long metal hurdles, with another hurdle cut in half to create the ends of the rectangular pen. One end was able to swing open whilst the other was fixed, the whole construction relying on the amount of bailer twine available at the time of assembly. Harry decided the lamb wasn't going very far for the time being and left it to investigate its new-found world. Instead he decided to concentrate on the first of the two lambing sheds.

The farmyard was set out in one main block, with its centre an open concrete square. To the left of the square stood the main farm building, to the right two smaller barns, at the back of which stood a lean-to that gave cover to the stored hay and straw.

Below the main barn stood a set of sheep-races that allowed Harry Sinton to sort and hold his sheep whenever they needed to be handled. The farmyard was set off the main road that ran through the small village of Ilton. The farmhouse was set behind the yard, giving it a secluded position.

The system Harry used for his lambing was very labour-intensive in the mornings but allowed time in the afternoons to concentrate on other jobs. All the lambing tasks made the farmyard a hive of activity in the mornings, but it calmed down for the afternoon. That was the way Harry Sinton wanted it, and that was the way it had been done for as long as he could remember.

Harry Sinton checked that the chambers of his shotgun were empty and therefore safe and propped it against the outside wall of the first lambing barn. He walked up to the metal entrance gate, opened it carefully and made his way into the midst of the flock, closing the gate behind him. All his movements were done slowly and carefully, so as not to startle the sheep.

"Morning ladies, what have you got for me this morning?" He whispered the same question each morning.

Looking around he could see the seven ewes already penned up with their lambs, and at least four others that had lambed since the last inspection around eleven o'clock the night before. The four that had lambed were spread out nicely, he cautiously ventured toward the closest.

"Good girl," he murmured as he saw the two healthy lambs the ewe was standing over, the lambs stumbling near her hind legs looking for their mother's milk.

He opened the nearest pen, laying down some fresh straw as bedding, and returned to the ewe. The ewe was eyeing Harry with some suspicion. She tried to back away from the advancing Harry and take her lambs with her, but the lambs were unaware of the farmer and Harry managed to grab their hind legs without causing the old ewe too much concern.

"Good girl," he coaxed, as he dragged the lambs towards the open pen.

The ewe followed and when Harry put the lambs into the pen while standing on the outside himself the ewe rushed in, allowing Harry to close the gate and secure it with a length of bailer twine.

"I wish they were all like you," Harry declared. The ewe, for her part, still eyed Harry apprehensively, oblivious to the compliment she had just been paid.

Harry performed this task on the three remaining ewes that had lambed, one more twin ("good girl"), one big single ("old faggot"), and one that was a twin; but the ewe had only paid attention to the first born, leaving the second to suffocate in its embryotic sac. To this Harry did not say anything; the live lamb was strong and dry and had therefore been born a while ago, Harry's early cup of coffee had not sealed the dead lamb's fate. Harry considered putting a pet or orphan lamb on to this ewe to bring her complement of lambs back to two, the optimum number for a ewe with two full working udders. He discounted this idea although he had three pet lambs in the main barn, two were over a week old and he was waiting for a ewe that had lost all of her lambs to put those on to, while the third pet lamb was tiny (by name, as well as stature, every year there was a "Tiny") a throw-back to a set of triplets that had lambed a couple of days before. He would have to wait and hand-feed Tiny for a number of days before she would be strong enough to look after herself with a ewe.

When he had made sure all the ewes had enough milk in their udders for their lambs and had placed a bucket of water in each pen (thirsty work this lambing lark) he continued to the second lambing barn and repeated the procedure with the six ewes that had lambed in that barn. When he was satisfied all was done in that barn he ventured toward the main barn to recapture the escapee.

The pens in the main barn were built in columns of ten on each side of the entrance, back to back, with a passageway between the fronts to allow access. In the middle of the barn stood Harry's quad bike with a trailer attached. This was his third machine in as many years, the other two having been stolen over a period of eighteen months. He usually kept it locked up in the workshop but believed that at lambing time, when there were so many people about at all sorts of times throughout the day and night, it would be safe enough left in the main barn. It was also easier to fill up the trailer with the sheep feed the night before and so have an immediate start in the morning.

Harry caught the escaped lamb and reunited it with its mother. The lamb immediately dived under its mother's hind legs in search of some milk. The ewe nudged at her lamb and, smelling her scent, stopped her distressed bleating.

Harry made a final inspection of the main barn, checking that no other lamb was out or in the wrong pen, and then left to retrieve his shotgun and continue on to the paddocks.

Having left the M27 and continued up the A34, Stevens took another couple of turnings on to minor roads, and then the first words were spoken in the front of the transit van.

"We're nearly at the first farm. This prick keeps his quad in a shed next to his workshop, and there is only a poxy padlock there so it shouldn't take too long."

Turning off the village road down a track they drove toward the farmyard. The gates, or what may have resembled a pair of wooded five-bar gates some years ago, were open and the workshop stood straight in front of the van. Stevens aimed the headlights at the shed next to the building he knew to be the workshop from past "farm visits", drenching it with light.

"Come on then," he called as he shouldered his door open, the other two jumped out and headed for the shed. Stevens went to the back of the van, undid the padlock that secured the doors together, opened them and pulled out his toolbox, carrying it to the shed door. Now that they were getting down to the real work of the morning, his mood started to lighten.

"You would think these pricks would learn their lesson, eh Seanie. What's this, the third or fourth time here?"

"Third easily," Sean replied quickly, relieved that Stevens had finally acknowledged them. They would always laugh at the stupid yokel farmers and their attempts at security on their farms.

Stevens produced a crowbar from the toolbox and, holding it in his gloved hands, proceeded to lever off the padlock holdings, gaining entrance to the shed in less than ten seconds. There were no light fittings in the shed so they moved out of the beam of light from the transit van to allow the light in. Parked in the middle of the shed was a second-hand beaten-up quad bike, it looked as if its previous owner had used it in a banger race. The seat was covered by a number of plastic Tesco's carrier bags, foam padding disgorging from rips in the plastic, some of which had been mended by lengths and lengths of black insulating tape strapped around the body of the seat. Mudguards were at strange angles, the tyres were all bald, dents and scratches ran from the front to the back, and it was covered in rust and mud. Stevens' mood immediately blackened.

The farmer, George Hollis, had bought the quad "sold as seen" from a local agricultural engineering firm. He had got fed up with buying new quad bikes just to have them stolen six months later. He decided to buy a cheap bike that would not cost him too much if it got up and walked off one night, and he had regretted his decision ever since. It had been costly to repair, temperamental in the mornings, and downright stroppy throughout the day. He was now hoping that someone would steal it, so he could get a new, reliable one, which he would then secure in a burglar-proof barn, (or so he told himself).

"The tight bastard!" Stevens stormed, he threw the crowbar at the machine, continuing to swear at the farmer's inconsideration in buying a second-hand quad bike. "Bollocks! We would be doing this bastard a favour pinching this thing."

Stevens searched around for anything else to take his anger out on, while both Sean and Paul found something that grabbed their attention at the far end of the shed rather than meet Stevens' eyes.

"Well, get the bloody thing in the back of the van, standing around like two tossers," Stevens ordered.

Sean and Paul did what they were told, pleased to have something to do rather than wait for Stevens to fully explode. They pushed the quad to the back of the van, produced two planks of wood from inside, positioned the planks to give the bike an easy push up and proceeded to man-handle the machine into the van.

Stevens had retrieved his crowbar and replaced it with a torch, he walked over to the workshop and inspected the padlock on the door.

"That wouldn't take long," he murmured to himself and continued to inspect the workshop building.

To the left of the door was a window, Stevens shone his torch in and peered through the glass, trying to make out the shapes of the tools as the light flickered over them, distorting them with shadows. The presence of a beaten-up quad bike had more than halved the amount of money Stevens had expected from this farm stop, he was now trying to decide whether to help himself to some tools to make up the difference or continue on to the next farm. The tools in the back of the van would cut down the space for another quad bike, where the real money was, and he knew from his reconnaissance trip last week that the next farm had a new bike.

Stevens would drive up to the area a week in advance to check the lie of the land and the farms that had the bikes. He had seen this quad bike from a distance and had not realised it was in such a shabby state, but he knew the next farm had a relatively new bike as he had passed it on the road. Stevens used his four year old BMW for these reconnaissance trips as it looked less suspicious than an old blue Ford transit van with its rear windows blacked out and a padlock to secure the back doors together. This type of planning had served Stevens well for the last four years.

Sean and Paul appeared from behind the van and made their way towards Stevens.

"Have you secured it?" Stevens asked

"Yeah," replied Sean. Of course I bloody have, he thought to himself but decided not to tell Stevens.

"Get back in the van," he ordered and the two boys did as they were told.

Stevens picked up his toolbox and placed it in the back of the van, closing the doors and locking the padlock. He was pleased at the warmth that hit him as he climbed back into the driving seat, having not noticed the chill of the outside air due to the nervous excitement of the job. He turned the van around and headed out of the farmyard onto their next stop. The whole operation had taken less than ten minutes.

It took Stevens twelve minutes to drive to the next farmyard, which was at the end of the village lane. From the lane he could see into the yard and it became obvious that this was not going to be his morning. He knew from past experience that the farmer kept the quad bike in the workshop, which lay to the left of the entrance, but since his last visit the farmer had invested in some new security measures. The entrance was barred by two twelve-foot metal gates that were fixed together by a thick metal chain secured by a large padlock. The hinges of the gates were attached to the straining post in such a way as not to allow the gates to be lifted from their hinges, the top hinge had been turned upside down preventing such actions. On the left-hand gate was a large sign declaring:

UPPER PINHILL FARM

PRIVATE PROPERTY

KEEP OUT

Stevens drove up to the gates and stopped the van. He got out and immediately felt the cold wind snatch at his hair and face. The light from the van allowed him to identify the main buildings in the yard, and in front of the workshop he could make out an old cabless tractor parked at right angles and nudging up to the double doors. Behind the tractor, attached to the three-point linkage, was a counter-weight of concrete resting on the ground. In front of the tractor was a front loader with a set of forks attached, the forks were stabbed into the ground. It was clear to Stevens that the farmer had purposefully left the tractor in such a position as to prevent it being pushed away from the entrance to the workshop. It would need the tractor to be started to allow the hydraulics to lift the forks and counter-weight from the ground.

Ian Gordon, the owner of Upper Pinhill Farm, had decided to invest in some extra security measures after his farm workshop had been broken into last September. He had kept a look-out for an old tractor that had a set of forks on the front and a sizeable counter-weight at the back for the sole purpose of parking in front of the workshop's double doors. He had also installed three security floodlights, moved his sheepdogs from the kennels next to his house, to the barn next to the workshop, and adjusted the entrance gates to prevent burglars from by-passing the padlock and chain by lifting the gates off their hinges. He hoped this would deter any passing crook that happened to be in the area.

Stevens decided to take a closer look and climbed over the gates, while Sean and Paul looked at each other, unsure whether to follow or to wait for him to gesture them forward. Before they could decide, the farmyard was flooded with light. Stevens had walked across the beam of a security light, and three floodlights saturated him in halogen brilliance. At the same time dogs started to bark, their howls coming from the building to the left of the workshop.

"Bastard!" Stevens shouted and turned back towards the van.

As Stevens jumped into the van, Sean and Paul tried to shrink into the bench seat. Stevens stamped down on the clutch, and jammed the gear stick into reverse.

"I'm going to come back here and burn his fucking barns down! Wasting my fucking time."

Having turned the van around, Stevens sped off down the narrow village lane until he believed he had gone far enough to safely pull over and consider his thoughts. Stevens acted as though the other two were not there. This was fine to both Sean and Paul who were starting to think that the sooner this morning's work was over and they were back home in Southampton, the better.

Stevens had to decide whether to knock the whole morning's work on the head and return to Southampton, or go on to one more farm were he knew the farmer kept a good quad bike. He had known the last farmer had a good bike but that had not helped him in stealing it. To go back now, dropping the knackered bike off at his mates, on the outskirts of Winchesters (so as not to carry it around half of Southampton in the early hours of the morning) would mean a loss of around two and a half grand on the night, and that didn't include paying the boys off. Well they could go whistle for that, he thought to himself. He checked his watch, it read five forty-eight, it was getting light around the six-fifteen mark now, and he would rather be heading home as the sun came up, always preferring to do his work under the cover of darkness.

"Sod it," he growled, and without further explanation to his two passengers whether that statement meant he had given the morning's work up as a bad job, or thought he had nothing left to lose by going on to one more stop, Stevens put the van in gear and headed for Downlands Farm.

Harry Sinton checked his watch, five forty-eight. He looked up into the deep, inky blackness of the sky to see if any signs of the new day were breaking through. Silver-fleeced shadows raced overhead, illuminated by the bright moon that peeked through breaks in those clouds.

"Not long now," he thought to himself.

Harry loved this time of the morning on these cold crisp days, the pale, grey light forcing the clutches of darkness away to reveal a new day. He was alone with his thoughts at such times, before the rush of the morning work stifled them. The rest of the workforce would be arriving at seven: Ken and George the full-time staff on the farm, and Andy the lambing student for the season. Ken was the shepherd-cum-tractor driver, whereas George was the foreman-cum-tractor driver, shepherd, mechanic, builder, plumber, fencer, forester, and anything else he was asked to do. All four would work as a team for the morning, getting the bulk of the days work done before lunch, and then Andy would be left to check the lambing barns, Ken would check the outside sheep, and George and Harry would get on with whatever needed doing or whatever Harry had dreamed up while relaxing with his morning cup of coffee in his Aga side armchair.

Harry was heading back towards the barns. He had not seen his erstwhile victim while out among the ewes and lambs in the paddock, but he had seen the evidence of its existence. He had discovered another lamb lying dead on the ground, its mouth and tongue eaten away, and its tail gone. Harry was considering calling in a neighbouring gamekeeper who specialised in killing foxes using a night light and high-powered rifle. He had refrained from this course of action before, but it was getting to the stage when something had to be done; his livelihood was being eaten away before his eyes.

Harry hunched his shoulders, keeping his hands stuffed firmly in his coat pockets, his shotgun held safely under the crook of his arm, broken in the recommended manner. He kept his chin to his chest as he walked into the stiff breeze that was carrying the wisps of snow flakes toward him. He was recalling his evening the night before, his "church meeting" as he and his fellow devotees called their Sunday evening gathering in the *Pig and Whistle*. The group consisted of a hard core of five of his contemporaries, local farmers he had known for over twenty years, and now and then the numbers would be swelled by one or two more, all connected with the agricultural industry. The talk always revolved around farming or farmers, only changing tack slightly in the summer months when the various village cricket teams and their performances would be dissected; but it was usually the price of various foodstuffs, the actions of another local farmer, the rumours of farmers further afield, or the bungling of the government over agricultural policies that kept the evenings going. Sometimes a big news story of the week was reviewed, but it would always return to farming talk. It was a chance to meet his friends and catch up on the gossip of the week, all of which he would repeat to Betty as she had her own church to go to, a church that had 'proper services, sang proper hymns, and whose congregation didn't get pie-eyed in the evening' she would tell him with a grin.

Betty would drop him off at the pub before going on to the evening service at St. Mary's, returning later after she had had a cup of tea and a gossip with other Christians attending the service. She would catch the end of the proceedings at the *Pig and Whistle*, but she was usually the only wife there, which made Harry proud to think he could share these evenings with her while the other "devotees" would rather be on their own. They would then wend their way home, for Harry to have a last look around the lambing pens before the early morning shift. It was usually the job of the other three men in the lambing crew to arrange the late night shift but on a Sunday night Harry would always do it, saying he was up anyway. The other three were not about to argue.

Last night had been a good evening, most of his friends had been there, discussing the lambing, the weather, the local gossip: shaking their heads at bad news, grinning and laughing at someone's misfortune and generally enjoying each other's company. There was a time when he could have walked into the pub on any evening and known everybody there, but as times had changed, and the village had grown away from the agricultural background he could only guarantee meeting people he knew on a Sunday evening.

The sky had got lighter as he neared the farmyard, a break in the lower lying scattered clouds gave way to a bank of heavy snow clouds to the East, ahead of the rising sun, the combination of the two producing a beautiful blanket of red, orange and amber trailing off into the distance, a stunning reverse sunset scene in the early morning.

"Red sky in the morning, shepherd's warning," Harry mumbled to himself, "there will be snow later I know."

Stevens entered Downlands farmyard and stopped in front of the workshop, he jumped out and made his way to the back of the van. As he did so he looked into the main barn where Harry Sinton had reunited the escaped lamb with its mother not three-quarters of an hour earlier and he noticed the quad bike sitting in the middle of the barn.

"At last," he thought to himself, "maybe this trip won't be a complete waste of time."

He returned to the front of the van and climbed in, just as Sean and Paul had decided they had better get out and see what Stevens wanted them to do.

"Where the fuck are you two going?"

Without a word the two of them got back into the front and waited for the next development in this morning of let-downs. Stevens reversed the van back into the wide open gateway and then turned the van to the right and drove parallel to the main barn until he reached the entrance to the concreted yard, where he turned left and drove past the entrance to the main barn before stopping and reversing the van inside the barn, backing up to the quad bike.

The entrance of the blue transit van into the barn caused an increase of noise from the resident ewes, bleating their requests for their morning feed and water. Stevens was oblivious to the change in volume.

"Unhitch the trailer from the bike, we haven't got enough room for both of them."

Sean and Paul hopped out and set about their job; it needed both of them to lift the trailer off the quad's ball hitch, as it was loaded with the morning's rations of sheep feed. Stevens walked around the van and unlocked the padlock holding the back doors in place, and groped about for the planks of wood to allow the quad to be pushed up into the back without too much effort.

"Billy, look," Sean shouted. "The silly sod's left the keys in it."

"Well drive the bloody thing into the van then. Just get on with it."

To accommodate two quad bikes in the back of the van, the second had to be up at an angle, resting on the back of the first, on its rear wheels.

Stevens could see the first pale blue streaks of light outside and knew that the farmer would not be far away. Facing the farmer did not bother him and the chance of the farmer taking down the number plate and ringing up the police also meant little. The van was stolen over a year ago, and a new set of number plates had been fixed to the bumpers. The numbers and letters of the new plates coincided with a similar van from Reading. Stevens had taken these numbers on purpose, noting them on a visit just after he had acquired the van, so that if he was ever stopped, the police would find the van registered to a house in Reading, not stolen, and Stevens would say he bought it from that address last week, the documentation being in the post. He would then sell it on immediately, cash for scrap.

Before Stevens had acquired the battered blue van, he used to drive up to these "farm visits" in an old Escort van, which he drove about until he found a likely four-wheel-drive car to steal and use for the night, hoping to pick up a trailer on the way. Usually the farmers who had a quad bike also had a trailer to ferry it from place to place. After loading his haul of the morning, he would drive the stolen car, trailer and loot, to his accomplice on the outskirts of Winchester, leaving the lot. He would then be picked up by Sean who had been following on behind in his Escort van. The possession of the transit van meant that Stevens did not have to worry about discovering a suitable four-wheel-drive vehicle, or a trailer, and therefore cut down on the hassle of the night, not to mention the chances of being caught.

Sean drove the bike into the open rear of the van, ducking his head as he entered. Paul followed and together they manoeuvred the quad onto its rear wheels and rested it on the back of the first, securing it with straps. Paul then headed back to the passenger seat. Stevens waited for Sean to get out of the back and then shut the doors and locked them with the padlock. Sean had jumped in beside Paul when Stevens returned with two lambs, one under each arm.

"Here, payment in kind, give them to your mums." He grinned as he threw them towards the two passengers. Stevens had purposefully picked up two lambs with the dirtiest backsides he could find to throw at his companions. His mood had lightened again now that a second, almost new, quad bike was safely in the back of his van. The two boys caught the lambs and held them at arm length looking startled, not knowing if Stevens was serious or not. Stevens climbed into the driving seat and closed the door.

"Throw the little shits out you stupid sods. It was only a joke."

Sean opened the door and tossed his lamb out into the nearest pen, alarming the ewe that was lying down with her own lambs. The newly arrived lamb tried to stand but its legs were unsteady and its body shook from the fright of the fall; Paul held his lamb up and turned it towards him, looking it in the eyes.

"I don't know, my mum might like it, it's Mothers Day soon."

"Well you keep hold of it, but if it gets any of its shit on my seats, I'll throw you out as well as him."

"Maybe not then," Paul decided and propelled the lamb out of the still open door along the same route as the unfortunate first lamb. It crashed into the metal hurdles and fell awkwardly onto the straw-covered concrete floor of the pen.

"Close the door, let's get out of here." Stevens commanded.

As Harry Sinton walked back towards the farmyard he heard the sound of a vehicle somewhere near the barns; the wind was blowing into his face and he was not sure of what he could hear, and he could not see the yard as yet.

"Maybe Andy had come in early" he thought.

Harry then followed the bend in the track and could see the farmyard in front of him. Andy's car was not in its usual place, so Harry doubted the validity of what he thought he had heard. Then he heard the sound of the quad bike come to life and he started to look at the yard with more suspicion.

"Who would be starting that up now?" he wondered. "We always walk around the lambing barns first thing in the morning."

Harry increased his speed as he approached the yards, breaking into a trot. He then heard the sounds of doors slamming in the main barn. As he neared the main barn he noticed the front of a dark blue transit van. Rounding onto the entrance he saw a lamb being thrown out of the passenger's side door and the door being slammed. Behind the slammed door he could now see his quad bike trailer discarded at an oblique angle, unattached to the quad.

"'Ere!" he shouted at the van, he could not see the three figures in the front of the van as the overhead lights from the barn reflected from the windscreen into his eyes.

"Just what I fucking need," Stevens roared. He had turned around to see a figure of a man dressed in wellingtons, waxed jacket and flat cap, holding a shotgun under his arm. The man's face was pink from the bitter cold of the morning, but could not hide the broken veins and weather-beaten features of his face that made Harry Sinton look his age.

"What does this old bastard think he's going to do?"

Stevens put the van into first gear and started to drive towards Harry. Harry, in a state of shock and anger at the sight of these intruders, raised his gun in reflex, but accidentally pulled the first trigger, the barrels now pointing at the radiator grill. The sound of the shotgun being fired in the confines of the barn, and the shot striking the radiator grill, the radiator and the bonnet amplified the noise to a deafening crescendo. The sheep in the barns started to bleat and raced up and down in the close confines of their pens.

Stevens slammed on the brakes; he could not believe this was happening, what was this stupid old sod trying to do? The van was now knackered, would it make it back to Southampton? Would he get the quads to his mate or himself back home for that matter; the whole morning had turned sour, again.

Stevens opened his van door and climbed out, glaring at the man in front of him.

"What the fuck do you think you're doing?"

Sean opened his door and followed Stevens' lead. Stevens had reached back into the van and produced a baseball bat from under his seat. Paul looked wildly from one man to the other, not knowing what to do.

"You stupid old sod. Why didn't you let us drive off? Then no one would be hurt. You stupid old bastard." Steven's rage made it nearly impossible to spit these cries of fury out.

Harry was now starting to shake, frightened by the sound of the shotgun going off in the confines of the barn, the yelling of the man walking purposefully toward him, baseball bat in hand, and the appearance of another figure from the front of the van. He broke the shotgun, the spent cartridge automatically ejected, and he scrabbled in his pocket for a new shell to replace it.

"Put that fucking gun down, you senile old git, before you shoot yourself," Stevens warned as he advanced towards Harry, his words coming out slower, in a deep growl. Sean was on Stevens' left now but started to fall behind as they advanced towards the old man.

"What are we going to do?"

"We are going to teach this old bastard a lesson."

Harry fumbled a new cartridge into the chamber, snapped his shotgun together and raised it at the advancing men. Even firmly held, stock snug in his shoulder, the gun was visibly shaking. He tried to tell them to stay where they were but his throat was dry and no words came out. He saw two men striding towards him, the first with wild unkempt shoulder-length hair, three days of growth on his chin, a menacing grin and evil glint to his eyes, his massive gloved hands wrapped around the handle of a wooden baseball bat, thickset shoulders enhanced by the padded checked coat, zipped up over his chest. The other was younger; baggy black jeans, and windbreaker jacket did little to hide his skinniness. Limp blonde hair protruded from beneath his ski hat, gold earring in his left ear. Paul watched from his seat in the front of the van as his two partners moved towards this man with a gun. He could not move from his seat, he did not know what was going on or what was needed of him. He just sat stone still and watched the events unfold. The man with the gun was not aiming, head low looking down the barrel, but had his head high, it seemed to be shaking.

The noise in the barn fell as the sheep started to calm down, but Harry Sinton was oblivious to all around him, he just watched the two men coming towards him, less than ten feet away.

"What the fuck do you think you are doing?" Stevens repeated. "Put the fucking gun down now!"

Harry Sinton pointed the gun at the first man, shaking his head. No words were coming out of his mouth. He wanted to tell them to go, he wanted to tell them he would not press charges, he wanted to tell them sorry, he wanted to go back to the warmth of his kitchen and start all over again.

Stevens was eight feet away; at least this would get some of this morning's frustration out of him he thought, the stupid old sod should have just let us go.

"You stupid old bas . . . "

The roar of the shotgun exploded inside the barn again. Stevens was hurled back off his feet, his arms reaching forward, the baseball bat dropping to the ground. The whole scene was being played in slow motion to Harry. He could see the surprised, pained expression on the man's face as he fell backwards, the deep red stain on his chest suddenly appearing, increasing in size, around the fist-size hole the shot had created. Stevens' arms flung forward in some grotesque form of welcome. Even before he had hit the floor, Harry turned onto the other man. They were both rooted to the spot, the second man watching his mate's slow descent towards the cold concrete floor. As Stevens hit the floor the second man turned back at Harry. All colour had left his face, total shock and astonishment could be seen in his eyes. Harry, still shaking his head, tears forming in his eyes, pulled the second trigger.

The force of the five-shot cartridge hitting Sean from nine feet mirrored Stevens' decline. He was driven back against the pens behind him, his arms stretched forward, head bent into his chest. His hat catapulted from his head. Harry watched the young man hit the pen behind him, flip over the top rail and crash to the straw

21

floor on his back, his feet jammed up in the air resting on the inside of the pen, arm flung wide. The ewe in the pen, splattered with blood, bone, skin and cloth, tried to squeeze herself into the furthest corner away from this intruder, her two lambs on the other side of this man, trembling in fear, their bleating being lost in the cacophony of sounds inside the barn.

Slowly the senses returned to Harry; he was staring at the body of the second man, it reminded him of an unconscious drunk fallen off a gate. He still held his gun in his hands, stock tightly forced into his shoulder, pointing to where the second man had been. He turned and looked at the first man; there was no sign of life in the prone body, blood seeping out from underneath him. He looked up at the transit van, the dents and damages from his first shot contorting the grill and bonnet into an ugly disorder, beads of blood glinting on the bonnet's blue metalwork, along with the sharp silver scars of torn metal. Shreds of cloth from Stevens' clothes stuck to the bodywork.

Harry started to hear the sounds of the barn, the bleating of the sheep, the cries of the lambs, and the rustling of the straw. He started to shake, he let the gun drop to the ground. He looked around him, bewildered at the sights and the sounds he was now sensing. His legs buckled and he made a grab for the nearest stanchion, holding himself up as he searched for something to sit on. He found a bale of straw next to the stanchion and lowered himself onto it, still shaking, feeling faint, unsure of what had just happened. He dropped his head into his hands, elbows rested on his knees, and he started rocking backwards and forwards.

Paul sat as still as a statue, sweat drenching the small of his back. He dare not breathe in case this man in front of him would notice. He could not see Stevens' body lain on its back to the right of the bonnet through the blood-splattered windscreen, but he could see Sean's legs in the air, the left leg twitching slowly. It had all happened so fast for him, his mind was racing to the cause, the action, the next move. He watched as the old man in front of him swayed, dropped the gun and grabbed at a stanchion, then eased himself onto a bale of straw. Still Paul dared not breathe, his heartbeat deafening his ears.

An uneasy peace settled inside the barn, the ewes nuzzled their lambs while surveying the world outside their pens, lambs regained their innocence and started to dance and prance about under the watchful gaze of their mothers.

Paul eased himself forward so as to see the rest of his friend's crumpled body. He saw the hole ripped in Sean's chest, the blood weeping from the wound, the twitching of the leg slowing down. He then looked to his right to see the prone body of Billy Stevens just in front of the van, blood seeping onto the concrete floor framing Stevens' upper body in a pool of crimson fluid. Paul eased himself back into his seat and stared at the figure on the bale of straw, rocking back and forward. He still did not want to show himself. Should he make a run for it? Where to? He did not know where the hell he was. Who would he tell if he could escape? They had broken into the farm, threatened the farmer. The police would arrest him.

Give himself up? What would stop the madman in front of him from killing him, leaving no witnesses to his crime. He could not stay here, he knew that.

Try and escape, he told himself; the light was increasing, he could make his way to the nearest village, the nearest telephone box and ring his mother. He would make up any story, as long as it released him from this nightmare. Yes, run for it, he decided.

Paul started to slide across the bench seat towards the open passenger door, the same door he had thrown the lamb out not two minutes before, now light years ago. The slightest noise Paul made sounding like a screaming alarm to alert the figure sitting on the bale. He slipped down off the seat, carefully easing his feet onto the floor, not taking his eyes off the rocking figure. Still he could see the lifeless remains of Sean in his line of sight as he concentrated on the figure of the farmer. Feeling his way with an outstretched arm behind him, he started to step backwards toward the walk-through passage from the main barn to the entrance of the farmyard. He glanced around to check his path, and when he was certain of his route and that the madman could not catch him, he bolted through the passage, crashing into the trailer as he ran, up past the entrance gates, never looking back.

Harry heard a different noise to the constant bleating of the sheep, a jar of metal on metal and the sounds of someone running. He looked up from his hands towards a fleeing figure running out of the barn, still he was bewildered. What had just happened? Could it be real?

"Oh God" he whispered." Oh God no, please no."

He sat staring at the scene in front of him, clasped his arms around himself and started to rock back and forward again, unable to tear his eyes from sight. Repeating his plea to an unanswering God.

Betty checked the time on the kitchen clock again, a quarter-to-seven. She had moved to the kitchen after clearing up Harry's pyjamas in the bathroom, picking up bits of hay and straw brought in from the barns the night before, and making the bed. She was now pacing the kitchen, wondering what was keeping her husband. She had cooked him his breakfast of bacon, two eggs and a slice of fried bread, keeping it warm in the Aga. He was usually back in the kitchen by now, announcing the morning's news; how many twins, triplets, or singles. In fact, he was usually ready to go back out to the farm by this time, after having his breakfast, meeting up with the rest of the staff for the morning's second shift. Bracken eyed her from her basket.

"Where has he got to lovie?" she asked the dog. The only reply was the wagging of the tail.

She had heard the shotgun blasts earlier, three in all. She would have some fun with him over that, three shots at a fox, it must have been a slow one. The shots sounded as if they had come from near the barns, the cheeky blighter must have been in the yards, she thought.

George Stone was the first of the staff to enter the farmyard that morning, as every morning, at five-to-seven. George lived in a tied cottage on the farm, only fifty yards away from the entrance. He had been in the employment of Harry Sinton for the past seventeen years and had no reason to look for a new job. They had had their disagreements, but he had worked on other farms and estates before Downlands Farm and he realised that Harry Sinton was an easy-going fellow who worked as hard as he expected his employees to work. He would be quite happy to see out his last fifteen years of employment here and retire in this area where he had been born and bred.

Entering the yard he felt nothing amiss, but as he made his way towards the walk-through entrance of the main barn he noticed a difference to the usual morning sounds. There was more noise, as if the sheep had been disturbed, or they had heard the rattling of the feed bucket, and they were bleating their impatience. Passing through the walkway he saw the reason for the change in the morning's sounds. He could see an old blue transit van parked where the quad bike should have been, and the quad trailer knocked into the pens to his left, sheepfeed nuts strewn across the floor from a dislodged bag off the trailer. He slowed as he walked around to the front of the van. He saw the prone body of Stevens lying in a pool of blood, a baseball bat at his feet. He recognised the rocking figure of Harry Sinton looking up at him from a bale of straw, noticed the shotgun lying on the ground.

Harry watched as George entered the barn, walk around the van and stop at the sight that greeted him. Harry wanted to tell him it was all a mistake, he did not mean to do it, but no words came out of his mouth.

The sounds of two cars entering the yard broke the men's gaze from each other. Andy and Ken had followed each other into the farmyard and were now getting out of their cars, doors slamming, morning greetings carrying through to the two men in the barn.

"Are you alright Harry?" George asked tentatively.

No reply came from Harry. George started to walk towards him and only then did he notice the body collapsed in the pen.

"Bloody hell."

"I . . . I . . . It . . . I . . . didn't . . . I." Words spurted from Harry's mouth.

George spun round to the two men now entering the barn.

"Ken, go to my house and ring the police ," he shouted.

"What?" Ken said just before he noticed the van. "What's happened?"

Ken and Andy rounded the van and stopped dead in their tracks, questioning looks on their faces as they took in the scene before them.

"Go to my house and phone the police , don't touch anything," George repeated.

"Er, yea," Ken replied. "Er, what do I tell them?"

"I don't know, just tell them to come here!"

Ken turned and made for George's house. George's wife would still be there, before she drove into Carlton for the day's work. Andy stood and stared at Harry.

"I didn't mean to, they kept . . . they kept . . . ," Harry said, pleading for forgiveness, understanding, both.

George was next to Harry now, trying to get him on his feet. He wanted to get him to the farmhouse, get him in the warm, get him away from the scene of carnage. He had a good idea what had gone on in the barn but did not want to think about it at the moment. He wanted the police to be here, he wanted to be relieved from the situation.

"Give me a hand," he asked Andy, and Andy was pleased to have something to do. They pulled Harry up, and with one on each side of him walked him to the farmhouse. Andy kept trying to catch George's eye with a questioning look, but George ignored him, concentrating on keeping Harry Sinton moving towards his house. The daylight had got a grip of the morning but the stark light of the winter sun gave little heat to the ground as the three men made their way towards the old farmhouse, their wellington boots slipping on the smooth frozen mud surface of the path.

Betty saw the three men from the kitchen window, saw Harry being supported on either side by the two others, and hurried to the back door.

"What happened?" she cried, looking at George for an explanation.

"There has been a bit of an accident."

Betty looked at her husband in between the two men, a mixed expression of hurt and sorrow on his face, as if he wanted forgiveness for what had happened. Had he shot himself? She could not see any blood on him. Had he had a heart attack? He looked dealy pale.

"Bring him in, what sort of an accident?"

"I'm so sorry love, I'm so sorry. I didn't mean it to happen," Harry implored his wife.

"What to happen, George what happened?"

They took Harry to the kitchen and dropped him into his armchair. George told Andy to go back to the barns and wait for the police. To tell them where they were, and repeated not to touch anything. He then turned to Betty, she was at her husband's side, holding his hands, whispering things were going to be alright to him.

"Betty, I think you should sit down as well" he said, pulling up a chair from the kitchen table to where she was standing over Harry.

"Please tell me what happened Harry, are you alright? Did you have a heart attack?" Her attentions were all on her husband. Harry did not reply, he just looked into his wife's eyes, his voice had failed him again.

"Betty, please sit down," George asked.

She did as she was told, and then watched as George went over to the Aga and took the frying pans off the stove, replacing them with the kettle. It was an action of keeping himself busy rather than a need for any hot drink, he was trying to formulate his answer to Betty's pleadings. Bracken had jumped out of her basket and was now at her master's feet for the second time that morning.

"I don't know what really happened Betty, but I think Harry stumbled across a couple of burglars in the barn." George did not want to continue, but Betty's eyes begged him to.

"There were two of them and I think, I don't know, I think they were after the quad. I think they came at Harry when he disturbed them."

"The gun shots?"

George did not want to tell her the two burglars were dead in the barn, that her husband had killed them with his shotgun, her husband the murderer. He could not believe it himself, but he had seen the evidence in the barn, what else could it have been? He hated being here, he had come to look upon the Sintons as his friends, always the employer, but still his friends. They had been good to him over the years, always trusting him and making him feel welcome, they were easy to talk to and always ready to help. Now he was about to tell his boss's wife that her husband was a killer. It would break her heart, shake her world to the core. Then again he would rather say it than let a stranger tell her, even if it was the police .

"I think Harry must have defended himself."

"What do you mean?" Betty did not understand.

"I think Harry must have defended himself, with the shotgun."

Harry had started to cry, he had pulled his hands away from Betty's and stuffed his face into his palms. Betty felt weak, she still did not understand George, but she sensed something terrible had happened.

"I don't understand, George."

"He must have defended himself Betty." He did not know what to say, how to put the truth to her.

"What happened? Please, George."

"Betty," George went to her and took her hands. "I think he shot them, in self-defence. I think Harry shot them."

Betty stared at George, unable to comprehend his last statement. She looked around at her husband, saw this proud man crying into his shaking hands. He was always so strong for her, always had the answer in his slow unflustered manner. She looked back at George hoping he would say he had it all wrong, it was all a mistake, but all she heard was George saying he was sorry.

The police arrived at the farmyard twenty minutes after they had been called, they had driven straight to the farm, knowing the way from two previous visits: once to check on Harry Sinton's shotgun cabinet, and the other to survey the scene of yet another farmyard break-in. They had often driven through these villages to show their presence to the locals. They had been told it was another break-in, with possible injured parties. The caller had given a rather garbled message but at least told them where it was. As soon as they saw the scene in front of them they called for back-up in the form of the CID.

The more senior officer inspected the two bodies, finding no signs of life. They talked to the two men who were waiting for them in the barn, both had little to say. They had just turned up to find the same scene as the police could now see. No, they had not touched anything, no they had not heard anything, no they did not know the time scale of the killings, no they did not recognise the two intruders. The older of the two had rung the police from the house they passed as they approached the farm, the younger one had helped carry the owner to his house on the other side of the barns with another employee who was still there. No, he had not noticed any injuries to Mr. Sinton. They had then waited for the police to arrive, not knowing what to do. Feeding the sheep had fallen in the list of morning priorities.

The more senior of the two policemen told his colleague to wait for the back-up, and repeated the order not to touch anything, while he went to the farmhouse. In twenty years of policing this area he had never seen anything like this. He had attended road accidents with the horrors of bodies mangled with metal, seen the aftermath of pub brawls, but never a fatal shooting. These things just did not happen in the quiet villages of rural southern England, he could hardly believe it. Then again he had long ago learnt not to be surprised by anything.

There was a knock on the front door, Harry Sinton visibly jumped at the sound, while Betty and George exchanged looks.

"Police. Sergeant Phillips," the policeman called as he knocked again.

"Do you want me to let him in, Betty?" George offered.

"Please," she replied.

George made his way from the kitchen, through the hallway, to the front door. He unlocked the door with the key that was already in the lock, and opened it to reveal the police sergeant.

"We are all in the kitchen," George explained as he turned to show the way.

Sergeant Alex Phillips had been in the house before, when he had checked up on Harry's shotgun cabinet. He had been struck by the ease of the surroundings, and the pleasant nature of his hosts, offering him tea and cakes and talking comfortably. Now as he walked through their hallway, looking at the family pictures hung on the wall, the ornaments of a life in farming on the shelves and tables, he could not help but wonder at the story behind the scene in the barn. How had this mild man come to kill two men, and what was this whole episode going to do to this family? He then corrected himself, telling himself not to jump to conclusions, just record the facts and locate the truth.

Entering the kitchen he saw Harry and Betty Sinton looking at him with dread. He had been in many difficult situations before, having to break bad news to families, but the look on the two faces before him was pitiful. The elderly couple were holding hands, trying to reassure each other that all would be alright. Where to start? He thought to himself.

Start he did, introducing himself, asking if everybody was alright, and then he began on the statements. What had happened at first, trying to get the general picture. Harry's answers were clumsy, as if on telling the story he was looking for the reason or absolution in his own words. He described the reason for taking the shotgun, the walk in the paddocks, and then the realisation of intruders in the barn. Betty and George looked on in silence as Harry described the events leading up to the confrontation in the barn. It was now that Harry started to shake, his words coming awkwardly. Betty tried to comfort him, George offered to find a glass of whisky for the shock, but Harry waved the suggestion away with his shaking hands.

"The van, it . . . it . . . started to come at me, it . . . it . . . I . . . couldn't see the driver. It . . . it . . . just started to come at me. I . . . I . . ."

"Take your time Mr. Sinton," Sergeant Phillips assured him.

"They . . . I . . . The . . . The shotgun went off, at the van. Oh God I don't know how, I was frightened, they were coming towards me." Harry stared at the Sergeant, imploring understanding from the figure of justice standing in front of him.

"Go on," was the only reply.

Harry took a deep breath, turned his eyes away from the faces in the room and looked at his dog instead. The dog that would always adore him whatever he had done. What would people think of him now? What did his wife think? George? His children didn't know yet, what would they think of this stupid old man killing two human beings? What had the man called him, a senile old git. He was not a bad man, he kept telling himself, he had never been in trouble before, and all the time he worried what people would think. Especially his wife.

"I'm so sorry Betty" he said, still looking at the dog, unable to meet his wife's eyes. Tears were welling up in Betty's eyes, not for the two men lying outside, but for the torment she could see on her husband's features. Sergeant Phillips urged him to continue again.

"There . . . there were two of them. Two men . . . got out and came at me. They . . . they . . . threatened me, they wouldn't stop, they kept coming. What was I supposed to do?" Harry paused "and then they stopped."

He fell silent, he could not go into detail of what happened. He did not want to talk any more, he wanted to be left alone. Harry Sinton wanted to turn back time and start the morning again. He wanted to be out in the yard moving ewes and lambs around like any other morning. He wanted anything but what was happening now. Why didn't I just let them go? he kept asking himself over and over again.

Sergeant Phillips finished scribbling in his note book, realising that was all he would get out of Harry Sinton for the time being, and turned his attention to the man who had let him into the house. He was as helpful as the two in the barn, only knowing the time he had entered the barn and very little else, Betty likewise. Sergeant Phillips wanted the CID to turn up now. He had done all that was possible for the moment, taken the initial statements from all those present, obtaining the general picture. It would be up to the CID to work out the details.

"There was another one," Harry Sinton whispered.

"Pardon?" Sergeant Phillips turned back to face Harry.

"There was another one. Another man. In the van. He ran away."

Paul Allen had kept running for what seemed like an age; he had run through the entrance to the farm, passed a row of houses to his left, down the road, past fields and wooded belts, and still he ran. He came to a T-junction and instinctively took the left-hand bend. He did not know where he was going, he did not recognise any of the surrounding countryside. He had taken no notice of the directions they had followed to reach the farmyard, it had been dark with no street lamps to shine the way, all the fields looked the same to him, God he hated the countryside. He ran down to another bend in the road and stopped, his chest was heaving, his face burning from the bitter morning air, he was lost. He wanted to cry, he wanted to be back home, anywhere rather than here. He looked around him, there was nowhere else to go but to follow the road, so he started to jog, no longer able to run, the pain stabbing at his chest hurting too much.

The morning's events kept filling his mind. The whole thing was a complete cock-up, even before the shooting. Why had he let Sean persuade him to go? Now look at him, miles from anywhere, alone, scared out of his wits. I know, he told himself, I'll say Sean bullied me into it. No, I'll say Stevens bullied us both, yea blame the mad bastard who got us into this trouble.

Then doubt crept into his mind. What if they were not dead and I ran out, what if they are still lying there, waiting for help? He was going out of his mind with worry, every possible scenario was being played out in his brain. Sean's mum, their mates, Stevens' mates, what would they think? What would they do to him? His mum, oh God his father. Why had he let himself be talked into coming on this trip? He was forgetting that he had badgered Sean to be able to go, he wanted a part of the action. He had listened to Sean's boasts of night raids in the countryside, the easy money, the laughs, and wanted in. Why had he let Stevens bully him, he kept trying to convince himself? Still he was in the middle of nowhere, he could not see a house anywhere.

His legs finally failed him, he slowed down to a walk, he could not hold back the tears any more, he was lost, alone, cold, and frightened. He had seen his best mate shot dead, the image of Sean's twitching leg burnt into his memory, Stevens' blood splattering against the windscreen. He started to shake, feel the cold. He was so alone, and there was still no sign of any human life near him, no signposts to direct him. He stumbled on.

He heard a car coming towards him, unable to see it from the bend in the road. He looked wildly around: hide was his first instinct. He scrambled over the wire fence on his right and lay flat on the ground, watching for the approaching car. He saw a white Ford Fiesta speed pass him, followed closely by a Subaru pick-up. Still he lay on the ground; he did not have a watch, he did not know the time, or how long he had been running. Unknown to Paul, he had just watched Ken Johnston and Andy Falks making their way to Downlands Farm.

Paul wanted to be saved from this mess, he wanted out. He would flag the next car down and give himself up. He got to his feet and climbed over the fence, and carried on the way he was heading. Still the anxieties flooded his brain. Should he go back and help his mate, who should he ring if he ever found a telephone box, what would he say to people? Sean's big brother: the thought of Sean's big brother suddenly filled him with dread, he would kill him for running out on his little brother, he would kill the madman in the barn. He stumbled off the road and collapsed, back against the wire fence, arms wrapped around himself. He could not go on any further, he would wait for the next car. It was light now, there must be a car along soon, even country bumpkins must go to work. Still the image of Sean's twitching leg filled his head.

He did not know how long he had sat with his back against the fence before he heard another car, this time coming from the opposite direction from the last two. He pulled himself up off the ground, and stood by the side of the road, waiting for the approaching vehicle. As it came into view he flagged it down, relief flooding his body as he noticed it slowing, coming to a stop next to him. A middle-aged man, wearing a shirt and tie, started to wind down the window.

"Are you alright lad?" he inquired, "you're a bit far from anywhere."

"Yea, me mates left me for a joke," Paul said, wiping the tears from his cheeks with the back of his hand. "Could I have a lift to a phone box?"

"Not a problem, let me shift the briefcase." The man leaned over to the passenger seat and moved his brief case from the front seat to the rear.

Paul scampered around the car to the passenger door, opening it when the man had unlocked it, and jumped in. The warm air hit him in the face and he shivered, feeling himself cold to the bone. He pulled the door shut and the man started down the lane.

"I wouldn't call them mates if they left me out in this."

Paul tried to make conversation with this man but could only nod in agreement. The middle-aged man kept looking at him, asking questions. How long had he been out in this weather? Where had his mates gone to? Was he a local lad? At college? He had not seen Paul about before, he said, but he had only been in the village for a month, moved from the local town after being posted there from his army days.

Paul tried to keep up with the man's chat but found it easier to sit still and try to warm up. The man seemed happy to talk to himself, only bringing Paul into the conversation now and again. Asking questions, not waiting for the answers, telling Paul his thoughts of the type of mates he was hanging around with, the reason he moved to the countryside, his house, wife and children. He asked for Paul's name.

"John," came the easy reply.

"Right, where do you want to be dropped off John? I know there's a cafe on the high street in the next village, you could call your so-called mates from there and keep warm while you wait."

"Yea, thanks," Paul muttered.

"Not a problem. I've been left in the middle of nowhere before and had to flag down a local for help. Not in weather like this mind!"

The man drove up to another junction and turned left. Suddenly the road grew wider, it had defined edges, no longer bordered by grass but by paved stones, signs of life were evident. Houses came into view, and people. The man pulled up next to the pavement and pointed towards a building with condensation-filled windows.

"It's in there, they are bound to have a 'phone. Do you need some change?"

"No, thanks," Paul said as he got out of the warm interior of the car into the icy morning air.

He watched as the man drove off, a smile on his face, obviously pleased with his good deed for the day. Paul half walked, half ran, towards the cafe. He could not believe the difference in the area, there were cars rushing by, trailing white clouds of smoke from their exhausts as the engines warmed to the morning air. People walking this way and that, waiting at bus stops, wrapped up against the bitter cold, white wisps of breath being snatched away by the wind. It had only been a moment ago when he was being driven through country lanes with no sign of life, and then one turning brought him back to more familiar surroundings.

He entered the cafe, the smell of cooking filled his nostrils, deep fat fryers mixed with the whiff of cooking sausages. His eyes darted around the room, keeping from any long contact with the other customers sitting at their plastic tables. He put his hands in his pocket to reveal a handful of change. He could not afford any food, only a cup of coffee. Ordering his drink at the counter, he asked for the name of the village.

"You a bit lost son?" smiled the lady behind the counter, as she handed him a mug of coffee. "This is the village of Carlton," she informed him with a wry smile. She always laughed at the idea that Carlton was a village, more like a small town.

Paul also received directions to the pay-phone in the corner of the room, and he walked towards it, checking his change as he went. He had decided to call Andy, his friend who had a car and would hopefully pick him up. He looked around trying to find a clock. One hung on the wall behind the counter, above the smiling lady who had just served him and who was now in deep discussion with another women who had just entered. The hands, in the shape of a knife and a folk, pointed to different cooked foods. The knife pointed straight down towards two fried eggs, the smaller fork aimed its prongs at some baked beans to the left of the eggs, where the number seven should be. Seven-thirty. At least Andrew would be home, still deep in his pit probably, but he could not think of anybody else to call. His mother would ask him questions all the way home, his father would not even take time off work to pick him up, and no way was he going to call any of Sean's relations.

He dialled the number, praying that it would be answered. A woman's voice answered those prayers.

"375 283. Hello."

"Mrs. Goodman, is Andy there please?"

"Who is calling?"

"It's Paul, Paul Allen."

"You're up bright and early, aren't you Paul? I'll just get him out of bed, wait a minute."

Paul checked his change again, worried that he would run out of money before Andy made it to the phone. Andy took an age to get to the telephone, Paul kept jamming twenty-pence pieces into the machine.

"What do you want?" a groggy voice demanded.

Paul turned his back to the rest of the customers in the cafe, shielding his conversation from their prying looks, bending his head down, forming a cradle around the handpiece.

"Andy mate, I'm in the shit, you'll never . . . believe . . . what's happened," Paul babbled, he could not contain himself, he needed to tell someone, but he was still to frightened to confess all.

"Slow down, slow down. What's happened?"

"I'm in the middle of nowhere, I'm fucked up. Andy, pick me up for God's sake."

"What do you mean? Where are you?" Andrew Goodman could hear the despair in Paul's voice.

"I'm in a place called Carlton, please Andy."

"Where's that?"

"I don't know," Paul cried. "Just find me please. You will never believe what's happened, it's all gone wrong. Andy, pick me up for fuck's sake."

"Alright, alright, I'll come and get you."

The pips warning of the end of the paid line time sounded in their ears.

"I'm in the cafe," Paul blurted as the line went dead. He did not know whether Andy heard him, he would get a table by the window and keep a look-out for his friend's car. He trudged to an empty table next to the window, acutely aware of the looks he received from the other customers. Did they know? Did he look guilty?

He sat down next to the window, wiped the condensation from the pane and looked out at the world going by, all the figures shuffling along, making their way like any other Monday morning. He wrapped his hands around the coffee mug, trying to extract all the warmth he could, his stomach aching from the smells radiating from the kitchen. He closed his eyes, trying to blank out the images of the morning, but all he could see was Sean's crumpled body in the sheep pen, legs in the air, one slowly twitching.

Chief Inspector Anthony Kemp arrived at the scene of the crime after a lengthy detour around the surrounding country roads, unable to find the farm from the directions given by the station. Sergeant Collins, driving the Chief Inspector, had come to the rescue when he recognised the *Pig and Whistle* public house and had worked the directions out from there. The two of them were now inside the barn surveying the scene: nothing had been moved, they were assured by the uniformed officer in the barn. Kemp approached the first body lying on the cold concrete floor and shivered, whether from the sight of this man with a hole in his chest, or from the cold wind now picking up and swirling into the open barn entrance, maybe both.

He had noted the baseball bat at the feet of this body, and the shotgun about eight yards away discarded on the floor.

"Not a very fair fight," he mumbled to himself.

He turned the body over enough to extract the wallet from the body's back pocket, and still bending down, proceeded to examine the contents. Nothing, no cash, no driving licence, no credit cards, no video membership cards, nothing to tell the Inspector who this body was. He would run a make on the van but that would not guarantee any results. Leaving the wallet next to the corpse, he crossed over to the second body crumpled inside the sheep pen.

"I think we can move these animals to another pen," he told the uniformed officer who had been following him about like a shadow since Kemp had arrived.

While he waited for the sheep to be moved by the two farm workers who were by then desperate to do something, unsure what would happen to this morning's chores, Kemp inspected the front of the van. The passenger's side door was open and it revealed a chaotic interior. Crisp packets, cans of beer and soft drinks, cigarette packets, tabloid newspapers, chocolate bar wrappers were all strewn about the floor, leaving little room for the passenger's feet to rest on the original surface. He was hoping to find a discarded petrol receipt that could shed some light on the area these people had come from, but a more detailed search could be carried out later; he was still gathering his thoughts from the initial picture he was inspecting.

Returning to the second body now that the excitable sheep and her lambs had been moved, he extracted the wallet from the back pocket and proceeded to find the details that he wanted. A pink driving licence, and a cashpoint card confirmed that the body in the sheep pen was one Mr. Sean P. Robson, of 135 Knight Drive, Southampton, and that was the start Chief Inspector Kemp had been looking for. He ordered a check on the name on the driving licence, a check on the van and on the first quad bike in the back of the van; he assumed the second quad was the property of this farm, but he asked for a check anyway, never wanting to assume anything.

Wheels would now be put into motion, the CID from Southampton would check the name against their records, find out if this body had any known associates in the farm break-in business, or any other criminal activity for that matter, and slowly a solid background picture would be compiled. From the quick briefing he had received from the officer on the scene, Kemp believed this would be a very quick case to solve. They had the bodies, the weapon, and even the suspect, sitting in his kitchen with his wife. It would be up to the jury to thrash out the rights and wrongs of the situation; all Chief Inspector Kemp was concerned about was finding out the truth and processing another crime. At least this one he could get his teeth into, it was not the run-of-the-mill burgling or late-night brawl, this had a bit of meat to it. A simple case of a disturbed break-in and self-defence, he told himself, two less toe-rags to worry about.

Arrangements then had to be made to take the farmer down to the station to be formally interviewed on the morning's events, solicitors would need to be called, next-of-kin informed, media coverage to contend with.

"A good start for a Monday morning," he thought out loud as he surveyed the scene before him.

Paul Allen had waited nearly an hour inside the cafe, eking out the coffee, before he could no longer take the inquiring looks from the lady behind the counter. He left the warmth of the cafe and waited by the side of the road, propping himself up on a lamp post, hunched against the wind, still aware of the looks he was receiving from the passers-by. After the second hour was up he was trying to decide what to do, who to ring, Andy had either gone back to bed, or could not find this place. Then he saw Andy's car coming down the road, waves of relief flooded his whole body. He could not wait to get into the car; he had opened the door and climbed inside before his friend had come to a halt.

"What the hell are you doing in this place? It's bloody miles away, it took me ages to find it and then I think I went wrong. What have you been up to?" Andy bombarded Paul with questions. He continued to drive, looking for a place to turn around, and start to head back home.

"I'm in the shit Andy, big shit."

Paul could not contain himself any longer, he was swaying back and forth in the front of the car, staring at his friend, begging for help, pouring his revelations out. What should he do? He was scared, petrified. He had seen his best friend blown away, the local villain shot dead. It was the first time he had been out with them, he could not have done anything to stop it, he was lucky to be alive, it could have been him. If he had not been sitting in the middle he would have got out before Sean. Paul continued to rant, arms crossed in front of him, swaying back and forth.

Andy Goodman could not believe what he was hearing. Sean shot dead, Stevens the local crook killed as well. First he thought it was all a joke, but the sight of Paul, tears in his eyes begging for help, convinced him something really bad had happened. What had Paul got himself mixed up with?

"What the fuck were you thinking of, you stupid little shite."

"What should I do Andy?" He pleaded.

"Change your bloody story for a start."

"What . . . what do you mean?"

"Are you going to tell the police that Sean went for this bloke. That's self-defence, the bloke will get a medal for taking Sean out. You're in serious trouble. What about Sean's Mum and Dad, bloody hell, what about his brother, what are you going to tell him?"

Paul stared at his friend, he did not want to hear this, he wanted to hear that he could not have helped it, that he was not at fault, that everything was going to be alright. He tried not to think of the consequences of the morning's events.

"It wasn't my fault, it wasn't my fault," he kept repeating.

"Mate, you know you have to go to the police don't you. You can't run from this. Go to the police , admit you were with Sean, but tell them Sean surrendered, or tried to stop Stevens, anything but he went for this bloke."

"Stevens bullied us into going."

"Shit, you're in it bad man." Andy shook his head. "You're in it bad."

"You will back me up won't you Andy?"

"Back you up on what?" he cried. "I wasn't there, I didn't know anything about this. Don't you bring me into this. This isn't a little joke, if this actually happened, this is serious, it's not pinching a couple of car radios, or joy riding. This is murder. You'd better get your story straight now. Shit, we had better get our stories straight, they will question me an' all."

The full implications hit Andy like a hammer blow, he was now mixed up in this, he would have to lie about what Paul had told him. At least he had nothing to do with the deaths, he told himself, he just had to say what happened when he picked up a mate who was lost. He knew Sean had been going out with Stevens on these morning raids. Sean could not keep his mouth shut for long, flashing his new-found wealth at the pub, laughing about how easy it was, boasting about his friendship with Stevens. So Paul had been bullied into a "farm visit". He did not believe that for one minute. Paul loved himself, and would have loved to think he was tough enough to run with the likes of Stevens. The stupid little sod was in the shit now.

Silence had fallen inside the car, Andy was speeding back to Southampton, he would drive straight into a police station and get it over with. Both teenagers were deep in their own thoughts, all the different scenarios being played out inside their heads.

It took Andy half the time to get back and enter the outskirts of Southampton, he then drove up a side street and parked the car.

"Right, what are you going to say?"

"I . . . I . . . That the man shot Sean and Stevens."

"You will have to do better than that, you will have to tell them you saw Sean giving up, or pulling Stevens back."

"Yea, yea, Sean tried to pull Stevens back," the idea sparked Paul's imagination. "Yea, Sean was trying to stop Stevens from beating up the bloke with the gun, and . . . and . . . and when the man shot Stevens, Sean tried to give himself up, but . . . but the bastard shot him anyway. He . . . he would have shot me if I hadn't run."

The thought of being able to twist the story around against the man who killed his mate appealed to Paul. He could get away with it, the man in the barn would get done, he would be alright. Yea, he would be OK and the bastard in the barn would be sent down.

CHAPTER TWO

ANNAVALE INQUIRIES

Events were running away from Harry Sinton, sweeping him along, it all seemed a blur. He had been asked to go to the station to be formally interviewed by the Chief Inspector. He would be met by a solicitor from the firm of solicitors he had dealt with all his life for boundary and right-of-way disputes, making out of Wills, indeed anything that needed the skill of a high street solicitor. One of the original partners of the firm, Gerald Evans, was an old school friend and Godfather to Harry Sinton's son.

Betty had been left at the farmhouse, being watched over by George. She was going to ring the children, and hopefully they would all rally round and help out. Betty was in a daze as he was led away, still fussing over him, asking if he needed his coat and hat. Harry had wanted to organise the morning's work, the feeding of hay, the movement of the sheep, the reason for the holding back of some of the ewes, while others could go out onto the frozen ground. All the usual morning chores. He still did not understand that the morning's events would change his life for ever, that forty miles away in a police station in Southampton, he was being accused of murder. Harry Sinton believed (or hoped) he would be back on the farm in the afternoon, catching up on the work he had missed in the morning.

He recounted the story to the two policemen sitting across from him in the interview room, he managed to distance himself from the two killings, talking almost matter-of-factly about taking the lives of the two strangers who were coming towards him, threatening him, swearing. It was obvious he was still in deep shock. He told them how he accidentally fired the first shot at the van, how the older man had threatened him, the younger one backing him up. He said he had told them to stop, to leave him alone, at least he believed he had.

He looked a sad sight in the artificial light and confined bare walls of the interview room, hands in his lap, grasping his flat cap, eyes cast to the ground, dishevelled working clothes clad around his body, only looking up at the men across from him when hoping for some sign of comfort, talking in his slow Hampshire drawl. A man taken out of his natural surroundings and thrust into a completely alien environment.

The policemen were polite, offering coffee, which Harry declined, not wanting to put them to any trouble. They asked questions about time, reasons for having the gun out in the morning, if he knew the two men, seen the van in the area before, going over and over the morning's events, asking for clarifications on points already made.

"You say you asked them to stop, Mr. Sinton?"

"They kept coming at me, I didn't know what to do. I wanted them to stop, leave me alone. I was scared. I didn't mean to hurt anyone. I asked them to stop, go away."

At the end of the interview they explained that he would have to be kept in custody for the time being whilst further inquiries were made. They were very interested in the third man, the one who had run away. Had he seen him? Noticed what he was wearing? Harry could not be sure.

Harry had listened to his solicitor as he was told of the repercussions of his actions, but it did not really sink in. He was told he would be kept in custody until the police had finished their inquiries, or had enough evidence to charge him with a crime. (It was obvious that they had enough evidence, Harry had admitted to it himself, the solicitor refrained from stating that point.) The solicitor tried to comfort Harry, telling him he would probably face the Magistrates Court in a couple of days' time, if not tomorrow, depending on the speed of the police inquiry, and be bailed to attend trial at a Crown Court. He could be home in twenty-four hours. The solicitor also said he had called Gerald Evans, knowing they were old friends, and that he would be in later to see him. Still Harry couldn't comprehend the situation. The police themselves were wondering if the old man should be charged with murder, manslaughter, or be given a medal.

It had been three hours earlier when Harry had noticed the van in the barn. Now he sat on the edge of the solid bed in the cell of Annavale police station in shock, not believing the morning's events, expecting to be back home in the afternoon.

Paul Allen and Andy Goodman walked into the police station and told the officer on the desk that they had information concerning the deaths of Sean Robson and Billy Stevens. This was the first that this officer had heard of the killings, but he did know of Billy Stevens. He looked the two teenagers up and down and decided he had better follow up their story, there was something about their manner that spoke of fear. They were not the usual sullen, cocky type he saw slouching around on the streets and shopping malls of Southampton every day. They had the latest fashion clothes on, earrings in, and the younger of the two had his hair greased forward as was the wont of teenagers of today, but something in their manner made him suspicious. Then there was the reference to Billy Stevens, Mr. Big, small-time crook, or Mr. Small, big-time crook. Whatever you called him he was an evil man, often using young impressionable youths to do his dirty work for him.

The desk officer asked them to take a seat in the lobby and he would call someone to take their statements. He called up to the CID office on the second floor on the internal line and was staggered at the speed of the response. Two plain-clothed policemen came jogging down the stairs, only to slow-up (to give the appearance of calm) before they entered the foyer, through the electronically locked door, which led to the heart of the building. The two officers invited the teenagers into the nearest interview room and closed the door. The desk officer got on to the internal 'phone line again and succeeded in getting through to a friend who filled him in on the morning's goings-on.

"It has been an interesting morning. We had a call from Annavale police that one Sean Robson had been shot at the scene of a farm break-in, along with another man. Now you call up saying that you have two youths who say they have information on the deaths of Sean Robson and Billy Stevens. It looks like someone has finally taken-out Stevens."

When the two teenagers were seated and everyone seemed ready, the tape recorder was switched on. After the formalities of the time, date and who was present, one of the plain-clothed policemen asked the youths to expand on their statement given to the desk officer. Although a solicitor was offered, Paul and Andy decided against it, both wanting to get on and tell their stories.

Andy started the talking, hoping to show to Paul what he had to say to tie-in with his version. He told of a frightened phone call, a morning mercy-dash to a friend, the story (revised story) the friend had given him and the speed with which they had made it to this police station.

Paul, after his initial worry of making-up the main parts of his story, told of how he and Sean had been bullied into going on the job with Stevens. He stressed it was his first time, and then added it was Sean's first time as well. At this point the senior officer again offered the younger boy the use of a solicitor to sit-in on his statement if he wished, but Paul wanted to get the story off his chest, and declined. He told of the two farmyards they visited first, of how Stevens was in a black mood after the second, but livened up at the last. He needed no prompting from the two officers to carry on. Paul told of how Stevens had shouted orders at them to get the quad bike into the back of the van and then jumped into the front just as the farmer turned up.

"We tried to get out, but the farmer shot at the van and then Stevens got really mad, I mean real mad. He grabbed a baseball bat and was heading toward this bloke who had the gun. He was mad, out of his mind. Sean tried to pull him back but before I could go and help, this bloke shot Stevens, I mean blew 'im apart, I couldn't fucking believe it." Paul was caught up in his side of the story, he could give his version of events, get it off his chest, and it was all being recorded, that in itself must make his story true!

"Sorry," Paul apologised for his language "but he was ripped apart, and then this bloke turned the gun on Sean and . . . and . . . shot him too. Sean was trying to give up, he didn't need to be shot.

The bastard shot him. I ran like hell out of there. I wasn't going to hang around to be the next victim, this madman had killed Sean for no reason. He was trying to give up, I tell you. Sean was shouting and had his hands up. The bastard killed him for no reason."

"And then Andrew here picked you up?"

"No, no I had to hide from the man in the barn." Paul was enjoying himself, he was being listened to, he was the centre of attention, it didn't matter if he stretched the truth a bit more. "I had to get to the nearest phone without being caught. I didn't know if he was following me or not, I was scared man! But I kept my head, I got to Clayton, and then rang Andy."

The officers exchanged glances, realising the young man had finished with his story. They told Andrew Goodman he could go, as long as he left them his address and telephone number, and made himself available if they needed him again. They told Paul that he would be kept at the station while further inquiries were carried out, but his parents would be notified and were welcome to come down to the station to see him.

The two officers left the interview room and reported back to their superior, leaving the desk officer to attend to the two youths. They now had some serious work to do, not the least was to tell the next of kin that their loved ones were lying on their backs, in some farmer's barn, with their chest ripped open. The bodies would have to be identified before a post mortem could tell everyone what they could see for themselves. That the two intruders had died from a close-range blast from a shotgun, opening their chests to the cold morning air. They would have to liaise with the Annavale branch to verify the two versions of events, and then charge the necessary people with whatever they could stick on them.

First they would go to Stevens' flat in the high-rise block of flats north of the city. They knew the flat of old, either picking up Stevens to "help with inquiries" or to see what stolen property Stevens had forgotten to hide somewhere else rather than in his flat. This would not be a happy task, they knew Wendy Stevens would be there to greet them, and they knew she would not welcome them with open arms. So it was with no small amount of apprehension that they knocked on the door of number 126

Tamworth Flats, and waited for it to be opened.

"'Es not 'ere," Wendy informed them as soon as she saw the suits. She knew what they were, recognising the older one.

"We know that Wendy."

"Then why are you 'ere?" she demanded. She leant on the frame of the doorway, arms crossed, cigarette in her hand, dressed only in a bathrobe to keep her warm. At one point in her life she would have turned men's heads, thought the younger officer, still might do if she brushed herself up, he thought.

"We have some bad news Wendy, can we come in?"

"Not bloody likely, not if you ain't got a warrant. Anyway, bad news for me must be good news for you."

"You're not wrong there," thought both officers, but declined to tell Mrs. Wendy Stevens.

"Go on then, spit it out."

"We have reason to believe that your husband was involved in an attempted robbery . . . "

"I know nothin' about it," she injected.

"Please let me finish. We believed he was disturbed, and in the attempt to leave the scene he was shot."

"What?"

The officer had decided that there was no point trying to be subtle, to try and break the news easily. He had known the Stevens family for a long time, he knew what Billy could get up to, and how Wendy always protected him, even encouraged him on some of his worst offences. He felt no remorse in breaking the news to this woman, he even felt a little sensation of triumph in telling her.

"Billy is thought to have been shot dead in a bungled raid on a farm on the outskirts of Annavale."

"Piss off, you're windin' me up."

"We need the body identified, we were hoping you could assist us."

"I don't need this. Even if 'e is dead you lot know what 'e looks like, you've been 'assling 'im long enough. You identify 'im."

Even as she shouted this at the men standing in her doorway, her mind was racing. Billy had not returned from his morning's farm visits. She had not started to worry yet, he often stopped off at Bob's place after his morning's work, especially if it had gone well. She was damned if she was going to stand there and have these bastards gloat at her. She slammed the door shut in their faces and returned to watch her morning television, listening to Richard and Judy extolling the virtues of a holiday in St. Lucia. She snubbed out her now lifeless cigarette and lit another, she decided she would ring Bob later, give the police enough time to get away from her door, and find out were the bloody hell Billy was.

"Well, that was the easy one over," the senior officer grinned at his partner.

"If I didn't know you better, I would say you enjoyed that."

"Not me," he assured him as they walked back towards the car, wrapping his coat around his body in a vain attempt to keep warm.

"She turn you on with that outfit?" the younger officer asked.

"Oh, she was a looker at one time, but always an evil bitch, even before she hooked up with Stevens. Why, did it turn you on?"

"I've had worse," he joked as they descended the litter-covered stairs back to their squad car.

The address given for Sean Robson was not far away from the Stevens' flat, but in a much better part of town, in a terrace house over-looking a park. Ringing the door bell, and knocking loudly on the door brought no reward. A work-place visit was on the cards. They traced Mr. Robson to his painting and decorating firm, his wife was the secretary and the force behind the business. Mr. Robson was out on site, not far from the office, and a call on his mobile phone had him driving back. Mrs. Robson was polite and courteous to the two officers, she had nothing to worry about, her records were up to date, no wrong-doings were going on that she knew of, and she would know of them alright, she ran a very tight ship.

The officers accepted the offer of coffee, and waited for the arrival of Mr. Robson before they revealed the reason for their visit. Mrs. Robson expected it to be regarding one of the employees, some of whom had attracted the attention of the police before, nothing major, but enough to keep a closer eye on them.

They all heard Mr. Robson's diesel van pull up outside the office, and a moment later he entered the room from the outside door, at the same instant the two officers stood up.

"This must be serious."

"Mr. and Mrs. Robson, I'm afraid we have some bad news concerning your son."

This was going to be harder than he had expected. It was apparent from their manner and surroundings that they had worked hard for what they had got. An honest, hard-working family. Now he was going to tell them that their son had been shot dead in a farm raid, in the early hours of the morning, almost forty miles away.

"Sean was involved in an incident earlier this morning."

"Sean!" she cried in disbelief.

A car crash was the first thought through their minds. Incident, accident, they heard it in the same way. Sean had told them he was out early in the morning, with his mate Paul Allen, to check out a second-hand trails bike for sale on the outskirts of London. They needed to leave early to see the bike first, and also to be back in time for college. Sean was taking his A-levels, Paul was on a work experience programme. A friend with a transit van was going to help bring it back if they bought it. They had seen nothing wrong with this, Sean had worked hard with his father over his school and college holidays, and had always said he would buy a trails bike with the money he made. It was not the first time he had travelled in the early morning up to London, Bristol or Reading to look at a second-hand bike. Although, he still had not found one he liked.

Mr. Robson stared in disbelief, Mrs. Robson shot questions at the officers.

"What sort of accident? Is he alright?"

"Incident, Mrs. Robson, Sean was believed to be in an incident. We believe he was in a bungled raid on a farm, on the outskirts of Annavale. It happened in the early hours. Do you know where Sean was earlier this morning?"

"You must have the wrong lad, Sean was off up to London, looking for a motor bike." She looked at her husband for confirmation.

"Do you mean Mark?" Mr. Robson asked cautiously. It couldn't be Sean, he thought to himself, not young Seanie.

The two officers looked at each other before continuing.

"The name we have is Sean Robson, from your home address. I'm sorry we have to break it to you like this, but there is no other way. We need to have his body identified."

"Body!" she shrieked "body, what do you mean, body?"

The younger officer winced at his partner's last statement, he could have handled that a bit better, he thought to himself. The elder officer once again realised there was no easy way of breaking this news softly, it had to be hard and fast, but unlike last time he gained no satisfaction from the thought of doing it.

"At a farmyard outside Annavale, earlier this morning, we believe an attempted break-in was disturbed by the farmer. The result of which was the death of two of the burglars, one of which was a young man who the police at the incident identified from information in the wallet found on the body as one Sean Robson."

The Robsons stared at the plain-clothed policeman in bewilderment.

"You must have the wrong lad, this can't be right. Sean will be at college" Mr. Robson argued.

"Where is the body?" Mrs. Robson asked, her voice shaking. She wanted to get this cleared up, the matter-of-fact statement the officer had given had frightened her.

"It is at Annavale Hospital, we can arrange for a car to take you there."

"If you are wrong about this . . . " Mr. Robson left the threat unspoken.

Betty Sinton was in a state of shock. George had stayed with her as the police took her husband away, offering coffee, tea, words of encouragement. Finally, in desperation, she offered to ring the Sintons' friends and farming neighbours Mike and Sarah Cairns. Betty agreed to this with a slight nod of her head and continued to stare at the Aga, Bracken at her side, head in her lap. George found the number in the small address book by the telephone in the office. Sarah Cairns answered the phone and without too much information on the morning's events agreed to come over and comfort Mrs. Sinton who 'had just received some bad news'.

"Mrs. Cairns will be here in a minute, Betty," he told her.

George would stay with her until his relief came, and then he would return to the barns and get things sorted. Questions swamped his mind. Should he ring the Sintons' children? What work would the police allow him to do in the barn? When would Harry Sinton return? Should he let his wife know? What had Ken told her? He felt helpless as he sat across from Betty Sinton; he needed to go back to the farmyard and get the morning's work under way.

He decided against ringing the Sintons' children, Sarah Cairns could do that when she got here. He wanted out of the confines of this house, he wanted to do something, anything, as long as it was familiar. Feed the sheep, move the ewes and lambs, bed up the pens with fresh straw. He longed for normality, but in the same instance knew that life on Downlands Farm had taken an irreparable turn for the worse.

Sarah Cairns arrived five minutes later, at the back door of the house. She had circumnavigated the police by taking a side track which led parallel to the barns and on to the farmhouse. She opened and walked through the doorway as she knocked and was met by George who ushered her into the back kitchen.

"What's all this about, George? I saw some police vehicles in the yard, where is Harry?"

George held up his hand to stop the flow of questions; he gave Sarah a quick summary of the morning's events, Harry's disturbance of the break-in, the shooting, the police arriving, statements taken, and finally Harry being taken away. Sarah Cairns' colour drained from her face.

"Mrs. Cairns, could you please look after Betty, I have to get back to the farm. Could you see if you could get hold of their children, I don't really know what else to do."

"When is Harry returning?"

"We don't know. I'm sure Martin will be able to get here to help, he is based at Dartmouth I think, and Ann is only just up the road, I'm sure she can come over. I really do need to get back to the farm."

"Yes, yes, you go and organise that, I'll look after Betty and ring her children. What an awful thing to happen." Sarah Cairns did not expand on who had her sympathy, the Sintons or the two dead burglars lying on the cold concrete floor of the main barn.

"Thank you Mrs. Cairns."

"Don't be silly, get on and go, please keep me informed if anything else happens." And with that she pushed past George and disappeared into the kitchen, looking for her friend and confidante.

George retrieved his wellington boots, only then realising he had left his coat on through the morning proceedings, and opened the back door to escape back to the farmyard. As he closed the door he could hear the sounds of a kettle being filled and encouraging words from Sarah Cairns.

It was not that he did not trust Ken and Andy to get on with the important work, but George liked to be "on hand" and able to supervise, especially if Harry Sinton was away for any reason. He took the responsibility left to him by his boss very seriously, never slackening off if he was left in charge. Harry Sinton would sometimes comment that he should go away more often, but all on the farm knew he could not leave the place for longer than a weekend, maybe a week now two grandchildren had turned up.

George entered the yard, to be met by a uniformed policeman he did not recognise from earlier.

"Sorry sir, this is a restricted area, you shouldn't be here. How did you get through the cordon?"

"I've come from the farmhouse, I don't know of any cordon. I'm George Stone the foreman, I need to know what we can do here, the sheep need feeding and moving."

The policeman asked him to wait there and left to find a superior and see what the answer would be. He returned moments later and asked George to follow him into the main barn. George was struck by the number of people inside the barn, all milling about with a purpose (or so it seemed). Some of the people had white overalls covering their body from head to toe, others had green overalls. There were a number of uniformed policemen and just as many wearing jackets and ties underneath their thin raincoats. The bodies had been moved, only a chalk outline giving any evidence of their final position. The chalk mark showing the position of Billy Stevens could be identified as an outline of a figure, but the chalk mark for Sean Robson was a semi-circle at the bottom of the sheep pen he had fallen into, with two arrows pointing towards that pen. Now and again camera flashes lit the barn as the police photographer recorded the scene for posterity.

As George took in the spectacle before him, another uniformed officer broke from a group of men standing around the front of the van and walked over towards him.

"What needs to be done in this barn?" he asked without any introduction.

"Er, the sheep and lambs on the left side need to be moved out," George answered, waving towards the left-hand side of the barn. He was about to continue until the officer interjected.

"Why?"

"To make space for the new-born lambs from the other two sheds."

As he was answering the questions, he was looking around hoping to see his workmates, but to no avail.

"We want to disturb the crime scene as little as possible. Can you keep the sheep where they are for today at least?"

"I suppose so, I would need to have a look around and see the numbers that have lambed. We need to feed the ewes that are penned up; they could last another day without being bedded up." George was talking more to himself than the policeman in front of him. The policeman had heard his first comment and had then switched off to the expanded explanation.

"Good, do what you need to, ask before you disturb anything in this barn, and if you find anything that you think might be of interest to us, even if you think it might be insignificant, tell us straight away." And with that the officer spun round and returned to his colleagues by the van.

George was left with the policeman who had stopped him in the yard.

"Could you tell me where the two lads that were here have gone?"

"Annavale Hospital morgue I would think."

George took a while to understand the answer: why would Ken and Andy be at the mortuary? He then realised the policeman had referred to the two bodies.

"No, sorry I meant the two farm workers. I need help to get

things done and there were two men here earlier, waiting for you lot to arrive."

"They were probably told to wait outside," he informed George, and then left to resume his cold patrol of the farmyard.

George headed out of the barn in search of his colleagues, working out the tasks that needed to be done as he made his way to his cottage. He would bet that Ken had returned there, taking Andy along, saying that that would be the obvious place to find them, sitting in the kitchen with a cup of coffee, gossiping over the mornings events, bringing George's wife Sandy up to date with the news, enjoying their new-found fame. They probably had not been off the telephone since they got there, and Sandy would have put off going to work; but when she did, boy would she have some story to tell.

George's hunch was rewarded by two pairs of wellingtons left outside his kitchen door: Ken had not disappointed. George found them around the kitchen table, cordless telephone resting in the middle, coffee mugs on place mats.

"How are they?" Sandy asked.

"Harry's been taken down to the station to be interviewed, Sarah Cairns is with Betty, she is going to call the kids, Betty is in a bad way, shock I think." George tried not to look too upset at the picture in front of him, he knew people would gossip and speculate, but it didn't make it any easier to swallow. He just wanted to busy himself with work and keep the farm running until Harry Sinton returned, hopefully later that day.

"I'm not surprised, poor dear."

"We have work to do, come on you two." He mustered the two workers who were looking guilty, caught deserting their duties.

"Yes, I have to get going myself, I'm nearly two hours late." Sandy had purposely hung around hoping for some more information to arm herself with before spreading the story around the convenience store in nearby Clayton, where she worked.

George led the others back to the farmyard. He had to check around the lambing barns in case any more had lambed, to count how many isolating pens were left, hopefully enough to take the number of ewes that would lamb in the next twenty-four hours. If not, the stronger lambs and ewes would have to be put straight out into the paddocks, by-passing the main barn completely. The paddocks themselves had to be emptied of ewes and lambs to make way for the new batch. The sheep not lambed would have to be let out and fed their supplementary feed in the two "park" fields, which meant the sheep-feed would have to be transferred onto a trailer pulled by one of the tractors, and if the police wouldn't let them move the already bagged sheep-feed, a new load would have to be bagged-up from the bulk bin. The ewes and lambs inside the main barn would need their morning's supply of hay, sheep nuts and water. The hay racks in the lambing sheds would need restocking before the return of the sheep in the "parks". New straw bedding was needed in the lambing sheds; that may have to wait until tomorrow, he thought to himself. He also kept reminding himself not to forget the three pet lambs that would need feeding with milk that had to be prepared from specially powdered milk for lambs.

That was George's immediate list of chores and didn't include putting the rubber rings on the lambs' testicles and tails, numbering the ewes and lambs for easy identification when they were finally let out into the fields, and generally keeping an eye on anything that might need extra attention. He had plenty to keep himself and his workmates busy, even without any interference that may come from the police; but still his mind would wander, conjuring up images of Harry Sinton in an interview room, huddled in a stiff chair, answering question after question on the morning's killings.

Telephone calls exchanged between Annavale and Southampton police stations showed a difference in the two stories being told by the respective parties, and a second interview was set up for each person who was being held, "helping with inquiries".

Harry Sinton stared in disbelief as the officers told him of the accusations being made against him. Murdering an unarmed teenager, who was surrendering at the time. A teenager, he thought to himself; seventeen to be accurate they had said. He remembered his only son Martin at the age of seventeen, he was at college doing his A-levels, hoping to go to university, and Ann, two years younger, following her brother in the same hope. He remembered their happiness and love of life. His shoulders slumped, his body seemed to deflate. His will to clear up this nightmare deserted him. He sat on the edge of his chair, head down, staring at the table top before him, he didn't want to meet the eyes of the two accusers before him.

"I didn't want to hurt anyone," he whispered almost to himself.

"Do you want to change your statement, Mr. Sinton?"

Harry's solicitor, accompanied by Harry's old friend Gerald Evans, had been summoned back for the interview. He told him not to answer if he didn't feel up to it, and complained to the officers about the treatment of his client.

"All we are asking is if Mr. Sinton would like to change his statement in the light of new evidence."

"What new evidence?" the solicitor for Harry asked. "The word of a member of the gang that carried out this raid. This is preposterous, my client does not need to change his statement as I see it. He has told you what happened in the farmyard early this morning, it is a simple case of self-defence against violent criminals who had already carried out one theft and were in the process of stealing Mr. Sinton's property."

"That may be the case, but we have a witness in Southampton who says that Mr. Sinton fired at an unarmed teenager who was giving himself up at the time."

Harry continued to stare at the table top; all eyes were now on this man waiting for some sort of response.

"I, he didn't give up. I didn't want to do it. They were coming at me. I didn't mean to do it, I wanted them to leave" he mumbled to himself. It was dawning on Harry the seriousness of the situation, he was being accused of murder. "What are you going to do with me now?" he asked.

"You will be held here for the time being while we continue our investigations. Your solicitor will tell your family of the situation."

Gerald Evans smiled weakly at his old friend and gave him a comforting pat on the back as Harry was led away back to his cell. He knew he had a lot of work to do for his friend; he had to select a Barrister, and get a team of people together to formulate a defence, whatever charge they brought against Harry Sinton. Gerald Evans just hoped that Harry's version could be shown to be the truth, but he also knew the quirks of the law and its fickleness. This was far from an open and shut case.

Paul's parents had been summoned to the police station; they arrived separately and cold looks were exchanged between them. They had been separated for four years and it wasn't an amicable parting. They sat in on the interview, hearing the morning's events summarised by the police, and with each statement the police would ask Paul if this was right, if he remembered anything new. Smug looks on the two officers' faces showed Paul they knew something different and were just playing with him, letting him dig a bigger hole for himself. Mrs. Allen sat solemn-faced, Mr. Allen seething with anger against his son.

"You had better not be lying boy, you're in enough trouble as it is."

"Do you want to change your statement Paul?" the senior policeman asked for the second time.

"Answer the man, boy."

Paul looked to his mother for comfort; he was too scared to change his statement. He had had time in the cell to realise the trouble he was in: not from the police but from his dead colleague's friends and relatives. Sean's brother for one, and any of Stevens' dodgy friends; not that Paul knew any of them, but he imagined them all in a shadowy, smoke-filled room, discussing Paul's ability not to talk to the police. What to do if he did.

"We have a witness saying that your friend Sean Robson wasn't giving himself up, in fact he was backing Stevens up, threatening the farmer. The farmer is well over sixty you know Paul, not much of a match compared to Stevens, a man of his reputation."

A witness: the words stung Paul like an electric shock; a witness. He was sure it was only him and the mad old man in the barn. Could there have been another person in the barn all the time; why hadn't they shown themselves when they first got there?

"Did you back-up Stevens as well Paul, three of you against one old man? That's better odds, isn't it Paul? Did you show Stevens you were up for the big time?"

"You can't talk to Paul like that!" Mrs. Allen came to Paul's defence. "He told you what happened and you're treating him like the criminal, like the murderer. You should thank him for being so honest and coming to you, telling the truth: not like that farmer and his stories. Why don't you believe my boy?"

"Shut up, woman." It was Mr. Allen's turn to put the pressure back onto Paul. "He is a criminal, he admitted being at the barn . . . "

"He was bullied into going, he said so."

"Don't be so bloody stupid. He is a little idiot, I bet he followed like a lost pup. You are in serious trouble boy, and you had better start telling the truth or you will regret it."

Mr. Allen blamed Paul for all his woes. Before Paul, he and his wife had a good relationship, both with good jobs, money coming in. As soon as Paul arrived unexpectedly, his wife lost all interest in him, and concentrated her love on her new baby. Income went down, and expenditure went up. Paul could do no wrong, and Mr. Allen just got in the way. This led to his downward spiral of drink, and advances to any female that was available (and some not available), both of which contrived to lose him his job, his house and his wife. And now she was backing Paul up, even though he had admitted his part in the raid.

The two officers were happy to let the Allens fight it out between themselves, Mr. Allen doing their job for them, pressurising Paul, threatening him.

"What's the charge for this sort of thing?" Allen senior asked. "Obstructing the course of interviews or something."

"Obstructing inquiries: it is very serious, especially in the case of murder. You do remember there have been two killings, Paul?"

"'Course I fucking know, I was there, I saw it. I saw Sean blown apart." Paul was now in tears, he didn't know what to do. He couldn't change his statement now, the old man would have won if he did. He saw this as a straight fight between him and the madman in the barn. But they had another witness they said, could they be lying? He would still have to face Sean's family and even some of Stevens' friends. But if they found out he was lying, would he go to jail? He couldn't risk asking, they would then know he was covering up something.

"Mum, I've told them everything. Make them stop, please."

"Don't you go crying to your mother, boy; if she had been harder on you from the start you wouldn't be the toe-rag you are now."

"Don't you start blaming me; if you had been about more, been more of a father."

"This isn't getting us anywhere" the duty solicitor for the Allens cut in warily, he was tired of listening to the two parents fighting.

"I think we will take Paul back to his cell and let him think this thing over a bit more. Interview stopped at," the policeman checked his watch, "twelve-thirty."

Wendy Stevens dragged herself away from the television and to the telephone. She knew Bob's number off by heart, she had to. Stevens never left any incriminating contact numbers around the house, he believed himself too smart for that. Nothing to connect him with his various fence friends or any other undesirables. He would never ring them from the flat, always on a public telephone, usually in the *King's Head*. He liked to think he was too smart for the police, it massaged his ego.

The telephone rang for what seemed like hours to Wendy before it was picked up. She could picture Bob Richards at the other end of the line, standing in his workshop which passed for a garage-cum-scrapyard, podgy hands covered in grease and oil, overalls smeared with the same lubricants, hair slicked back, three days growth of stubble covering his double chins. She had been to the 'Garage' a number of times, usually to pick up Stevens after he had dropped off a stolen car that Bob had ordered that week.

"Richard's Repairs and Recoveries," he announced on the other end of the line.

"Bob, 'ave you seen Bill this mornin'?"

"That you Wendy?"

"Course it's me, 'as Bill been in this mornin'?"

"I've been expecting him all morning, I had some stuff on order with him, he said he would be dropping them off this morning. Phoned me a couple of days ago saying he would be in."

"But 'e 'asn't?"

"Not yet. What's your problem Wend?"

"Nothin'," and with that she put the telephone down. Where is he? She thought. She looked over to the wall clock and noted the time, twelve-thirty, the *King's Head* will be open by now. She had to get out, she decided to walk to the pub and ask around there.

"I bet the stupid sod's ballsed up the mornin's work and is now suppin' at the bar," she muttered to herself.

Chief Inspector Anthony Kemp slumped down in his chair behind his desk at Annavale police station, and picked up the telephone and dialled the Southampton police department he had been liaising with all morning. At the same time he started to unwrap the sandwich he had just bought from the station's canteen. As he waited to be connected through to his colleagues handling the Southampton end of the investigation he surveyed the scene through his office internal windows onto the "shop floor" of the Criminal Investigation Department, his department. Plain-clothed officers were in constant motion, either behind their desks writing reports, on telephones, or striding from one area of the office to another. There was a constant buzz about the room.

"What have you got?" Kemp asked as soon as he was through.

The police had been busy at both ends of the inquiry, taking statements from anyone connected with the main players of the crime.

"The youth Allen isn't changing his statement yet; we have left him in the cells to sweat a little, we will give him another go later. I'm sure he is holding something back, if not completely lying through his teeth. He was in above his head and he is scared shitless. Give us a little time and he will squeal like a stuck pig."

"The next of kin have been informed, the dead boy's parents are on their way to your town's morgue now. As for Stevens' next of kin, she wasn't particularly forthcoming, so we got the next best thing, the publican of his local, the *King's Head*. A Mr. John Smith believe it or not. He hasn't said much, probably waiting to find out what he should be saying before he does, but he has agreed to go and identify the body."

"We know who they are," Kemp told himself more than his

colleague on the telephone. "We know who killed them, he admitted it himself. What we have to work out is who we charge with what."

"We can charge the boy with burglary for one, he had entered the barn with the intent to steal the quad, or whatever the thing is called. He has basically admitted it, although he said he was bullied into it. He has no former convictions on record, although he is quite well known with the boys on the beat around his home estate apparently; nothing major, just graffiti, criminal damage, and a spot of joy-riding. That sort of thing. Always got away with a slap on the wrist. We could try fleeing the scene of the crime as well, maybe?"

"I don't blame him for that. OK, remind him of those little misdemeanours in the next interview. What else have you got?"

"The van was stolen around a year ago from somewhere outside Bristol, but the number plates had been changed to a set that tallied with a blue Ford transit from the Reading area that hasn't been stolen. So if it was ever reported looking suspicious in an area, it would come back clean on the police computer."

"William Stevens is a well-known crook, small time, nasty man. A string of convictions dating back as far as you like, mostly with aggravated assault. Lately he has been moving into auto theft, again small time. Likes to use local youths to help, boosts his ego. They look up to him or something."

"Sean Robson is a different matter, no former convictions, good wholesome lad, from all accounts given by his teachers at the local college. The workmen at his parents' business back up the description, saying he was a hard-working lad. No angel, liked a beer or two, but nothing serious. We haven't really worked out how the two boys got in with Stevens, maybe at the local watering hole. We will ask Paul Allen later. The Robsons have an older son as well, one of their workers told us. They don't like to talk about him apparently, not a nice man. They don't know where he is, and don't care."

"Well, follow up anything, there is a difference in the two stories that could mean a hell of a lot to the people on trial."

"The difference between going to prison, and not?"

"I think this one is going to go down to the wire," Kemp sighed. "Judge, jury and all. The old boy farmer will plead self-defence and will probably get it with Stevens, but he could go down on the second body. An unarmed teenager, who his mate says was giving up at the time, could be a tricky one."

"So you think manslaughter for Stevens and murder for Robson?"

"I'm not thinking anything at the moment."

"Can the forensic tell you if the boy's arms where up at the time of being shot?"

"What, like in a surrender? I don't know. But even if the boy had his arms down he could have been walking backwards, trying to tell the old boy sorry. No, it's Paul Allen's word against Harry Sinton's as far as I can tell. Try and sweat Allen a bit more, see if he changes his story at all; there is no rush on this, we don't have to charge anyone for another twenty-four hours. I believe the farmer as far as his statement is concerned. I think that is what he honestly believes happened, but a shock like that can do funny things with your memory. Perhaps the boy wasn't given any time to back-off, Harry must have been scared out of his wits with Stevens bearing down at him."

"I bet the two youths weren't full of courage after Stevens was taken out either."

"No, I expect not," Kemp agreed. "Anyway it is not up to us to sort this thing out, we just have to bring them to Court, let the jury decide. Keep me informed on any changes."

Kemp rang off and stared at his sandwich. I really could do with something hot, he thought to himself, something to warm my bones with.

Mrs. Robson collapsed on seeing her son's pale face staring, unseeing, back at her. All the way to Annavale she had been telling herself it couldn't be Sean, maybe they had got it wrong and it was her oldest son Mark. She had long ago stopped feeling guilty of wishing her oldest son dead. Sean would be at college studying for his A-levels, she told herself, he had his whole future ahead of him, they had such high expectations for him. He hadn't done anything wrong in his life, or so she had thought. But now she didn't know. What had he done before this break-in, what hadn't he told them before? How well can you know your own son?

Mr. Robson managed to keep his emotions hidden by caring for his wife, putting his arm around her and guiding her out of the cold, sterile mortuary towards the closest seat he could find. The accompanying police officers kept a respectful distance.

Mr. John Smith arrived just as the Robsons were leading each other out. He took in the scene before him without breaking his furrowed expression, the Robsons took no notice of him. The police officers exchanged knowing looks. On seeing the body, John Smith said, "That's Stevens" without emotion. He had known Stevens almost seven years, but never really changed his first impression of him, a horrible, nasty man, capable of most things and ably backed-up by his wife. Certainly a man who you wouldn't like to be against you even less than be on your side.

Smith had always walked a fine line with Stevens in his pub, especially if the man had had a lot of beer on board, mixed with a bad day. He couldn't ban the man without some sort of repercussion, broken pub window or slashed car tyres; he had found that out to his cost, although he could never prove it. Nobody else in the pub would ever have backed Smith up, fearing their own well-being. At the present time John Smith honestly believed he could not feel less emotion towards seeing another human being lying dead on a metal slab.

John Smith had not been told the full story of the morning's events, only that the body of William Stevens needed to be identified, therefore it was no fault of Smith's that he didn't connect the couple sitting down on the row of seats outside the mortuary with the body he had just seen. Smith knew Sean Robson from the pub, a nice enough lad, but keeping the wrong company with Stevens. He had never met Sean's parents. As he walked back past them his eyes connected with Mr. Robson's. Smith realised these people must have lost someone very dear to them; Mr. Robson wondered how a man could show so little emotion in a place like this.

Wendy Stevens entered the *King's Head* and could not see her husband, there was only four other people in the pub, two youths she didn't know playing pool, old Archie Barns sitting at the bar reading the racing page, coughing, and the latest bar girl looking bored behind the bar.

"John 'ere?" she asked the apathetic bar girl.

"Na, he went out. Dunno when he's back."

"You seen Billy this mornin 'arry?"

Harry stopped studying the form and noticed Wendy for the first time.

"John will be back soon Wendy," he wheezed.

"That's not what I asked, 'ave you seen Billy this mornin'?"

"No." Archie Barns didn't elaborate on his answer. He had been in the bar when the police turned up and asked Smith to identify the body of William Stevens. He was going to hang around the bar, putting off his trip to the bookies, to quiz Smith when he returned. He thought better of it now, he didn't want to be around when Smith returned and told Wendy where he had been, and why. He wondered why the police had not asked Wendy to identify her husband's body, then dismissed the idea when he thought of Wendy's likely reaction. He would finish his pint of stout and shuffle away, returning later to hear all about it.

"You two know Billy Stevens?" Wendy shouted to the pair at the pool table, only to be met by shakes of the head.

"Billy Stevens?" the bar girl asked, looking interested for the first time.

"Yea, my Billy."

Archie Barns shrank in his seat, this woman behind the bar was going to blunder into the conversation and reap the full fury of Wendy Stevens.

"He was in last night," she said, hoping this would help the woman in front of her. She had not been at the bar when Smith was called away and didn't know the reason for her boss's sudden departure. She had been out at the back, disposing of the empties from the night before when Smith asked her to mind the bar while he was out.

"I couldn't give a toss about last night, I want to know where 'e is now!"

"I was only trying to help," she said indignantly.

Wendy's response was halted as John Smith entered the bar, having just been dropped off by the police. He stopped in his tracks, staring at Wendy.

"'As Billy been in?"

"Do you want to come through to the back Wendy?"

"Why can't any of you wankers give me a straight answer? Has Billy been in this morning?"

"No he hasn't Wendy. If you will come with me to the back I'll tell you why."

"Tell me now."

"Please Wendy, let's go through the back."

"Look I've had enough of this crap. The police and now you lot. Just tell me where Billy is."

John Smith sighed, he knew the police had been around to Wendy before him, and that she had been her usual helpful self. It was now up to him to back up the police's story.

"I was asked to identify Billy's body this morning Wendy, The police took me to Annavale and I saw Billy in the morgue . . . it was him."

Silence hung in the bar, Wendy stared at Smith, and then looked from person to person, defying them to say anything. They all looked away from her glare. She then pushed past Smith and walked out of the pub, heading for the police station. She knew the way well. John Smith resumed his position behind the bar, ready for the questions of his morning's exploits, the first of many inquiries he expected as the day wore on and the story did its rounds.

The news of the two killings at Downlands Farm was spreading like wildfire around the villages. Farmers' wives rushed out to find their husbands to tell them the story, husbands working in their farm office rushed to tell their wives. All work stopped on local farms as farmers and farm workers discussed possibilities and probabilities. Telephone conversations were exchanged, everyone wanting to be first to tell the grisly news. Anyone who 'phoned found no answer at the Sintons' home, (Sarah Cairns had left the telephone off the hook after she had called the children). Some thought about going over, on the excuse of offering help, others thought it better to stay away and wait for a while before offering their sympathy and support.

George Hollis had just left the telephone, reporting a break-in and a stolen quad bike to the police (he had to wait until nine o'clock to report it to his local station as they didn't start work until then), when his phone rang. It was Tom Whitworth, a farming friend for many years. Had George heard the news? After listening to the mornings revelations, he rang the police again to tell of his suspicions of a connection between his break in and the alleged shootings at Downlands Farm. He was told officers would be around shortly.

The local newspaper was first to hear about the double-shooting. Whether they were told by a member of the local police, or by a helpful member of the public was not divulged, but the news network started to get to work. The local paper was only printed once a week, and then on a Friday. It had an arrangement with the local radio station that any and all information would be shared between the two; it was the local paper, therefore, that put the local radio station on to the story. The local radio station first rang the police for verification, and were rewarded with some very sketchy information. Yes, the police had been called to a farm on the outskirts of Annavale that morning; yes there were reports of casualties; no, no further information was available at the present time.

The local radio station then despatched an outside-broadcast van and reporter to find this farm, meanwhile broadcasting that:

> '. . . unconfirmed reports are coming in of a double murder, on a farm on the outskirts of Annavale . . .'

It did not take other newspapers, radio and television stations long to get wind of these reports, and more reporters, backed up by their technical support teams, hurried off in search of this farm that could give them this morning's lead story. They were rewarded at mid-day by the police media-liaison officer making a statement at the farm entrance gates:

> *'The police can confirm that an investigation into the deaths of two men in relation to an attempted break in at this location is continuing. The names of the two men are being withheld until their next-of-kin have been informed. I can report that two other men are in custody helping us with our inquiries.'*

A barrage of questions was aimed at the officer from the assembled pack of Press men and women, the officer held up his hand in resignation to ward off the questions, he had nothing further to add, and walked back to the barn. The assembled media pack then turned and scuttled back to their respective positions and filled in any gaps to the story they could. The whole circus of events was watched by inquisitive villagers who had emerged from their homes to observe the drama being played out on their doorsteps.

Wendy stormed into the police station and challenged the young officer at the front desk.

"I want to see someone about Billy Stevens."

"Popular bloke today," the young officer replied coolly. "Please have a seat, I'll get someone for you. Who will I say is here?"

"Wendy Stevens."

The young officer took this in his stride and rang the message up to the second floor. After a few moments the same two plain-clothed policeman that had visited Wendy earlier that morning appeared through the doorway.

"Hello again Wendy, would you like to come through?"

Wendy was now wondering what she was doing there, what help could the police give her, they had hassled her and Billy all their lives. She started to feel unsure of herself, the idea of being without Billy slowly creeping up on her.

"I want to see my 'usband," she couldn't bring herself to say husband's body.

"Please come through Wendy and we will go through

everything with you." The officer hoped Wendy would fill in some of the missing pieces to the morning's jigsaw, but he knew he wouldn't get much, not from Wendy Stevens.

They ushered her into an empty interview room, told her it wasn't a formal interview, just an informal chat to bring Wendy up-to-date with the morning's events. They told her of the break-in, and the killings, how John Smith at the pub had identified the body.

"I want to see the . . . I want to see Billy," Wendy repeated. She was starting to shake, but she held back the tears. She would never let these bastards see her cry, she told herself.

"We can arrange that Wendy, can you add anything to the morning's events?" he asked in a vain attempt to extract some additional information from Wendy Stevens.

She just looked at him and repeated her request.

The Robsons had been dropped back at their home, neither wanted to be dropped at the office, not wanting to drive, not wanting to do anything that involved thinking. Mr. Robson supported his wife from the police car, into the house, and on to the sofa in the front room. He promised her a cup of tea, and left her staring at the blank black screen of the television in the corner of the room. He filled the electric kettle, set the teapot ready to be filled and made his way to the telephone. He rang the office without thinking and started to listen to his wife on the answer machine before putting down the receiver and dialling a second time, getting through to his foreman on his mobile. The conversation was laboured, the foreman already knowing the background to the morning's events from the police inquiring on Sean Robson's character. They skimmed around any real conversation, Mr. Robson just asking for his and his wife's cars to be brought around and the office to be checked in the evening and morning for any messages. He would try and get to work as soon as possible. His foreman reassured him that they could cope, and to take his time.

Mr. Robson then returned to the kitchen, made the tea and took it through to his wife. She was still sitting on the edge of the sofa, staring blankly at the lifeless television set, still with her coat on.

He sat next to her, put his arm around her and sat quietly, both not touching the tea. Their world had been shattered, the reason they worked, the reason they saved, the reason they lived had just been snatched away from them. Nothing could bring him back, nothing could change the past, and now they could see no future.

When Wendy Stevens was returned to her flat after being driven to see her husband's body, she could contain her anguish no longer, she thrashed and kicked her way through the flat. Smashing plates that had been left on the cluttered dining table, overturning chairs, picking up ash-trays and hurling them at the walls, kicking out at anything in her way, tearing at posters on the wall, curtains, anything she could get her hands on, screaming at the world against her. She stumbled into the kitchen, pushing the dirty pots and pans, piled high on the work surfaces, onto the floor, kicking at them as they fell, the noise giving body to her wails. It wouldn't be until much later that she would notice the gash on her right arm, blood spilling down to her hand.

She staggered back into the sitting room and fell onto the sofa, whimpering. She curled up into a ball and lay shaking, tears staining her face. She knew her so-called friends would desert her now, they had only stayed loyal before due to fear of her Billy. She had nothing, they lived from one crime to another, dole money and housing allowance both relied on Billy, both fraudulent. She would be kicked out of this almost luxury flat compared to what she had been in before she had hooked up with Billy. She had laughed at the people she had left behind in their cramped, dirty, dangerous bedsits, mocked them. Now she would be sent back there, at the mercy of her vengeful neighbours. She knew she was completely alone.

George Stone stood still for what seemed like the first time that day. He had busied himself with the day's chores, always keeping Ken and Andy occupied with something, trying to keep them away from the mounting number of Press reporters that were hovering at the farm gate. The police guard kept them off the property, although you always thought you were being watched, listened to, filmed. They had worked through their lunch-break, Andy and

Ken kindly offering George some of their sandwiches (maybe in return for the countless number of cups of coffee they had consumed at his kitchen table). He had worked around the police the best he could, giving them a wide berth, not noticing anything suspicious to call their attention to.

They all had been formally interviewed, but could shed little light on the actual events of the morning, only repeating what they had seen and done when they arrived at seven that morning. George had confirmed that a fox had been taking some of the weaker lambs in the nearby paddocks, and that Harry Sinton had been talking of taking his shotgun out with him in the morning for a couple of days.

The sun was now setting, the promised snow had not materialised, the banks of clouds had dispersed, leaving a clear sky showing the first stars gleaming out of the dusky heavens, threatening a hard frost for the night. He had sent his two colleagues home, organising who would take which watch of the barns that night. No one mentioned their apprehension in returning to the farmyard in the dead of night, but the promise by the police that a guard would be stood by the gate eased their worries a little.

The police and their entourage had left some time earlier, taking the van with them, leaving only the two policeman at the farm gate, sitting quietly in their squad car, offering thanks to the villagers who had kept them supplied with coffee and cakes most of the afternoon (the villagers had ignored the hopeful looks of the reporters and photographers as they delivered the steaming coffee pots to the two policemen). They had asked George not to disturb the main barn too much as they may need to return as the investigation continued. They had roped off the main area of concern, containing the chalk figures of William Stevens and Sean Robson, with their yellow plastic police tape, congealed blood evident on the floor.

George Stone surveyed the scene of calm before him. Ewes were laid down on the straw, munching away at the latest round of hay placed in their pens, lambs were either settled down next to their mothers, or bouncing around in the confines of the pens. Now and again a bleat could be heard from one of the lambing barns over the noise of ewes rustling straw and chewing hay. He had been around to the farmhouse earlier that afternoon, pleased to be met by Sarah Cairns, not Betty. She had told him Ann had appeared, along with the twins, and they had contacted Martin's commanding officer who would pass the message along. Martin was finishing an exercise in the Scottish Highlands and was due back at Dartmouth the next day. The C.O. would recommend compassionate leave. She said Betty had expressed her thanks to everyone, especially George, and she hoped it would all be back to normal soon. George doubted that very much. She said Harry was still being held, helping police with their inquiries.

George listened to the soft noises of the barn; he always enjoyed this time of the day. You could look back on the work well done, and relax for a short time before it all started again the next morning. He heard the bleat of a pet lamb under the warming-lamp and reminded himself of the need to give them their evening feed.

"Whilst I feed them little mites, that ewe in the barn might have had her second, and I can get on and put her in a pen," he told himself.

George knew that sooner or later he would have to return home and face a torrent of questions from his wife. He understood she would like to be brought up-to-date with all the latest news, but he would just give himself a small amount of time on his own, just himself and the sheep, gathering his thoughts.

The follow-up interviews with Paul Allen did little to change his story, he stuck rigidly to his version of events, making himself and Sean Robson out as the innocent parties in the whole affair. The questioning officers made a play at the difference Paul had mentioned at the time of Sean's death. In the first interview Paul had stated that Sean was trying to hold Stevens back, while in the second he said that Sean was giving himself up and was nowhere near Stevens. To hide the mistake, Paul said it was a bit of both, Sean started to hold Stevens back and then walked away and was on his own, giving himself up. Paul was secretly pleased with the way he had got himself off that hook. His mother had complained, what did the policemen expect after bullying her son? He was bound to get confused. They couldn't expect him to remember everything perfectly, the poor dear was in a state of shock.

His father eyed him suspiciously.

The police charged Paul with burglary and attempted burglary, and processed him through their computers. He was given police bail and left with his mother, ignoring the cold looks from his father, and was driven home in time for dinner. Paul managed to keep still long enough to eat his mother's offering, but couldn't wait to get out of the house and meet up with his mates, especially Andy Goodman, to tell his side of the story. He was a hero in his eyes, he had survived the questioning by the police, keeping to the story the two had agreed on, and he hadn't squealed on anybody. He made sure people knew that Paul Allen wasn't a grass. Andy Goodman asked the question Paul was fearing the most.

"Are you going to tell Mark?"

"Would you?"

"I don't know, but it's not me that saw his brother die . . ." He didn't have to say ' . . . and didn't do anything about it.' Paul knew what he meant.

"I don't know where he lives at the moment."

"Don't worry, when he finds out, he will come to you."

Paul did not want to hear that, although he knew it to be true.

Harry Sinton had yet to be charged. Chief Inspector Kemp was careful not to jump the gun and charge the old man with murder, before all the evidence was available. He allowed himself a further forty-eight hours to get to the bottom of the investigation, and then he would decide. What he did know was that there were two dead bodies, an old man admitting he killed them, stating it was self-defence in the face of provocation, and a young man, an accomplice to the two dead raiders, stating that the second killing was cold-blooded murder. He knew that to pin a murder charge on the farmer he would have to prove malice aforethought, and the farmer couldn't have done that unless he knew the raiders were coming, or that he carried the shotgun with him each morning in case he happened to bump into some unsuspecting villains. His other concern was with the force that the farmer had used to protected himself. Blowing two attackers in half was certainly at the extreme scale of self-defence: a warning shot, or even one directed at the attackers' legs, may have been more appropriate. He wondered if he would have reacted the same way, with a person like Stevens bearing down on him. He came to the conclusion that he wouldn't have had the time to think and that he would have defended himself first, and worried about it later, much like the old man.

The telephone was still off the hook at the Sintons when Sarah Cairns made her way home, promising to be back tomorrow if needed. Betty's daughter Ann and her eight-month-old twins remained. They had busied themselves the best they could through the day, and now with the night firmly set in, the emptiness of the house started to surround them. Harry should have been sitting in his chair now, with Bracken's head resting on his feet in front of the wood-burner, recalling the day's events. A number of local farmers and their wives had been around, giving promises of help, words of encouragement. Betty listened to them politely, offering hospitality as usual, all the time believing that Harry would soon be walking through the back door with a sheepish grin on his face, as if returning home later than he had said from the local pub.

The knock on the door was answered by Ann. Gerald Evans stood, looking apologetic, in the front doorway. Gerald Evans had retired some two years earlier but still kept a keen interest at the firm he had helped to set up, still making himself available for consultations. He and Harry Sinton had known each other since their school days together and he took it on himself to tell his friend's family, in person, the recent events concerning their father. After being summoned to his old offices, pulled away from his potting shed, and the situation explained, he had gone to see his old friend. Later he spent the afternoon and early evening using all his old contacts to furnish his friend with one of the best Barristers he knew, and a legal team to go with it.

He was ushered into the front room and offered a coffee; he asked if he could have something a bit stronger. Betty came out of the kitchen where she had been occupying herself baking cakes, for all the people she expected to call round the next day. She brushed at the flour on her apron and started to make small talk with Gerald, he tried to continue with the light conversation, answering questions about his wife's health, his children's work, and his new-found retirement. Eventually he asked Betty to sit down, and for Ann to accompany them.

"I thought it would be best if you heard the latest news from me."

Both Betty and Ann looked at Gerald blankly.

"Harry has been kept in custody overnight while the police continue their investigations. It is my belief he will be charged with manslaughter of one, possibly both of the men he . . . who broke into the farm this morning."

Ann took a sharp intake of breath, covered her mouth with her hands and started to weep, Betty continued to stare at Gerald.

"I am not a Defence Barrister as you know, but I have managed to put together a good team of solicitors, and an excellent Barrister for Harry's Defence. Harry will have to be charged within seventy-two hours of being detained, and then he will be summoned to appear before a Magistrate's Court where he will be committed to trial at a Crown Court. At the committal hearing we will be able to apply for bail. At the moment we believe we have a good case for self-defence. I would be foolish to promise you anything, but believe me when I say it does not look as bleak as you may think."

"Is Harry coming home tonight?"

"No Betty, Harry is still being held at the police station, we hope to have him back as soon as possible."

"Oh," was her only response.

"Please do not hesitate to call me or my firm if you have any worries whatsoever. The Barrister's name is Patrick Parker, and I will get him to introduce himself to you both as soon as possible. Leave everything to me and I will organise things my end. I cannot express my and my family's sympathy strongly enough to you both. We just hope we can get this ghastly thing cleared up as soon as possible."

Ann sat next to her mother and held her hand, she tried to hold back the tears and reassure her mother things would work out. Betty was starting to realise things were far from alright, she had tried to tell herself all day that things would work out and they would be back to normal soon, but now she was realising the truth of the matter. Things were very bad indeed, and would never be the same again.

Gerald finished his whisky, and wondered if he should leave these two women alone. He offered his house for them to stay in, but they declined the invitation. They assured him they would be fine, and thanked him for coming over personally. He left with a deep sense of foreboding. He hoped he had fortified them but at the same time not raised their hopes unduly. He knew it wasn't as clear-cut as he had expressed.

The Robsons had sat alone in their front room as the light faded and the night took over, with only the sound of the passing cars to accompany them. Mr. Robson tried to get his wife to move up stairs and into bed, but to no avail. Eventually he laid her down on the sofa and brought the duvet down and covered her with it, tucking her in for the night. He knew he couldn't sleep, he couldn't stay still. He wanted to get out of the house and lose himself in the night, but he wouldn't leave his wife alone. Instead he poured himself a large whisky, just the one he told himself, and sat across from his wife, watching her shallow breathing. He knew she wasn't asleep either, she had just shut her eyes to the world, wondering what they had done to deserve this life, who they had betrayed to have this punishment against them: why it couldn't be their oldest son lying cold in the mortuary.

Wendy Stevens laid curled up on the sofa; she didn't know when she had fallen asleep, it was light the last time she was awake, now darkness invaded the flat. Only the artificial lights of the city, alive outside the window, showed themselves in the night. She felt the blood around the cut on her arm for the first time, and in a state of shock she made her way to the bathroom, stepping and stumbling over the aftermath of her rage. In the bathroom she turned on the light and looked at herself in the mirror, the harsh light accentuating her haggard, pale, tear-stained face. She was sickened and frightened by the sight. Who would have her now? There were no bandages in the flat, no first-aid box, so she took an old towel and wrapped it around her arm. She had more important things to look for.

She made her way back to the main room and opened a cardboard box that was lying in the corner, it was full of assorted spirit bottles. Billy had been paid off with the spirit for helping in a job well done the week before (the spirits themselves having been 'spirited away' from a nearby off-licence). A little 'knocking job' he had particularly enjoyed. Knocking on an old couple's door and persuading (bullying, threatening) them into buying some Tarmac which they didn't need, for their drive. Three hundred and fifty pounds for half an hour's work, Billy was pleased with that. Wendy opened a bottle of vodka and took a swig. Unlike Mr. Robson, she didn't tell herself "Just the one".

Betty Sinton made her way up to her bed, hot-water bottle in hand, at her usual early time. She had left Ann in the sitting-room listening to her child-intercom. It all seemed wrong to Betty. It was the first time, for longer than she cared to remember, that Harry had not been with her in the house, already in bed, reading a few pages of one of his many Western novels, one that he had read many times before. When she had got into bed she would often watch him read for a while and then whisper, just loud enough for him to hear, 'A man's got to do, what a man's got to do', usually when she thought it was time to turn off the lights. Harry would sniff at her mocking, put down the book and turn off the light. Ready for a night's sleep, ready for their early morning ritual the next day. But not tonight.

The bedroom looked bigger to Betty, lonely. The bed was colder, and the room too quiet. As she lay down in her bed she started to weep, she turned off the light and very quietly, so as not to disturb anyone, for the first time that day, she allowed herself to cry.

Harry Sinton lay on his side on the bunk, wide awake in the cold, sterile cell at Annavale Police Headquarters. He had a blanket wrapped around him, and was still wearing his old work clothes. He could hear some voices echoing down the passageway, the sound of the night shift coming and going. He had been brought down to the cell after his last interview. Gerald Evans had followed him down, explaining the proceedings, the wait for the charges, the appearance before a Magistrate's Court, only to be committed to trial, the application for bail. All this washed over Harry; he was more concerned with the farm, how they were coping without him, and for Betty, what this would do to her. He had sat in a trance for most of the evening, unable to stomach any of the food brought to him. He had tried to sleep as night arrived, lying down on the thin mattress that covered the hard bunk, but sleep eluded him. He did manage to drop off in the early hours of the morning, only to be woken by his internal clock at four-thirty, ready for the morning shift. How he yearned to be on the farm now, to be able to re-run yesterday's events. Turn the clock back twenty-four hours and he would change everything. He would lose a quad bike and regain his life. If only he could start again.

CHAPTER THREE

MAGISTRATE'S COURT

The following morning light on the barns of Downlands farmyard showed no evidence of the owner's absence or troubles. It revealed only the continuing labours of George Stone and his colleagues, constantly moving, working to get their chores completed for another day. The police guard was still in place, the early morning media scrum had subsided after the initial reports *'Live from the scene of the double killings'*. They were now awaiting further information concerning the charges.

Behind the scenes additional tasks were being completed. Harry had been told he may have to spend another day in the cell as the police continued their investigation. Wendy Stevens had regained consciousness, and with a thumping headache, cracked open another bottle of vodka. She wanted to hide herself in a pool of self-pity and intoxication, it was far better than reality. Mr. Robson forced himself back to work, rarely speaking to others. He left his wife being cared for by her parents, and various sisters. Mr. Robson's network of family took over the arrangements for the funeral, organising the service, the wake, the flowers, even the announcements in the paper.

Betty Sinton had a number of well-wishers on her doorstep, and on the telephone. She kept herself busy with their hospitality, baking cakes, thanking them all for their kindness, fussing over the twins. She only ever ventured out of the house to visit her husband, accompanied by Ann (the twins being left with Ann's mother-in-law). Betty had selected clean clothes for Harry, and even brought along some angel cakes (the police guard whispered something about the cakes being too small to hide a file in, but the joke was lost on the assembly). The sight of her cherished partner in the cold, sterile surrounds of the police station demoralised Betty. No amount of reassurances from Ann, Gerald Evans, or her friends, could comfort her after the visit. Back home she hid herself away in the bedroom, only coming out when she thought she had worried Ann too much.

Mark Robson heard the news about his beloved kid brother from his rather nervous partner. She knew the esteem Mark held his brother in, he was the only one of his whole family that hadn't betrayed him. His parents, grandparents, aunties and uncles had all deserted him. They were never mentioned in his presence, and vice versa. He knew he had a habit, it wasn't his fault he got caught up on heroin. It was a vicious circle: his Defence Lawyer had said so. Truancy from school, unemployment, soft drugs, petty crime, all building up to the taking of hard drugs to relieve the boredom of life.

He knew he had done wrong by stealing his father's car whilst high, but he swore he never saw that little girl crossing the road. If he had killed her in anything but a car he would have got a life sentence and would still be in the cell, crawling up the walls, selling anything he had for the next fix. But three years of lost freedom later, he was out, rejected by all his family, except Sean. Sean had kept him supplied with cigarettes in the prison, kept him sane with his visits. All the time when he was telling his parents he was in London with a new girlfriend, or watching his football team, or simply out for a day, Sean was visiting his brother. It had not been easy, but his parents' desire to believe everything Sean said, and to see him as good, compared to Mark's evil, allowed him the leeway to get away with it.

After he was released, Mark Robson had tried to start a new life in London, but the streets were not paved with gold. He eventually returned to Southampton to be near the only person he could rely on. He changed his name to Spencer Marks, having decided on the name while walking passed a Marks and Spencer store, and moved to a different part of the city, away from his parents and his past. He found himself a circle of dope pushers and drug addicts, and created a thriving business for himself as a supplier of a new drug, with a new niche market. Sean had given him that opening, showing him the business opportunity with the latest drug craze, the Ecstasy tablet, for young school and college kids who wanted a bit extra for the night. Mark Robson backed-up his empire with his own brand of violence that he had learned the hard way, in prison, and in his failed ventures in London, but he knew he owed everything to Sean.

Mark's blood-shot eyes looked straight back at the now terrified girl's. She had heard the news a couple of hours ago, whilst on an errand for Mark, picking up some more tablets to be processed and sold later that week. He had run-out after a particularly good weekend. He had stayed in bed, a mattress on the squalid wooden floor, awaiting her return. Why have a dog and bark yourself, he would always say. She had wandered the streets, arguing to herself whether to tell Mark or not. If she didn't and he found out, she knew all along, the repercussions would be unthinkable; not just the violence, she could handle that, she had always been able to handle that, but the deprivation of her only need in life, her solace, her narcotics: that would be unbearable.

"What did you say?" He was now out of the bed, oblivious to his nakedness.

"Seanie's dead Spenc." He had revealed his real name only to a small select group of people in the area. She was one of them, but would never call him anything but Spencer. "Iain just told me. He saw it on the news. He . . . he was going to come round and tell you but . . . but."

"How?"

"I don't know," she lied. "He didn't say . . . Something about a break-in."

Mark grabbed her arm and swung her against the bedroom wall. She cried out in fear and pain.

"What did he say?" He screamed at her, their faces barely inches apart.

"He . . . he . . . said that Sean was shot . . . " She sobbed through frightened tears, she tried to turn her face away but he held her neck and jaw in a vice-like grip, forcing her head back and up against the bedroom wall.

"Where is he?"

"Don't hurt me, please."

He threw her on to the mattress and searched around for his clothes, pulling on his filthy jeans, jumper, and donkey-jacket. She was whimpering, saying it wasn't her fault, not to hurt her. He found his boots, laced them up in a frenzy, and then turned back to the crumpled figure on the mattress, and placed a well-aimed kick at her ankles. She reeled from the pain, increasing her pleas.

"Where is he?"

"Please don't hurt me, it's not my fault," she repeated over and over again.

He aimed a second kick at her knees.

"I don't know, I don't know," she whined.

"Useless bitch," he grunted as he gave her a final kick in the stomach. I'll find him myself."

"Don't go, don't leave me. I need some stuff, please, you promised. I need a hit."

"Useless bitch!" he spat as he walked out the door.

Iain MacDonald was his supplier and Mark had a good idea where he would be by now. He had just sold a load of tablets to Mark's runner, and money burned a hole in Iain's pocket. He would be at a bar somewhere, or more likely at a casino, at a card table losing all his new-found wealth. Mark hoped he wouldn't be at the casino, there would be no way he would be allowed in, dressed and smelling as he was. He would first look in the local pub, he needed a drink anyway.

The bar of the *Red Lion* was depressing, in a depressing pub, in a depressing area of Southampton. Grimy windows blocked out the daylight, wallpaper fell away from the walls, and a threadbare carpet told the story of spilled drinks, stubbed-out cigarettes, and sick. It was the perfect pub for Mark Robson and his sad empire. As Mark walked in, the barman started to pour a pint of lager; he needed no telling.

"Sorry to hear the news Spenc." Eddie Blackmore said as he passed the pint of lager to Mark

"Does every bastard know? Am I the last to find out?"

Eddie Blackmore was the barman of the *Red Lion*, he and Mark had a little sideline together. He also dealt in drugs, restricting his supply to marijuana, but if anybody came in looking for tablets of Ecstasy, he would refer them to Robson, and vice versa. It was obvious Mark Robson didn't have to track down MacDonald, anyone could fill him in on yesterday's events. Robson hadn't been out of his pit in those two days, spending his time with his girlfriend and a new batch of heroine. Time mattered little when he had those two to keep him company.

"I heard it on the TV man, it was all over the news."

The first news reports didn't mention any names, waiting for the next-of-kin to be told, but later reports expanded on the story and included the names of the two dead raiders. They added that two men were helping the police with their inquiries, one had been let out on police bail, the other still held in custody. Mark Robson listened silently as he was slowly brought up to date with the death of his beloved younger brother.

At two-fifteen that afternoon Chief Inspector Kemp, accompanied by Gerald Evans, charged Harry Sinton with the manslaughter of both William Stevens and Sean Robson. It was explained that he would be brought before the Magistrate's Court in Annavale as soon as possible, probably the following morning, where he would be committed to stand trial for the crimes he had been charged with. He was read his rights and then left alone with his solicitor, who once again explained the proceedings.

Chief Inspector Kemp had studied all the information he had received from his various colleagues, and had arrived at the conclusion that the charges of manslaughter were the only courses available to him. The charge of murder would not stand up to scrutiny as Harry could not have had the malice aforethought. He had not taken the shotgun out to the barn with the express purpose of killing the two raiders, but he did commit an unlawful act which led to their deaths, and that, Kemp believed, constituted involuntary manslaughter.

The slight quirks of the criminal law irritated the Chief Inspector; he would like things to be a lot simpler. Guilty or not guilty, black and white as far as he was concerned. Harry had caused the death of two human beings, but did so while protecting his life and his property. Simple self-defence: the villains shouldn't have been there in the first place. He knew however this wasn't how the legal system would look at it: intent, force of defence, provocation. All these extenuating circumstances would be brought up in Court, examined in minute detail in the cold light of day. It was enough to make his head spin. It was not up to him any more, he had passed it all on to the solicitors and barristers, Judge and jury. They could fight it out between themselves, making their money as they haggled over the future of the unfortunate old man sitting forlornly in the cell. The only thing Chief Inspector Kemp could do was not oppose bail when Harry Sinton went before the Magistrate in the morning. He saw the shattered old man in the cells as no threat to the general public.

Martin Sinton arrived at Downlands Farm around mid-afternoon on the day his father was charged with the double killings. He drove through the now depleted media scrum (having got all the footage they needed, the majority had retired to the warmth of the studio, only the die-hards remaining). He then stopped and explained who he was to the police guard that was still present at the gates of the farm before continuing on towards the house. Martin had arranged for a week's leave on hearing the news of his father, and as soon as he had returned from the Scottish Highlands, he drove the three and a half hours home. An announcement on the car radio as he passed through the farm gates told him that his father had been formally charged with the manslaughter of the two burglars.

Driving past the yard he noticed George Stone climbing into a tractor. Martin stopped and walked over to the foreman. They chatted briefly, Martin asking questions and thanking George for all the support he had given: how were the men coping? Did they need any help? George answered honestly and said he was pleased to see Martin home. Martin then continued to his family home. Parking behind Ann's car he retrieved his small clothes bag from the back seat and made his way to the back door. This was the first time he had seen his mother since the Christmas festivities over two months ago, and these certainly weren't the circumstances he wanted to return to.

On opening the back door he heard the familiar bark of Bracken, warning of a new arrival, and then Ann appeared, giving a tired smile in welcome. It wasn't in their family make-up to hug and kiss on meeting, so they stood across from each other with awkward smiles on their faces.

"Who is it Ann?" Came a call from inside the house.

"Martin's home," she called back.

Martin followed Ann through the kitchen and into the front room, dropping his bag en route. He asked after the twins, her husband and anybody else he could think of. Ann replied that all were fine. Betty, hearing that her son had arrived, had stopped her polishing in the front room (she had only completed the same task three days ago, anything to keep herself busy) and greeted her son with a loving hug, holding him for longer than normal, and then stepped away, her hands shaking, tears forming in her eyes. Bracken was circling with intent to be patted. Martin, on seeing the distress his mother was in, reached out and pulled her in for a second embrace, whispering in her ear that everything would be fine, things would work out. He decided now was not a good time to tell that his Mother that her husband, their father, had been formally charged with two accounts of manslaughter. Ann patted the dog.

The bodies of William Stevens and Sean Robson, after undergoing their post-mortems, were released to their next of kin. Sean's body was picked up immediately by the funeral staff that had been hired for the burial. His grandparents had wasted no time in arranging the funeral, setting the date for the coming Saturday afternoon in their local parish church. Stevens' body went unclaimed. Wendy Stevens had shut herself in the flat, eating little, drinking lots. She didn't answer the telephone or door bell, she was petrified it would be someone from the council trying to evict her. The police had been around, following up their inquiries, but had had little joy from the conversation, conducted through the door, with a drunken, hysterical woman. Wendy had refused to open the door for them, and when they mentioned that Stevens' body was ready to be picked up, she hurled the half-finished bottle of vodka at the door and ran whimpering back to the solace of the sofa. The two policemen flinched as the bottle bounced off the inside of the door, and gave the interview up as a bad job. They decided to return later, when things might have calmed down.

The follow-up interview with the Robsons also shed little light on recent events. Mrs. Robson stared blankly back at the two officers as they asked their questions. Mr. Robson's answers were monosyllabic. Had they ever met Stevens? No. Did they know Sean was out with Stevens? No. Did they know if Sean had been out with Stevens before? No. And so on.

The police believed they had built up a fair picture surrounding the affair, that Stevens had done this sort of thing before, although they hadn't tracked down where he sold the stolen equipment. They believed Sean and Paul may have been bullied into going with him, but more than likely went along for the ride, some easy cash, and for the ability to brag about it to their friends. A couple of Sean's friends had told the police he had boasted of these trips, while nobody knew if Paul had gone before or not. They believed the gang had broken into one farm, were thwarted at a second (according to Paul Allen's statement, although no other farmer had reported any signs of an attempted break-in), before they were interrupted at Downlands Farm. All the necessary reports were written up and new investigations were started.

The main body of media reported the announcement that:

'Mr. Harold Sinton, of Downlands Farm, Ilton, Annavale, has been charged with the manslaughter of one William Stevens, forty-five, and one Sean Robson, seventeen, both from the City of Southampton, following his disturbance of an attempted break-in at the farm.'

They found out the time for Harry's appearance at the Magistrate's Court the following day, and made plans for the coverage of the next stage to this news item. Some journalists decided to run follow-up pieces, commenting on rural crime: the bias of the law towards the criminal, as opposed to the victim, the dangers of such vigilante actions. Anything to fill the time-slots and interest the public. They tried to contact the Sinton family, but all 'phone calls received the engaged tone as the Sintons' telephone was still off the hook. Any advances towards members of the family of Sean Robson were turned away. They didn't bother Wendy, having been warned off by locals in the pub and on the estate.

There were a number of radio 'phone-ins, allowing the general public to vent their feelings about the case; many spoke of the right to defend yourself in such a situation, others stressing the need for the law to combat these so-called vigilante actions. Mid-morning television talk-shows mirrored their radio counterparts. The media were careful not to discuss the actual case, for fear of breaching sub-Judice regulations, but were able to recall other such incidents, all very similar. Although the commentators expressed sympathy and concern, none of the programmes did anything for the victims of the situation. The following day a new topic was discussed.

Martin busied himself with obtaining all the relevant facts concerning the case. He returned to the farmyard where he spoke to all the staff, again thanking them for all their help in these difficult circumstances. He drove into town and presented himself before his Godfather. Gerald Evans was now back full time at his old offices, directing the team he had assembled. After expressing his sympathies he pulled no punches as he brought Martin up to date with the situation. He stressed they had not received the full follow-up reports from the police, but at the moment they hoped they would have his father back home on bail by tomorrow lunch time, and then they would concentrate on his defence. He told Martin that even though they had a right to challenge the Prosecution's case at the hearing tomorrow, to try and get the charges thrown out due to lack of evidence, the evidence was in fact overwhelming. His father had admitted to the killings, and it would be futile to argue against it. Gerald then spoke of his fears that Harry Sinton could easily be sent to prison for what he had done that Monday morning.

"As the law stands, you should only use such force that is reasonable in the circumstances, and that would be up to the jury to decide. The use of reasonable force to prevent an attack is lawful but the use of excessive force indicates, in the eyes of the law, that your father may have acted unreasonably in the circumstances, therefore, there would be no valid defence and he would be liable for the crime he committed, manslaughter."

Martin kept running his hands over his close-cropped hair, shifting position on his seat as he listened to the solicitor, his mind was racing, running through the effect this would have on his family and the farm. He tried to blank those thoughts out for the time being and asked more questions.

"Will Dad get bail?"

Gerald Evans sat in his leather chair, behind a solid oak desk. He was wearing his tailored city suit that fitted his portly figure snugly. He had let the ever present junior solicitor go when Martin arrived. Whilst he had been explaining the vagaries of the law, Gerald Evans had been leaning over his desk, fiddling with his fountain pen. He now put the pen down, leant back into his chair and placed his hands in his lap, still twiddling his fingers.

"We hope so; the police are not opposing it, and we believe the Magistrate will see your father as no threat if he is released from custody, either to the general public, or from jumping bail."

"And then he will face a trial by jury?"

"Yes."

"When?"

"When the law courts can arrange it, also allowing the defence and the prosecuting services enough time to arrange their relative cases."

"How long?"

"Three months, maybe four. It has been known to go for over six months. We won't know until tomorrow."

"Where?"

"Probably, hopefully, Winchester."

Martin sighed, stood up, crossed to the office window, and looked down on the street below. Gerald Evans' offices occupied the second and top floors of an old, high street building. His own office, which he retained for his part-time consultation work and out of a little sentimentality, was on the top floor. Darkness had descended in the early evening, some shops had started to close. Street lamps shed light on passing figures below, all wrapped-up against the chill evening air, blissfully unaware of the troubles being discussed above them.

"How is Dad?"

"In shock mainly, appalled at himself."

"I'm going over to see him. Have you told him the situation?"

"Not in so many words. I have spelt it out very badly to you Martin, but have held back from the rest of the family. I think that would be . . . unproductive." Martin took in the advice.

"How long a sentence will Dad get?" Martin asked solemnly.

"How long will he get? How long could he get? Or how long should he get? How long is a piece of string?" Gerald Evans paused, took off his glasses and cleaned them on his silk tie. He thought about how honest he should be with Martin, and decided the bald truth was the only option. He replaced his glasses, straightened his tie, rested his hands in his lap, and looked up at Martin.

"How long will he get? I don't know and I wouldn't start to speculate at this point in time. We haven't got all the necessary reports in, and we haven't done the necessary research. How long could he get? If we are looking at the maximum sentence for a double manslaughter charge, there wouldn't be much change from thirty years. Saying that, I would seriously doubt that your father would receive the maximum sentence. How long *should* he get? I would like to see him walk free, but I am biased. Your Father has killed two men, who were in the process of stealing his property, and threatening him, maybe threatening his life. Now, a sympathetic jury, led by a skilful defence Barrister, may lean towards self-defence. The prosecuting Barrister, on the other hand, will question the force that your father used, he may say that you cannot allow people to take the law into their own hands, that this would cause a break down in the law itself."

Martin mulled over the last bit of information. His father didn't have thirty years in him to give. Five years in prison would damage him irreparably.

"When does a Barrister get involved?"

"After your father is committed to trial. We can appeal for bail at the Magistrate's Court, and do all the ground work, but we have limited powers in a Crown Court. I hope to get a Barrister by the name of Patrick Parker for your father's defence. I have dealt with him before and he comes on the highest recommendation."

Martin had been staring out of the window as he had asked the last couple of questions. He now turned and looked at his Godfather, a man who had been at all the major events in his family's life: christenings, eighteenth and twenty-first birthday parties, Ann's wedding. Martin had been building up to this question all through the meeting.

"How much will all this cost?"

Gerald Evans studied his Godson, he had nothing but admiration for this man. He had watched him grow up, giving him any advice he could, when he could. It was Gerald Evans who persuaded Martin not to be blinkered with farming, to look for an alternative career, he could always return to it later. He was pleased and proud when Martin had announced he had been accepted by the Royal Marines, and had followed his fortunes closely. He had watched the boy grow into a strong and reliable man.

"Your father instructed me to approach the A.M.C. (Agricultural Mortgage Company) with respect to the bail. Again I don't know what level they will set it at, if they do grant it tomorrow, but the A.M.C. have been most accommodating, and of course the amount is repaid as long as your father appears at the trial, which I could bet my life on! So all you have is a bit of interest to pay. As for the rest, I cannot put a figure on it at the moment. I will not be charging for my part, but a good Barrister and Defence team does not come cheaply." He paused before he continued, trying to deciding the best way to put the next statement. "I think you, and the rest of the family would agree that we should get the best Defence for your father. I don't know the farm's financial standing, but I would have thought that your father's freedom must be put first."

Martin did know the farm's finance all too well. A mortgage of forty-eight thousand pounds from when his father had bought-out his two sisters in the early sixties would be paid off after another six years. There had been a couple of insurance policies taken out to ensure the fact. The biggest worry was an overdraft that his father had arranged (arguing that was how everybody farmed), that had spiralled out of control when the bank interest rates climbed to seventeen and a half percent in the early nineties, reaching a peak of three hundred and eighty five thousand pounds. Harry Sinton had battled hard over the past five years to rein-in the borrowing, basically working for the bank, but had managed to do so without selling any land. He had brought it down to one hundred and eighty thousand, by tightening his belt still further, and mending some tired old machinery that really needed replacing. This could start it off all over again.

"What about legal aid?" Martin asked.

"Doubtful: as I said, I don't know about your father's accounts, but the mere fact that he is sitting on over seven hundred acres, and the capital asset that represents, would probably disqualify him from legal aid."

Martin had already thought this, but wanted to ask someone in the business, just in case.

"I don't have to remind you Martin, but your father is in a very serious position. I believe we must assemble the best Defence we can."

"At the cost of the farm?"

"I would think that would be a small price to pay."

Martin agreed.

Harry Sinton heard the echoing of footsteps coming down the passageway, and then sharp metallic sounds of the keys being inserted into his cell door. As the door crept open, he raised himself off the bunk, and waited to accept his evening meal. He was unprepared to see his son holding the tray of food. The custody sergeant explained that an officer had to stay in the cell while Harry received visitors, but he would stand at the back of the cell and remain silent, he would then escort Martin out, giving them about an hour. Father and son stood facing each other, not knowing what to do, how to react. A simple hand shake seemed inappropriate, while neither could remember the last time they had hugged. Martin passed the tray to his father with a simple "Hello Dad."

His father slumped down onto the bunk, shaking his head.

"I'm so sorry son, I'm so sorry."

Martin sat next to his father and rested his hand on top of his father's, squeezing it gently. Words of comfort seemed trivial. How could he tell his father that all would be well, that everything would work out, when both of them knew it was a lie. Martin swallowed and started on the sentence he had been running through his mind ever since he had heard the news from his commanding officer.

"I am so pleased it was them and not you."

Harry Sinton put the tray on the floor, and turned to his son, looking him straight in the eyes.

"I'm so sorry Martin, I'm so sorry. If I could change things I would, please believe me."

It hurt Martin to see his father like this. His father had never had any reason to apologise to him before. He had always been so strong, so patient. Always encouraging, congratulating Martin on whatever success he had achieved. Martin had never taken his parents for granted, but after he had joined the Marines and listening to the tales of some of the men below him, he had realised how lucky he was. Looking at his father now, he had nothing but contempt for the people who had placed him in this situation. He was pleased they were dead, two villains less to wander the streets. It was the effect the whole thing would have on his family that concerned him more. A hard-working, law-abiding family, shattered by the greed and meanness of two men.

"Mum and Ann send their love," he said lamely.

His father's eyes clouded over, this was going to be a long hour. Martin told of his meeting with Gerald Evans, careful not to mention any of the down sides, stressing that they hoped he would be given bail in the morning. Harry Sinton only nodded in confirmation that he knew of the forthcoming proceedings. By the end of the hour Martin was telling of how the lambing was going, and how all his friends had offered their help and support.

The police officer apologetically told Martin it was time to leave, noticed the food was untouched and said he would bring something down later on in the evening. Martin thanked him and said goodbye to his father. The image of this once proud and happy man, sitting crumpled and pale on the bunk, eyes imploring for forgiveness, would haunt Martin for the rest of his life.

Wendy Stevens crept up to the door and listened to the voice on the other side. She thought she could recognise it through her drunken haze, but wasn't sure. Someone had been banging on the door for the past five minutes, shouting her name, saying it was Bob. Then she realised who it was and, unlocking the door, she poked her head out and looked from side to side, grabbed Bob Richards and pulled him in, re-locking the door behind her.

Bob Richards took in the scene before him and swore.

"Bloody hell Wendy, has someone done you over?"

Wendy pulled him by his hand into the main room and then pushed him onto the sofa, leaving herself standing, cradling her ever-present bottle of vodka.

"'E's fuckin' dead Bob, 'e's fuckin' dead."

"Yea, yea I know Wend, that's why I've come over."

"What am I going to do?" Wendy Stevens was tottering just feet away from Richards. She had dried blood caked on her arm, her hair was matted and bedraggled, her clothes dirty and in disarray. "The useless bastard ain't left me nothin'."

"Wend listen to me, did you tell the police anything?"

"I ain't told them bastards nothin'."

"Are you sure."

"Don't you trust me Bob?" she asked softly, trying, with little success, to stand still, tall and straight. "Here, have a drink."

"Not just now Wend. You sure you didn't tell them anything?"

"You used to fancy me Bob, I remember how you used to look at me." Her swaying started to spiral out of control, she teetered to one side then decided to let herself fall on to Richards." I fancied you too" she slurred into his ear. "'Onest I did, still do."

Bob Richards had a number of reasons to visit Wendy, the main one was to see if she had told the police anything about his arrangements with Billy for the previous morning. He could see he was going to get little information concerning that from Wendy in her present state. The second was to see if he could get hold of Billy's four-year-old BMW. Bob knew it was all legal, the plates and the owners certificate. Stevens wouldn't have got thirty yards driving a flash car like that without the police taking an interest in it. He hoped Wendy could drive it over to his garage; that too had to be put on the back burner. His third reason was to see Wendy. He had lusted after her from afar, ever since she had picked Billy up from dropping-off his first stolen car nearly four years ago. He had often wondered what she was doing with a small-time crook like Stevens, but very wisely didn't pursue his desires any further. He knew Stevens' reputation.

"Wend, do you want to come back to my gaff, hide up for a while?"

"The stupid bastard got 'imself shot. 'e ain't left me with nothin'" she continued, eyes shut, not hearing his question.

Richards grabbed her by the shoulders and shook, Wendy's head flopping forwards and backwards, side to side. She started to giggle.

"Wend, listen to me, do you want out of this place?"

It was no good, she had lost consciousness, the bottle of vodka fell from her grip and onto the floor, dispensing the remaining liquid over the already stained carpet. Richards dropped her onto the sofa, scanned the room and decided to pack for her, hoping she would come round later. He enjoyed poking around Stevens' flat, trying to find some dustbin bags for Wendy's clothes. There were no personal possessions around the flat that he could see, no photographs of the happy couple, no little trinkets to remind themselves of a sunny day away somewhere.

He had found two black dustbin bags of clothes in the bedroom, and on inspection he established they were clean, just returned from the local launderette. He threw out what he suspected were Billy's clothes, and replaced them with Wendy's. He got an excited feeling as he rummaged through her knickers and bras, throwing them into the bag. With two full bags he ferried them along the passage and down the poorly-lit stairways to his car parked below, placing them in the boot. Darkness covered his activities. He had decided to take Wendy as she was, arguing that if she regained consciousness and started to scream at being abducted, he would say it was for her own good, that she could go back if she wanted. He hoped she would just comply.

He could not find any door keys in the chaos of the flat, so as he carried Wendy out he pulled the door shut, locking them both out. That wouldn't be a problem, he could always kick it in if they needed to return for something. Better to have it secure than to leave it open, he reasoned, you never know what sort of scum may be poking around. He would have to return for the BMW later, but that was alright, that was a bonus anyway.

Martin explained his activities to his mother and sister over dinner. He said that his father was well, looking good all things considered and, following from Betty's expressed concerns, eating all his food. He repeated Gerald Evans' words, skimming around the bad points, highlighting the good, completely ignoring the discussion about costs. Betty seemed pleased that Harry would be back for tomorrow lunch, Ann just looked tired. She excused herself after the meal and went to check on the twins, Martin helped his mother clear away the plates and stack the dish-washer. Betty was asking after his friends, what he had been up to, making small talk, Martin was happy to go along with this. They made some coffee and returned to the main room, Ann was on the telephone to her husband, explaining the latest details, asking after the lambing, reassuring him that she, the twins and the family, were alright. She returned to the sitting-room and accepted the coffee and collapsed into the nearest chair.

An uneasy silence filled the room, Bracken lay in front of the fire, one ear twitching. They had not switched the television on since the afternoon of the killings when they had been ambushed by news reports of their father's impending charges and Court case, likewise the radio. They all racked their brains for something to say to break the silence. Martin was first to think of something.

"I've got a week's leave Mum, and I could probably get that extended if need be." He declined from saying, "If dad isn't given bail."

"We're pleased you're here love," Betty assured him.

"When are you going to go back to Richard?" Martin asked his sister.

"I hadn't thought about it."

"Oh you mustn't stay away from your home for my sake dear, you should go back. I can cope, and Martin says that your father will be back tomorrow."

"Touch wood," he whispered under his breath, surreptitiously tapping the wooden table that stood next to his chair.

"Well, I'll come to the Court tomorrow, and we shall see from there," Ann said.

Again a painful silence developed. It was Betty's turn to ask a question, and it took Martin by surprise.

"Have you thought of what you're going to do when your time in the Army runs out?"

Martin had long ago given up telling his mother that the Marines were part of the Navy. Betty knew this, but after her first couple of slip-ups when she had said that Martin was in the Army, she continued to pretend that as far as she was concerned the Navy wore blue and white, with those nice bell-bottom trousers. It made her chuckle to think of her son tearing his hair out at his mother's feigned ignorance.

"I have been thinking about it, I was going to bring up the subject next time I had a long leave. I think I will get out of the Marines, I think you either leave now or stay for ever and make it a career. I would like to get back into farming, maybe do a quick course at the Royal Agricultural College."

"Richard went there," Ann put in.

"I know, he still has his rugby team photos on the toilet wall."

"He enjoyed it. Best days of his life he says, which upsets me a bit!" she said, giving a tired smile.

"I thought he said that you and the twins were the best things in his life?"

"He does now, but I still think he longs for his bachelor days now and again. Especially when the twins started to teeth," she chuckled.

The conversation continued, Martin being careful to steer it away from the initial question. Slight jokes and awkward laughter ensued. Nobody really wanted to sound too happy in the circumstances. When the time came for Betty and Ann to go to bed, Martin said he would be staying up for a while, said he had offered to do early morning check of the lambing pens, to ease the work load from George Stone and the others. He still wanted to stay up and reflect on the day's incidents. As he listened to them going up the stairs, he helped himself to some of his father's best scotch and collapsed back into the armchair. Bracken, seeing that Martin was staying, sidled up to him and placed her head on his lap.

"Hey old girl, what do you make of all this then?"

Bracken closed her eyes and leant into the affectionate strokes.

"It's a bit of a mess, eh girl," he continued, looking down on the family's faithful hound.

The committal hearing was set for tomorrow morning; they would all be attending, family and friends showing their support, praying for bail so that their father, husband, friend could return home. This was not what Martin had envisaged for his homecoming. He had planned to return home after the latest exercise in the Scottish Highlands to discuss his future with his parents. He had decided to leave the services, and he wanted to return to the farm he had grown up on. He also knew his father had a number of years left in him and would never really retire. It had been Harry's life since he could walk, and leaving it would take away all he lived for, and forcing his father out was the last thing Martin wanted to do. Now there was a serious possibility that his father would be sent to prison for a lengthy period of time, and that the Defence, with no guarantee of success, would put a severe strain on the farm's accounts.

He knew the farm may have to be put on the market to cover the legal costs, and that that would be the last straw for his father. He knew that he would blame himself, not only for the deaths of two human beings, but for the strain on his family and the shattering of their central being, the farm. The farm had given them a focus, from when Harry grew up on it, to when he watched his own children do the same. It had given them everything: an income, a way of life, a sense of freedom, of achievement, a work ethos, a standing in the local community. It had meant everything to all the family. Martin would often try to rationalise his feelings, arguing that it was only sentimentality that made Downlands Farm so important, that there were plenty of other farms, with better soil and more amenities. He would say things have to change, nothing remains constant, but he knew he loved the place.

It was thought for a while that they would have to sell the farm anyway, as neither Ann nor Martin could afford to buy each other out, and the farm was too small to support three families, their parents had to have somewhere to live after they retired. Betty had always said that it would be split evenly, not all going to the eldest son. Martin could have farmed the other half for his sister but he could only see complications with that set-up.

Ann then married the only child of another farming family. Her in-laws had given them six hundred acres as a wedding gift and it was widely acknowledged, although never discussed, that Martin would therefore inherit Downlands Farm. Perhaps now was the time to discuss it, he thought, bring everything to a head. But as he sat in his father's favourite armchair, drinking his father's best scotch, stroking the family dog, mulling over all the recent events and their likely repercussions, watching the flames flicker in the wood burner, he knew he would gladly swop the farm for his father's freedom.

The committal hearing at Annavale Magistrate's Court started at ten-thirty. Half an hour before, a sizeable band of media had arrived, standing in clusters, stamping their feet and hunching their shoulders to ward off the raw morning air. They cursed the weather, their editors, and the man on trial for bringing them out on this cold March morning.

Harry Sinton was brought to the Court House by two uniformed policemen, fifteen minutes before the start time. They had driven the short distance from the police station to the Magistrate's Court, parking in the allotted car park behind the Court building. They pushed through the awaiting media, Harry Sinton ignoring the questions being asked by the reporters. He looked startled and bewildered. His immediate family and friends had arrived earlier, and were now seated in the Court room. Television cameras were banned from the hearing, and therefore the operators had to wait outside. Here they continued to curse anything that had conspired to bring them out on this freezing morning, jealous of the reporters who sat in the warmth of the Court room.

The Magistrate's Court was a single-storey, functional building. Spent cigarette butts littered the pavement outside, tired-looking chairs cluttered the entrance hall. A drinks dispensing machine stood in the middle of the far wall, a shabby table with an assortment of magazines scattered on its surface to the left. The dull white walls' only attraction were posters detailing Court times and the layout of the building. The Court had been built in the mid-seventies and lacked any character whatsoever. Harry Sinton had expected it to be a fine old building, with a grand hallway and oil paintings hanging on the walls. He was sadly disappointed as he was shown through to Court number two.

Harry was led to his seat before the three Magistrates who had already arrived. The Magistrates, two men and one woman, all in their middle fifties, were lay Magistrates, an unpaid, part-time position. They were all somberly dressed, heads down, reading the summary notes on Harry Sinton's case. Gerald Evans and an ever-present junior solicitor sat in front of Harry, also deep in their notes. It would be a fast hearing, the Magistrates had little to decide. The legal process meant that they had to refer the case to a Crown Court due to the severity of the charges. All they had to do was announce the date set for the trial, and decide upon the application for bail and the amount, all of which they had been advised on earlier that morning by the justices' clerk. Still, they were going to enjoy their time in the limelight.

Slowly, one by one the Magistrates raised their heads from the notes, and studied Harry. He was sitting straight-backed, grey, thinning hair combed neatly and parted on one side, freshly shaven with his eyes fixed on the royal shield that hung directly behind and slightly above the middle Magistrate. He had his best tweed jacket and corduroy trousers on, a checked shirt, and a tie with a Suffolk sheep emblem in the middle. All had been recently washed and ironed by Betty, and had been passed on earlier that morning by Gerald Evans. This was the most unlikely killer they would ever see, they thought to themselves.

The Chairman of the Magistrates, sitting in the middle, cleared his throat and declared the hearing:

"The Crown verses Harold Charles Sinton, in session."

Harry had to speak only once throughout the proceedings, confirming his name to the Court. The Magistrate went on to state that the aforementioned man had been charged on two accounts of manslaughter, and that due to the severity of the charges, all he could do in his powers was to refer the case to the Crown Court.

This came as no surprise to anybody.

He now looked at his two fellow Magistrates, then back to his notes before he continued on to the next item on the agenda.

"A plea for bail has been submitted by the defendant's solicitors, and I see from my notes that the police do not object," he announced, looking up at Harry. "It is our view that a charge of such gravity would demand that, in the interest of the safety of the community, the accused be kept in custody until the main trial, when his innocence or guilt may be established."

The assembled body of family and friends held their breath, they had all hoped and believed that Harry would be given bail, the chance to walk out of the Court, and return to his home. The ability to offer such hope and then snatch it away was tortuous, sadistic.

"But after studying the notes before us it is our belief that the circumstances surrounding these charges must be taken into account, and along with the police's Counsel, we are willing to grant bail . . . "

A collective sigh of relief swept through the Court room, Betty sitting between her children, one hand in each of theirs, squeezed them hard, and smiled at the back of her husband. Harry Sinton didn't turn around to smile back, he didn't want to upset the Magistrates before him by showing any lack of respect in their Court. He gave out a sigh of relief, but kept sitting bolt upright, continuing to stare at the shield hanging behind the middle Magistrate. People muttered to each other under their breath.

" . . . It is our belief that the defendant does not constitute a threat to the public." The Magistrate paused to allow the muffled commotion die down. "The bail is set at forty thousand pounds."

A gasp went up from the Court, the majority had given no thought to the price of the bail, forty thousand pounds seemed a lot of money. Betty let go of her children's hands, clasped hers together, and sat shaking in her seat. Martin put his arm around her and whispered words of comfort to her, he told her it would all be taken care of, that the A.M.C. would be willing to put up the sum, at a much reduced interest rate, and that it would all be paid back when father arrived at the Crown Court. Still Betty shook.

"The trial will be held at Winchester Crown Court on the twenty-eighth of June. This hearing is now closed." The Magistrate had enjoyed his five minutes of fame, but now had to return to the usual mundane list of suspects he had before him, drunk and disorderly, and drink-driving making up the bulk of the charges.

Gerald Evans left his seat, shadowed by the junior solicitor, and walked over to where Martin, Betty, and Ann were sitting. He nodded in recognition to familiar faces in the crowd as they smiled their happiness of the verdict to him. He was a much relieved man, he knew the bail could have gone either way.

"I have to go backstage, as it were, to organise the details of the bail. Harry has instructed me on the payments. We shall see you at the front entrance. Martin, would you like to go and fetch the car and bring it as close to the Court house as possible. We really don't want to subject your father to the waiting Press, if we can help it."

Martin agreed, and left Betty and Ann in the company of many of their friends who were offering words of cheer at the verdict, while realising the hardest hurdle for Harry Sinton's freedom was yet to be challenged. Betty acknowledged their words, but the thought of such a sum of money kept troubling her. She knew the financial situation, she had managed to live with it, but now it seemed all their hard work in the past five years would be wiped away. She held on tightly to Ann.

The Court room emptied, leaving only the Magistrates, engrossed in the notes of the next case, and the Court reporter behind. As the assembled crowd spilt onto the outside pavement, the media cameras rushed in to hear the details. Some of the people refused to be interviewed, some denounced the huddle of media to their face, while others were only too happy to air their views. Tom Whitworth was one them.

"He should never have been on trial," he announced into the eager reporter's microphone as he walked towards his car. "You could not meet a more honest hard-working man. He should be given a medal," he added as he pushed through the converging reporters.

Betty and Ann stayed behind the smoked glass doors of the Court house, silently watching the spectacle before them. They noticed Martin in his parents' car pull-up to the pavement, slightly behind and unseen by the media scrum. Martin had chosen to drive his parents' car today; his own two-seater sports car, as preferred by bachelor Marines Officers, could not accomodate everyone.

Harry Sinton appeared from a side corridor and, accompanied by Gerald Evans, walked up to his wife and daughter, holding them both for what seemed like an eternity. He had sometimes wondered, as he sat desolate in his cell, if he would ever be able to perform this simple act again. Tears formed in all concerned's eyes.

After a time, when they broke up and wiped the tears away, Gerald Evans asked Harry if he was ready. Harry nodded his reply and told his wife and daughter to stick close to him. Gerald Evans then pushed open the smoked glass doors and hailed the awaiting media towards him. He had always thought of the media as a necessary evil, the need for unbiased reporting essential for a free and democratic country, but he disliked the growing number of Press reporters, and the clamour they produced. If he could shield his friend from such turmoil, he would. He also knew the need to keep them on your side, the power of the media was not lost on him. The plan he had suggested to his friend was a calculated risk, but one he believed well worth taking.

"If you would like to come this way, I have a statement to read out on behalf of my client."

This was unusual, usually the statement would be read out at the end of the main trail. The amassed media followed the solicitor as he led them away from the main doors. Martin edged closer to the building, Harry Sinton asked Betty and Ann if they were ready.

They nodded, unsure what they were ready for.

"The statement is as follows:"

Dictaphones were switched on, microphones lunged towards the solicitor, cameramen barged one another for a better shot. Harry Sinton motioned for the two to follow him and scampered towards their car. Martin, on seeing his father come out of the Court House, leant over and opened the back doors.

"My client, not wanting to attract excessive media attention, on what is a very painful and delicate case . . ."

Harry and Betty slid into the back seats, while Ann jumped into the front. Doors were slammed shut, and Martin, checking for any on-coming vehicles, drew out and headed home.

" . . . has already left the building."

Questions were fired at the solicitor. No one had noticed the Sintons' escape.

"Thank you, no further comments, thank you." Gerald Evans turned from the cameras and reporters and smiled to himself. He decided to give himself the afternoon off, get back to his potting shed. It had been a morning's work well done. They now had just under four months to prepare for the main trial, and he knew he would find himself under considerable strain. Take a break when you can, he thought.

"I'm going home for the rest of the day Timothy, could you tidy up what is left."

His junior solicitor complied and made his way towards the offices, just a small walk from the Court House. Gerald Evans took a deep breath, feeling the chill air in his lungs, and expelled any thoughts of the forthcoming trial along with his exhalation.

As Martin drove carefully back towards the farm, no one spoke in the car. Betty and Harry held hands while Ann stared straight through the windscreen. Finally Harry spoke softly.

"Thank you for coming. I'm so sorry all this has happened. I don't know if I could have coped without knowing you all were behind me. I'm so sorry."

Martin looked into the rearview mirror and smiled at his father, Betty squeezed his hands for the umpteenth time, Ann turned and smiled.

"We are all just pleased you are coming home," she said. She didn't know what else to say. Harry Sinton gave a weak smile and turned to look out of his window, Ann turned back around. Martin caught his mother's eye in the mirror and gave a resigned smile. They drove back in silence.

As they approached the farm gates Martin decided to take the parallel track beside the farm, the overgrown holly, laurel and black thorn hedge blocking views to the farmyard on the left-hand side, village houses dominating the right. They saw no villagers as they passed the houses. Martin then swung left into the drive that led them past the walled garden and into the parking area and garages of the farmhouse. This was the track Harry had taken not three days before, flicking his torch light onto the bays of straw and hay, on his way to look at the lambing sheds.

It was just after eleven as they stepped into the back kitchen. Bracken greeted her master loudly, barking and jumping up at his stomach.

"Hey, hey," were his simple words of greeting to his dog. He pushed her off, trailing his hand so Bracken could lick it, and made his way through the kitchen and into the main room. Nobody knew quite what to do. Betty put the kettle on the Aga, Ann excused herself and rang her mother-in-law, who was looking after the twins. Martin made his way upstairs where he changed into his work clothes. After a cup of tea he was going to head out to the farmyard to see what help he could give. He wondered if his father would venture into the yard today.

As Martin returned to the main room, his mother was bringing in a tray containing the tea things. Ann was explaining that she would be going back to her mother-in-law and would bring the twins back in time for her father to see them before they were put to bed for the night. Martin asked if his father was going out on the farm. He didn't want to force him back, but knew the longer he stayed away, the harder it would be for him to return.

"Not today I think Martin. Please explain to George and Ken."

"They'll understand. Why not take Bracken out for a quick walk?"

"Yes, maybe I'll do just that. Betty, would you like to come?"

"That would be nice, dear," she replied, passing him a cup of tea.

Again they sat in silence as they sipped their tea, nobody knowing quite what to say. Ann broke the silence.

"Dad . . . "

Harry looked up.

"You know that we all love you, don't you? Nothing has happened to change that. Nothing could ever happen to change that."

Harry Sinton was choked with emotion, what could he say to his daughter to make things better? He had killed two men, caused distress to all his family (let alone the victims' families), and threatened the existence of their farm. He could not think of a worse-case scenario. Yet here was his little girl expressing her love toward him. How often could he apologise? What could he do to make things better? He was powerless. He held his gaze on Ann and said a simple "thank you".

George Stone had been busily numbering and rubber-ringing the lambs in the main barn as he saw the Sintons' family car pull up outside their house. He had been keeping one eye on the driveway all morning, seeing the car pull out earlier, and now he waited to see if his boss got out of the vehicle. Andy, who was helping with the numbering, holding the lambs still as the rings were placed on their tails and, where necessary, scrotums, also looked over towards the vehicle. When they saw the unmistakeable stooped figure of Harry Sinton stepping out of the car and towards the house, George muttered, "Thank God for that."

George had spoken little to the two other workers about the recent events, he was more concerned about keeping the farm going, he didn't want to indulge in gossip. He had begrudgingly kept his wife up to date with what he knew which, if truth be told, wasn't very much. This didn't bother Sandy, she filled in any gaps herself when recounting the story to anybody who happened to ask whilst in the shop. Andy and Ken, on the other hand, careful not to mention anything while George was about, had a field day with the subject. When they were alone working together, or when they were out with their own group of friends, they discussed the events with gusto. They were in a prime position to tell the tale and were making the most of it.

They all had had an eerie feeling whilst working in the main barn. The thought of the two bodies as they worked, cleaning out the pen that one had fallen into or simply walking over the place where the other body had lain, sent shivers down their spines. The police had said they had finished with the section of the barn they had cordoned off, but if they found anything that they thought the police should know about, to tell them immediately. They had returned the quad bike after taking it away with the transit van, dusting it for fingerprints.

Now that the police guard had left, the late night and early morning check of the barns became a disturbing experience. George had suggested they did it in pairs, although they had all laughed off this idea, not wanting to look too frightened and feeble, arguing that it would defeat the object of taking it in turns to give the others more sleep. The checks were carried out at great speed with much looking over the shoulder. They were pleased when Martin had offered to take on the early morning shift; it was only the late night visit that they now had to suffer, once every three days.

Martin arrived in the yard and asked what needed to be done. George Stone, having asked after his father, and stated his pleasure at the morning's verdict, instructed Martin on the outstanding jobs. They continued to work, cleaning out the pens, moving the ewes and lambs from barn to barn, paddock to pasture, until around one o'clock. Lunch time was always flexible, dependent on when there was a break in the work. Ken and Andy sat in the workshop, and tucked into their packed lunch, while waiting for George and Martin to go to their respective homes before discussing the latest development in the saga of the double killings at Downlands Farm.

Martin, on returning to the farmhouse, found his mother in the kitchen on her own preparing his lunch, Ann had left to be with her children, while his father, Betty explained, had gone to lie on the bed for a while: he was feeling a bit tired. Martin sat down at the table and tucked in to the hot soup his mother had prepared for him. The weather was still bitterly cold and the soup warmed his bones.

When he had finished his food and thanked his mother for the meal, he had a leisurely cup of coffee. Having still taken less than half an hour for lunch, he headed back to the yards. The strawing up of the lambing barns, filling the hay racks, bringing in the lambing ewes, all needed to be done, and still the outside fields had not been checked. Making to leave, Martin stopped in the doorway.

"Mum, I think it would be a good thing if Dad got out for a bit this afternoon."

"I know dear, but I won't be forcing him."

Martin was satisfied with the answer and left for the barns. Betty watched him go, and reflected how nice it would be if he came back to the farm. She then thought of the impending trial and the very likely possibility that he may not have a farm to come back to. She knew the financial standing the farm was in, and she knew that Court cases cost money. She realised Harry, Martin and Gerald Evans had been protecting her from the harsh reality of the situation, and it warmed her to think they wanted to protect her, but she knew enough to be worried. She hadn't asked any direct questions concerning the likely outcome of the case, or the cost, believing that she would be told when Harry, or Gerald Evans thought it was right. Still, she knew she had a right to be worried. She tried to block these thoughts out of her mind, she had a strong belief in her God, and had even apologised to him one night for bothering him so much lately. She had been lying awake, alone in the bed, whispering her prayer, saying she was sorry for bothering him so much, saying she realised he had greater things to deal with, all the poverty, hunger, conflicts in the world, but she really needed his help now.

Harry Sinton came back down the stairs by mid-afternoon, saying he hadn't slept much, just lain there thinking, listening to the sounds of the farmyard as the men got on with their work. Betty suggested the walk and he agreed. They put on their coats, hats and wellington boots, and with Bracken leading the way, headed down towards the valley. Betty told her husband of all the offers of help she had received from their friends, the telephone calls, including those bothersome reporters, before they had left the 'phone off the hook. Harry listened, answering where necessary. He was concentrating more on his surroundings. He had never taken the beauty of the countryside for granted, enjoyed the changing of the seasons, the variety of sights, sounds, and smells. But now that there was a real risk of losing the ability to walk freely in the fields, through the woods, he cherished the fact that he could do so now. He didn't want to think about the uncertainty of his future, but to enjoy his present. He tried to clear his mind of all the thoughts of his trial and enjoyed the peacefulness of the countryside, the ability to walk across his own land. He knew he may not have the chance for long.

That evening the Sinton family struggled to make things as normal as possible; strained conversations, forced laughter, and difficult silences accompanied dinner. Ann had said she would be staying tonight, along with the twins, and returning home early the following evening. Harry Sinton was pleased to see his grandchildren, bobbing them on his knees, remembering how he did the same with his own children, but all the time the realisation that these pleasures may soon be lost, tainted his joy.

When the time came for Betty and Harry to go to bed, Ann having retired earlier, they left Martin nursing another tumbler of malt scotch. In the two nights Betty had tried to sleep alone in the big bed, she had longed for her husband. It was here that she felt his absence the most. She had missed the comfort of having him close at the end of the day. The rest of the day she could keep herself busy, tidying, cleaning, washing, baking, but lying awake, desolate in the vastness of the double bed, she could only despair at the thought of life without her husband being close. She would treasure these coming months with all her might.

Harry Sinton was thankful to be able to climb his own stairs, use his own bathroom, slip into his own bed. Two long nights in the sterile police cell made him foster these feelings closely. Ever since he entered the village, on the drive back from the Magistrate's Court, he had been intensely aware of his surroundings, and the ease at which they might be snatched away from him crystallised his thoughts.

When they had washed and changed into their night clothes, cleaned their teeth, and snuggled down into the folds of the sheets, they held each other close. Neither of them spoke of their fears for the future; they were relieved to have the chance to be together; They would worry about the future tomorrow.

Mark Robson watched the early evening news propped up on one elbow lying on his mattress, tapping ash from his cigarette in one hand, into an empty can of lager held in the other. He was alone in his flat, having kicked the screaming and wailing girlfriend out of the door, telling her not to come back, it was all over. He had plans to formulate, things to do, and he didn't want any excess baggage to slow him down, incriminating him. Anyway, he reasoned, he could always buy her back later with a promise of some more of her favourite white powder poison.

He had staggered out of the *Red Lion* and back to his flat early so he could catch this broadcast, and now the item he had been waiting for played before his tired, blood-shot eyes. He saw the man at the centre of his hatred. He was being escorted by two policemen, pushed through the crowd of reporters, on his way to the Magistrate's Court. He listened as the front man told the camera that this man had made bail and would be standing trial in four month's time. The fact that Harry was walking free didn't upset Robson, he had hoped that this man would get bail, and now his wishes had come true. With a cruel smile on his face Robson snarled at the television.

"Now you're out you murdering bastard, I can get at you!"

Harry Sinton still woke at four-thirty in the morning, but forced himself to lie still, listening to the sounds of his son making his way out towards the barns. Betty was also awake, but continued to lie with her back to her husband, not wanting to disturb him, just in case he was trying to get back to sleep. Both had only slept fitfully through the night, both still felt tired, both lay there in silence. The next sounds they heard were from Ann and the twins. She had changed their nappies, dressed them, and was making her way downstairs when Harry decided to get up, Betty following closely behind. They all converged on the kitchen at the same time, Martin arriving back from the barns with news of a quiet morning, ten twins and two singles. The atmosphere in the house seemed more relaxed, as if that, now they had had a night's sleep (if fitful) and dealt with the initial return of their father and husband, they could slip back into the old routine. They still refrained from switching on the television or radio, and left the telephone off the hook, just in case they were reminded of their situation.

Over breakfast Martin asked what his father had planned for the day. Hesitantly he replied that he might try and go through the post that had come for the farm. Betty had opened all the post but left the business letters on the desk for Harry to go through later. Then he suggested that he might accompany Ken on his afternoon rounds around the outlying fields to check on the already lambed ewes and their lambs. They could take the Land Rover and both drive in comfort; Ken usually took the quad bike and trailer. He mentioned nothing about visiting the farmyard. One step at a time, thought Martin.

The rest of the day rolled along easily Martin returned for lunch, bringing everyone up-to-date with the morning's work. Betty, Ann and Harry had taken the twins for a walk, avoiding the village and farmyard. Harry had checked the four-day pile of letters, consigning over half to the bin, placing the rest in his 'in' tray, on top of an already high pile of paperwork. Correspondence always fell behind during lambing, and he couldn't face working at it that morning. He had replaced the telephone receiver on the hook, deciding to screen any calls through the answering machine, but was still relieved that no one rang.

Ken picked his boss up after lunch and they drove around the fields, Ken being careful not to say anything to upset him, Harry constantly expressing his thanks to his shepherd. They had to drive through the village to get to the first fields, and Harry's heart sank when he saw two walkers in the middle of the road coming towards them. Ken noticed his boss tense, and drove by, slowing slightly, waving to the walkers he recognised as villagers who had moved in the Autumn. The walkers stood to one side and waved back. Looking in the rearview mirror, Ken noticed the two had stopped walking and were staring after the Land Rover, one of them pointing, both talking excitedly to each other. Harry was pleased to get to the first field and open the gate to allow Ken to drive in. He was back to the safety of his farm.

The sheep looked well, but Ken agreed they had to continue to feed hay whilst the weather continued to freeze the ground, holding the grass back. On their way back Ken, without thinking, swung into the entrance gates of the yard. Harry spluttering his words in a state of panic, asked if he could be taken straight back to the house. Ken, having had no intention of driving into the centre of the yard, suddenly realised his mistake, continued past the buildings and around to the farmhouse. Harry got out of the Land Rover, once again thanked Ken for all his help and work, and made for the back door and sanctuary of his house. Ken drove back to the yard, found Martin who was filling the hay racks in the lambing barns, and apologised for his stupidity in bringing Harry so close to the barns. Martin calmed Ken's worries and even said that it may have been a good thing: his father needed to confront his fears some time, and the sooner the better, he believed.

Whilst Harry was out checking his sheep, Gerald Evans had arrived and was now waiting, talking pleasantries with Ann and Betty. He had no special reason for coming over, he just wanted to see his friend, see how he was coping back at his home, and reassure him that they were working hard on his defence. He had been pleased to hear that Harry was back out on the farm, looking around the sheep, but he understood when Betty told him that he couldn't face the barns just yet. When Harry joined them they didn't talk specifics – that could wait till later; they had a quiet chat between old friends, remembering names and events from the past. This would be the first of many such visits from family friends throughout the remainder of the week. All offered their help; none, except for Tom Whitworth, touched on the events of that Monday morning.

Tom Whitworth never had the greatest sensitivity and started his visit by congratulating Harry on his courage, and for ridding the area of two criminals. He then continued by telling Harry he was as good as free, the Magistrates had patted him on the back, he said, and no jury in the land could blame him for what he had done. His boisterous manner was heard by Martin who, sensing something, had popped in on the pretence of a coffee. Before Tom could continue on his blunt appraisal, Martin, using the excuse of asking a question concerning a field they had sown with winter barley, took Tom into the office. Tom Whitworth was the local wheat and barley 'Baron', and he was always ready to dispense any advice on its production.

"Tom, can you go steady on Dad please?"

"What do you mean?" Tom Whitworth asked. He had been expecting to give advice on a field of winter barley, not to be admonished by a boy a generation younger than himself. He had not been reproached by anyone for a long time, and never by someone a generation younger. His eyes grew wide, and his face began to colour.

"I'm just asking you to calm your views. Dad has taken this whole thing hard. What he doesn't need . . ."

"I'm just telling it as I see it."

"What he doesn't need is someone, with the best intentions, reminding him of it so frankly, and also building up his hopes."

"Building up his hopes! The bloody Magistrate let him go, the police didn't contest his bail. Those two bastards deserved it."

Tom's voice was raised, Martin hoped that it wasn't carrying to his parents in the main room, awaiting their return.

"Tom, please listen."

Tom held back, his look challenging Martin to change his views.

"All I ask is to think of Mum and Dad a bit. They need time to get over this. It isn't finished yet, the hard bit is yet to come. They need gentle encouragement. The four months to the trial will flash by. They have taken this hard, they are not as strong as they were." Martin saw Tom's features soften, and changed his tack. "We can't thank you enough for your support, and knowing that you are there is a great reassurance, but Dad needs a bit of time to sort things out."

"It doesn't change my opinion."

"We don't want you to. We hope the jury will think the same, but we just don't know, and that is hanging over Dad all the time, it's bound to take its toll. On all of us."

Tom grunted his acknowledgement of this fact, and, not one for admitting he was wrong, or leaving a conversation without saying the last word, added "I still believe those two had it coming. We need more of this sort of thing to stop more of it happening."

Martin, very shrewdly, let Tom have the last words, and ushered him back into the main room. Betty and Harry were sitting down, cups of tea in hand, still in a slight sense of shock after Tom Whitworth's opening tirade.

"You sowed the wrong variety," Tom muttered gruffly, as an explanation for his and Martin's absence. Martin shook his head at this well-meaning, if rather tactless, friend.

Wendy Stevens woke in the unfamiliar surroundings of Bob Richard's bedroom. She had been placed in the bed, still fully clothed, the night before. Bob had resisted the temptation to undress her and had slept on the sofa using an old army sleeping bag as a duvet, his spare rooms were full of junk and stolen goods. He had been up and inspected his new visitor before making a quick tour of his garage and breakers yard. He then returned to his Woolaway bungalow, in the grounds of his yards, and armed with a cup of coffee, sat in his kitchen, waiting for the sleeping guest to regain consciousness. His work could wait for a day.

On hearing some muffled noises from his bedroom, he went over to the door, knocked and asked if he could come in. Wendy, still confused, her head thumping, body shivering, pulled the duvet up to her neck.

"Who's 'at?"

Bob slowly opened the door and poked his head into the room. Wendy tried to think back and work out how she could have got there. The last thing she remembered was seeing her husband's body lying still, pale and cold in the mortuary. She realised she must have started to drink, the pain in her head and soreness of her eyes confirmed that much, the taste in her mouth backed-up those conclusions. She remembered the feeling of dread at being alone with nobody to look after her. The worries of being evicted, of returning to the squalor of her old bedsits. She could not remember Bob's arrival at the flat.

"Do you want a coffee Wend?"

"'Ow did I get 'ere?"

"I brought you last night Wend, you were in one hell of a state."

He wanted to remind her of the fact that she had come on to him, but in the cold light of day, with Wendy sober and suffering from a hangover, he decided he would have to wait.

"I need a drink."

"You sure Wend? It's a bit early."

"Don't piss me around Bob, I need a drink."

She sat herself up on the bed and surveyed her surroundings through squinted eyes. Old clothes were strewn around the room, half-empty beer bottles, coffee mugs and half-full ashtrays fought for space on the chest of drawers. Old pictures of Bob in racing overalls hung lopsided on the tired-looking walls. Stained curtains held back the light of the day. Wendy had been in Bob's bungalow before, sharing a drink with her husband and Bob after a successful night's work, but she had never been in his bedroom. She knew the rest of the house was in much the same state, pieces of car and truck engines lying around on old newspapers, discarded take away food packaging festering in room corners.

She considered her situation; she knew she was alone in the world, she knew she had no possessions to speak of, no money except for a wad of cash hidden away in the flat which she intended to retrieve in the not-too-distant future. She had been in this situation before and had always got out of it by latching onto the nearest man, sucking-up to them, backing them up. Telling, and giving them, whatever they wanted.

Stevens had been her latest and, she had thought, her last. They had married seven years ago, Wendy revelled in the notoriety, she loved the fear he could instil in people, enjoyed the security he gave. Now she was back at square one, her looks fading and with no family or friends to help her.

"Where's that drink?" she asked softly, forcing a ragged smile at Bob.

Bob's heart raced, his loins stirred. She hadn't exploded, screamed abduction. She was sitting up asking for a drink. Wendy wanted a drink to forget, she knew Bob fancied her ever since their first meeting, it was so obvious she thought Billy was bound to notice, but he hadn't. Wendy used to flirt with Bob, lead him on, enjoying the thought of Billy finding out and what he would have done to Bob if he did. Now she was alone. She needed a drink to do what she needed to do, and to forget her beloved Billy. She shivered at the thought of Bob, his filthy, oil-stained hands on her skin, greasy hair and stubbled chin rubbing up against her neck. She knew she could manipulate him; Bob hadn't had a women ever since she had known him, her and Billy used to laugh about it behind his back. She could see no other escape; she needed him, but she needed that drink first.

Sean Robson's funeral was planned for the Saturday after his killing. His grandparents had arranged the service, the burial plot, and the wake afterwards. A good-sized crowd gathered to pay their last respects. At the head of the group, shuffling in slow motion out of the church, walked his parents, again Mr. Robson giving his wife the physical support she needed. Alongside them were the grandparents, both sets, and then various aunts, uncles and cousins formed the main body of mourners. Behind these came friends from school and college, dressed in an assortment of white shirts, black ties and jackets. Family members hung on to each other and wept, young girls buried their faces in each others shoulders and cried as the coffin was lowered into the ground.

The vicar finished his service and stepped back to allow the family to pay their last respects. At the back of the group Paul Allen and Andrew Goodman stood side by side. They had kept out of the way at the back of the church throughout the ceremony, not wanting to confront their friend's family, in case it caused a scene. They now turned to leave, not noticing the shabby figure watching from the church gates.

Mark Robson sniffed as he contemplated the spectacle in front of him, wiping his sleeve across his nose, leaning up against the graveyard wall. It was the first time he had set eyes on his family since he was sentenced at the Court for causing the death of the little girl. He had often wondered why his parents had come to the Court, they certainly hadn't shown him any signs of support. He suspected they had come for their own salvation, a form of punishment before they could console themselves and dedicate their lives to their favoured son.

"Now look at them, sad sods," he thought out loud.

He noticed the two boys break away from the crowd and start to walk back towards the church, to the main entrance where the cars were parked. He could make out the figure of Paul Allen, he had met him a number of times, he was always hanging around Sean, playing up as the big man. This was the person he had come to see. He didn't recognise the other boy with Paul; that didn't matter, he could soon scare him off, he had some questions he wanted to ask Paul. He would come back and pay his respects to his brother later, when everyone else had left. He had no intention of meeting his family, not now, not any time in the future. He pushed himself off the wall and made his way up the path, on course to intercept the two boys before they got to the main gate.

Paul and Andy were walking back to Andy's car, heads bowed, deep in their own thoughts. When one, and then the other, noticed the figure walking towards them, they instantly knew who it was, and their hearts sank. They stopped, there was no point in running, he would find them anyway.

Mark Robson caught up with the two boys, and immediately told Andy Goodman to "fuck off!" Andy didn't need telling twice and scurried away, glancing back only once, trying to convey his guilt at leaving Paul alone with Robson. Mark Robson then put his hand on Paul's shoulder and guided him after Andy. Robson looked back at the group huddled around the graveside and whispered menacingly to Paul.

"We have got some talking to do mate."

Paul walked with Robson out of the main gates and down towards the busy high street, they passed Andy who was sitting in his car, contemplating his next move. Mark Robson didn't talk as he guided Paul along the pavements, over the road and into the pub on the corner of a crossroads. Neither took any notice of the name of the pub, neither knew the area. Mark Robson pushed Paul into a secluded corner seat, walked up to the bar, ordered one pint of lager, paid for it with change from his coat pocket and returned to the frightened boy in the corner. He sat himself down facing Paul, his back against the wall so he could view the rest of the bar area, and made himself comfortable.

"Well?" Robson asked, taking a sip from his pint.

"I was coming to see you Mark . . . I didn't know where you were . . . I was going . . . "

"If you bullshit me, I'll slice your fucking nose off! Now tell me what happened that night, and don't give me that police report crap, I want the truth!"

Paul was now in a dilemma, he had repeated his and Andy's version of events so often he new it off-pat, almost forgetting the true events. Should he continue his tale of lies, or should he come clean to Sean's brother. The consequences of the police finding out Paul was lying was nothing compared to the fear Mark Robson invoked in him. If he strayed from his story, who else would find out? Where would it lead? At the moment he was being haled as a victim, even a hero to some of his friends, standing up to the man who murdered Sean. If he now told Mark and the truth got out, everything would start to crumble around him, no one would believe him again. He decided to stick to his story. He was trying to look away from Mark's searching eyes, but he was sat with his back to the bar, with only a floral picture hanging on the wall above Mark Robson to look at; he had never felt so intimidated in his life.

"Stevens bullied us into going . . . " Paul began, but before he could continue Mark stamped on his ankle under the table, causing the table to lurch, the pint glass tottered before Mark saved it from falling and spilling its contents. Paul cried out in pain and shock from the sudden, savage attack. Other people in the bar turned around at the sound, but soon averted their look when they saw the two figures in the corner.

"Didn't you hear me arsehole, I want the truth!" Mark Robson didn't let on that he knew Sean had been going on these farm visits with Stevens for years. Some of the money Sean had made from them was given to him to start up his little pill business.

Paul stared at his interrogator. Did he know he was lying, or did he just hurt him to see if he changed his story? Paul was getting more terrified by the second.

"It was my first time I swear!" Paul waited for another instalment of pain, when none materialised he continued warily. "We had waited for Stevens for ages, and when he did pick us up he was in a real bad mood. We drove up to some place near the place Sean was . . . well near that farm, and we went into the first farm which pissed Stevens off even more. The bike was knackered or something. Me and Sean could sense something was wrong even then." Paul was looking at Mark Robson for encouragement, but all he got was Robson leaning back against the wall, lighting a cigarette and fixing him with a cold stare.

"This happened again in the second place, we couldn't even get in through the gates. By this time Stevens was fuming, me and Sean just wanted to get out of there, it was all going wrong." Paul wanted to show that he and Sean were in it together, partners against Stevens. "Then we drove on to this Downlands Farm." Paul's throat was getting dry as he came close to Sean's death. Should he say he did nothing to help Sean, that he watched as Sean was torn apart by the farmer's shotgun.

"Can I have a drink?" he asked.

"Get on with it," Mark replied.

Paul fidgeted with his hands, rubbing them on his thighs, crossing and uncrossing his arms, looking around the room for any sort of distraction to keep him from continuing with his story.

Mark Robson leaned forward, close to Paul's face and hissed, "This is the part I want to know."

"The . . . the old farmer appeared from nowhere. We had just finished loading the bike into the van, we were all in the front. I was in the middle. We were just leaving when this farmer shot at us. Stevens just exploded, I mean he went crazy, screaming at the bloke. He . . . he jumped out with a baseball bat and went for this bloke, Sean got out too, I . . . I think to stop Stevens. Sean was unarmed, he had nothing on him. I . . . I . . . the . . . the bloke just shot them, shot them both, I couldn't do nothing, I didn't even have time to get out of the van. Sean was giving himself up, and the madman just shot him. There was nothing I could do Mark, you must believe me!" Paul was pleading for some kind of forgiveness, understanding.

Mark Robson stamped down on Paul's ankles again and pushed himself back against the wall; Paul cried out in pain. The barman looked over, undecided whether to investigate the situation.

"That's the truth I swear, I couldn't do nothing. I . . . I had to get out, I had to tell the police . . . " Paul was ranting, stumbling over his words. His ankles hurt, tears forming in his eyes. He wanted to know what to say to please the man opposite him. He had portrayed Sean as the innocent victim, showed that it was all Stevens' and the mad farmer's fault, what more could he say?

"I . . . I didn't know what to do, I . . . I . . . "

"You shat yourself and left Seanie dying in that place," Robson spat. He was disgusted at this whimpering, snivelling boy. Paul had backed-up all that Mark Robson had wanted to believe, all that he had wanted to hear. Sean was the good guy, trying to stop Stevens, giving himself up to the murderer, and this so-called friend did nothing to help, ran from the place. He continued to stare at the creature before him. What to do with him? What to do next? It was time to go, get back to his flat, he needed another fix after listening to the story of his kid brother's death. Time to think. He decided the waste of space before him wasn't worth any more effort, but he could always use another petrified dogsbody, you never knew when he might come in handy, especially one this age, able to get a foot-in-the-door with the younger market for his pills.

"You owe Seanie for running out on him, therefore you owe me!" he snarled. "And you'll pay!"

Paul trembled at the sound of the voice. He kept his eyes cast to the ground. Robson, holding the pint glass in one hand, grabbed the table with the other and rammed it into Paul's stomach, and stood up. Then, pulling the table away from Paul, Robson bent over the whimpering teenager and tipped the remainder of his pint into Paul's lap, letting the glass fall after the liquid. Robson then straightened up, glared at the barman who was looking over, defying him to intervene, and walked out of the pub. Paul was left snivelling in the corner, wishing he had died alongside his friend in the barn.

CHAPTER FOUR

THE PIG AND WHISTLE

The open log fire gave a welcoming warmth as you entered the *Pig and Whistle* public house. Smoke-stained pictures of various prize-winning pigs at various times through the ages hung on the walls, other comic cartoons of boars and sows littered the bar. The pub consisted of three rooms, two described as restaurants, although the menu could be ordered and eaten in any room, and a third kept aside for bar meals and drinking. The drinking bar was the original bar with a low ceiling and wooden floor, the extra rooms came from encroaching on the private area belonging to the Publican. The increasing demand for pub meals, and resultant increased profits meant the landlord was happy to see his old private lounge filled with customers tucking into his home-made fare.

Peter Squires leant against the bar and waited for his first customer of the evening. It wouldn't be long now, having just opened at seven o'clock he knew who would be the first in. As always on a Sunday evening, it would be the local squires, as he referred to them: the local squires at the Squires' pub was the running joke. Every Sunday night the resident farmers would congregate for an evening of reflection on the past week. Squires enjoyed their company, not to mention their regular patronage, but this week he was a bit apprehensive. The news of the double shooting at Downlands Farm had brought an influx of news reporters into the village, and true to form, the *Pig and Whistle* Public House had become their focal point. Again Squires was not complaining, but the thought of the Sunday evening farmers "Church Service", as the farmers referred to their weekly meeting, being interrupted by some news-hungry media hounds, still sniffing around for an extra "Human Interest" story to the killings, was not pleasant to him. He decided he would keep an eye on things and would ask any journalist to leave if they were upsetting his regulars: you always have to look after your regulars, he told himself.

"I don't think I'll go, dear."

"Oh mother you must, you can't keep hiding, you have done nothing wrong. Church is the perfect place to get out and be seen again. You can't lock yourself up for ever." As soon as Ann said it she flinched at her mistake, telling the wife of a man who was being charged with manslaughter she couldn't lock herself up for ever! Betty didn't seem to make the connection.

"Maybe next week, not just now dear, please."

Ann had driven over for Sunday dinner, as this was the last time all the family would be together for a while. Martin had to return to his regiment on Monday morning, and decided to leave early the next day. He had swapped his early morning shift for the late night check of the lambing barns with George Stone. Martin hoped to return before the trial, mainly at weekends, but his leave ran out tonight and he could see no way of extending it if he wanted to take more for the trial.

"You will have to go out sometime Mum. Would you like me to come with you?"

"Please, I know you mean well but let me do this in my own time." Betty had not been used to people fussing over her so much, that was her job, she felt confined by it all.

It was approaching a week since the fateful Monday morning, and all in the house were acutely aware of it. Harry Sinton had still not managed to set foot in the farmyard, restricting his activities to the fields, and woods. Martin had been a great help, but now that he was going the farm-staff would be stretched again. Harry had said he would do the outside sheep, freeing Ken for the afternoon, but he still couldn't bring himself to do either the late night or early morning shift. That would be shared between the three workers. They were sure the lambing would only be lasting for another fortnight at the most, and they believed they could cope with that.

"Are you going to the farmer's service dear?" Betty asked her son, making sure her husband was out of earshot.

Martin had wanted to spend the last night of his enforced leave with his parents. The thought of sitting in the *Pig and Whistle*, and listening to his father's contemporaries express their view on his father's likely fate did not change his mind.

"I don't think so Mum, I would rather spend the time here."

Betty smiled at this reply, and continued to prepare the evening roast.

"I'll just check the twins," Ann announced, and headed out of the sitting-room, towards her old bedroom that had been turned into a nursery eight months previous when Ann had given the Sintons their first grandchildren. She had decided to stay the night to make the most of the time they had left together. Her husband had agreed on this and sent his apologies, but was still in the middle of his lambing. The excuse was well understood.

Bracken, stretched out in front of the Aga, lifted her head at the sound of Ann leaving, twisted her neck to make sure no one else was leaving the room, and resumed her position. Martin looked across at his mother, she had seemed to wilt in front of him these last four days, her eyes red from lack of sleep, her face drawn and pale, forcing a smile whenever she thought it was necessary to show she was coping. She had hardly touched her food in the last week, nibbling away at bits on the plate, pushing the majority of it around until it was cold. The same was true of his father.

"You should try and eat more, Mum; Dad too."

"I know dear. In time."

Martin was truly worried about his parents; he knew that he couldn't stay, and that fussing around after them wasn't going to work. They would have to handle this thing in their own slow, methodical way. He knew Ann would be popping back as often as possible, and he had witnessed first hand the dramatic change the twins could have on his parents, bringing wide smiles and cheer whenever they appeared. Mike and Sarah Cairns, the closest of farming neighbours in terms of distance and friendship, would also be keeping a watchful eye on the situation.

When Ann returned, Martin left mother and daughter together and went to the front room where his father was sitting watching a documentary on farming without subsidies in New Zealand. Harry Sinton had always wanted to visit New Zealand, and was extremely jealous of both his children who had done so, Martin in a gap year before university, Ann in her first year after completing her degree. When the Court clerk asked for his passport as a condition of bail, along with reporting to the police station twice a week, he had been embarrassed to admit he had never owned one. He had never been out of the country but had always hoped that one day he may find the time and the money to visit New Zealand. He had now dismissed those dreams. They had resumed watching the television in the last two days, thankful for no mention of their case. New news items had taken its place.

At the dinner table the conversation was mainly concerned with the lambing, and the support that had been offered by so many. Then it concentrated on Martin's future. Betty asked Martin to repeat his plans on leaving the 'Army', and again Martin fudged his reply. Nobody pushed him for a straight answer.

"He should have taken all three of them out."

It hadn't taken long to get onto the subject of the killings, all the crowd at the long table in the corner of the drinking lounge of the *Pig and Whistle* had met each other individually through the week and had discussed the events at Downlands Farm, but they had never met 'en masse' and were now enjoying the chance to air their opinions to a larger audience. All the usuals were there, a hard-core of five, with a number of drifters to and from the table, all with the noted exception of Harry Sinton.

The 'service' had started quietly enough, inquiries into one another's health, the state of their farms, followed by grave voices expressing concern for the Sinton family, and then the beliefs and theories, judgements and conclusions started to flow.

"He would be in even bigger trouble if he had."

"It would be his word then, not this rubbish being spouted by some little thief. They got what they deserved!" Tom Whitworth was on his usual form, making statements that would place him slightly to the right of Attilla The Hun. He sat with his back up against the wall, arms crossed over his pot belly, the pipe in his right hand adding to the cigar and cigarette smoke atmosphere of the confined room.

"That's a bit harsh Tom." George Hollis liked to think of himself as more of a liberal, which wasn't difficult when facing Tom Whitworth, "a death sentence for stealing."

He enjoyed arguing against Tom, although was careful not to upset him too much. Tom Whitworth had a long memory for people who didn't agree with him wholeheartedly. Many locals were careful not to get on the wrong side of Tom, agreeing rather than defending an opposite viewpoint, but George had known Tom all his life and was happy to give as good as he got.

"You're only upset because you got your knackered bike back," cut in David Longstaff, a retired farmer who had sold his land three years previously, having no heir to pass it on to, and was now enjoying the comfort of being money rich, land poor, and not the other way around.

"Exactly," Tom Whitworth was back on track, "they had already pinched your quad, they are a bloody menace. They don't care two hoots about us."

"I was talking to a friend over at the N.F.U. the other day," Charles Renton broke in, "do you know how many quad bikes were stolen last year?" He waited for effect, all eyes were on him. "Fifteen hundred."

The answer was greeted by a general shaking of heads, and rising of pint glasses.

"He told me some incredible facts," Charles Renton continued, "four thousand four-wheel-drive vehicles, three thousand tractors!"

"Exactly!" Tom was off again. This time waving his pipe around for added effect, "These bastards get away with it. I've had my place broken into, and I bet you you couldn't tell me of any farmer around here that hasn't lost something."

"We are easy targets," someone agreed.

"And they are never caught," Tom continued, "and even if they are they don't get done. A bloody slap on the wrist and they're back on the streets that day."

Tom Whitworth had an opinion on most things, but this was closest to his heart. His face started to redden, spittle appearing at the side of his mouth. He wiped the back of his hand across his mouth and stared around the table, defying anyone to oppose him.

"What I don't understand is the mentality behind these people," Tom Whitworth's son broke in. He was sometimes embarrassed about his fathers opinions, and the way he would express them, but this time agreed wholeheartedly with his father. "I mean, they work bloody hard at thieving; if they worked just as hard on legal stuff they wouldn't run the risk of going to prison, and probably earn more money."

"That's what I've been saying boy. They have no deterrent. If we shot more of them, there would be less of a problem."

A ripple of disbelieving laughter broke out over Tom's last statement.

"You can't go around shooting people who you think are breaking the law Tom," George Hollis began.

"*Know* broke the law, we know these two broke the law. And if they were sent to jail, we would then have to pay for them being inside. And from what I've heard it's a bloody holiday camp in those places."

"I wouldn't like to try it," David Longstaff quipped.

"But where would you draw the line? A stolen quad bike is a death sentence. What's a chain saw worth? Lop off a right hand?"

The argument had centred on Tom Whitworth and George Hollis. The others around the table watched eagerly, not wanting to inject any comments in case it broke the rhythm of the discussion.

"I don't see why not. I know they introduced blinding burglars in one eye in some Indian province or somewhere, and the crime rate fell by sixty per cent overnight, or something like that."

"But who would police it? Now I know you've done some dodgy things in your time."

"I never pinched a thing!" Tom Whitworth screamed. "Don't you start accusing me of being like them Hollis."

"I didn't mean like that, I mean like . . . like say drink-driving. You have done that in your time."

"You too," Tom replied indignantly.

"I'm not saying I haven't. I'm just saying what would the sentence be for it. Amputate a leg?"

"It would certainly make me think twice about doing it," Charles Renton admitted.

Tom calmed down a little, sucked on his pipe in an unsuccessful attempt to draw some smoke from it and gave George a long, measured stare.

"So you're saying they should get away with it?"

"No, what I'm saying is your sentences are a bit harsh. Now if they had killed old Harry . . . "

"Which they probably would have," Tom's son broke in.

"If they had killed Harry, I'd be the first to say 'Hang 'em'. But thankfully they didn't. I agree with you Tom, these people get away with it and it's us who pays the bill, either by repairing things, or increased insurance premiums. The police's hands are tied, and the law is on the side of the criminal as far as I can tell."

A general air of agreement flowed around the room. Tom Whitworth concentrated on relighting his pipe, a regular operation when he had ignored it for longer than one minute. Sips were taken from pint glasses, cigars and cigarettes stubbed out or lit up, depending on their state.

Peter Squires accepted the smog from the farm meeting as one of the drawbacks from their patronage, but he would never asked them to refrain. The reason the "service" had moved to his pub almost three years ago now, was due to the landlord of Tom Whitworth's local asking the group to refrain from smoking, and perhaps keep the noise down. He had said some of the other customers had complained, especially ones that were eating, although there were only three couples in there at the time. He had moved into the pub not long before and didn't realise his mistake until the farmers, and their partners, never went inside the pub again. Now Peter Squires enjoyed their custom, not just on Sunday nights, but through the week when they brought friends or family for a meal. There was also a lot of mutual back-scratching, the duck, pheasant, or venison on the menu always being very local (and very cash in hand, if not put against the slate), firewood also being a mode of currency. If Peter needed the use of a tractor and trailer for any reason he only had to ask, the going price was two pints of the lender's preferred tipple per hour.

"I heard a bad story the other day," David Longstaff declared. "About a farmer from up in the midlands somewhere."

"A friend of a friend, sort of story?" asked George Hollis.

"Something like that."

All eyes were now on David; he took his time, it was his turn to revel in the attention.

"This bloke was up in Court for cruelty to a cattle beast he was transporting to the market, the market vet stated it was unfit to travel and this bloke found himself in Court. The upshot of it was he got fined about fifteen hundred pounds."

"So?" Asked Tom's son, "we've all heard stories like that."

The others around the table waited for David to continue, knowing there would be more to the story than that, knowing he had paused for effect, hoping to catch an impatient listener out.

"I was just getting around to that, if you will let me speak," he said, acting annoyed. "Anyway the next bloke up before the Judge was a youngster up for a charge of supplying drugs to school kids, aged about fourteen, fifteen, in the school playground. Guess what his sentence was?"

Slow head-shakes greeted David's question, more supping, more drawing on cigars and cigarettes. He had them in the palm of his hand and was enjoying the moment.

"Two hundred quid and a warning!"

"You're joking?"

"Bloody hell."

"Ridiculous!"

"I tell you, it's something when a farmer trying to earn a honest living gets fined more than a drugs-pusher preying on school kids. I couldn't believe it when I heard it."

"I could," Tom Whitworth muttered.

"You know what one of our problems is don't you?" George Hollis invited.

"Enlighten us George."

"Our image. How we are perceived. The general public see us as rich, bloated. . ."

"Squires?" Peter Squires prompted from behind the bar.

"Yes, squires of the land, so they fine us extra, or what they think we can afford."

"As far as I can tell," Charles Renton spoke, "the general public considers us as either Range Rover-driving, hunting, fishing and shooting millionaires, or thick, yokel locals with smocks on and straw sticking out of our mouths."

"Don't forget chemical spraying, hedgerow-ripping-out, cruelty-inflicting, villains," Tom's son added. "When exactly did farmers change from being the food-supplying saviours to the nation, and become the spawn of Satan?"

"About the time things began getting plentiful son," Tom told him.

"And when they started to realise how much of their coffers were going to our subsidies," George added.

Peter Squires had been giving the conversation in the corner one ear all evening, enjoying the banter, disbelieving some of the more blinkered beliefs he had heard, and mainly laughing to himself at the moanings of this set of farmers who always saw things as us against them. Either us against the government legislation, us against the European ministers, us against the urban population, or just us against the weather. It wasn't always doom and gloom at these services, although he believed that farmers had a high propensity to moan, but tonight the solemn air produced by recent events had brought with it a depressing conversation around the table in the corner.

"I don't know if I would have done what Harry did, if I found myself in that situation."

"I hope I will never find out."

"I hope I would have done the bloody same," Tom growled.

The conversation then turned to Harry, Betty and the family, how they were coping, how they had all offered help in some shape and form, but Harry being Harry, was too proud to accept.

Martin and Ann had said goodnight to their parents, Martin his goodbyes, and now they sat across from each other, slumped in their chairs, absently watching the television. Martin with his ever-present scotch in his hand. Bracken had swapped the warmth of the Aga for the warmth of the wood burner, and lay sprawled across the hearth rug.

"You're pretty evasive with your plans for the future Martin," Ann commented.

"Now is not the time. I do have ideas, plans, but a lot of them hang on what's going to happen in four months' time."

"Are you wanting to come back here?"

"That is an option, but I don't want to push Dad out. Before all of this mess I still couldn't really have come back here for at least five years, We would just be in each other's way."

"What rubbish! You could learn from him. You both get on with each other. You would learn more here than at Cirencester, and Dad needed to take things easier, even before this mess."

"There is more to it than that at the moment. There might not be a farm to come back to."

Ann looked puzzled, and Martin regretted his last statement.

"What do you mean?"

Martin sighed, swilled his drink around in the tumbler, and decided to speak of his fears. "I mean the farm might be the price of Dad's freedom. Even if we didn't need to sell the whole thing, Dad might not want to be around the place, being reminded of his horror for the rest of his days, and that's if he's found not guilty."

Ann sat and stared at her brother. She didn't want to think about the likely outcome of the trial, but knew she was listening to some harsh truths. She had found herself caught between two stools. She loved her parents and the home farm, but for the last six years, four of them in marriage, her loyalty had been moving towards her husband and his farm. Now that the twins had arrived, she had her own family to worry about. She hated the thought of her father being sent to prison, her mother left to cope alone. She would offer all the help in the world but knew her mother would refuse, not wanting to impose.

"I can't afford to buy them out, and even if they leave it to us I couldn't afford to buy you out. Then there is the overdraft, the mortgage. And even if I could afford to, what would Mum and Dad live on? Where would they go? Selling the place is the only option I can see."

"If Dad goes free."

"What do you mean?"

"Well if he is convicted, it would be better if you came back, looked after Mum, and ran the farm."

"I've still got eighteen months left to serve. That would leave Mum fourteen months left on her own."

"She could live with us, or you could come out early. The government want to get rid of half the Forces as far as I can tell."

"I think it is too early to say what is going to happen. I pray to God that Dad doesn't go down. That would kill him, and Mum. We just have to wait."

A silence filled the room. Martin swilled and stared at his scotch, Ann bent forward and stroked Bracken, who replied by giving a long, hard stretch.

"You know we haven't really talked about this," Ann began tentatively, "but Richard and I have a bit. We have come to the conclusion that it really wouldn't be fair if you had to buy me out."

Martin looked across at his younger sister. She was still stroking the dog, not looking over to him. He didn't know quite what to say, it was a massive gift. Half of seven hundred and sixty three acres, plus some seventy acres of amenity woodland, at today's prices, situated where they were between the M3 and the M4 (the M5 making what was known to the land agents the golden triangle, easy communications to the money of London) would have given little change from eight hundred thousand pounds. Then there was the farmhouse and the tied cottage George Stone lived in. House prices were restrictively high if you were a local on an average wage.

Martin had often wondered if Ann would have come to this conclusion. Richard was now sitting on a six hundred acre holding of their own, with the knowledge that they would inherit a further six hundred neighbouring acres when Richard's parents retired (retiring from life a more likely event, than retiring from farming).

He would never have suggested this, but now it was out in the open, at least he knew where he stood a bit better.

"I mean," Ann continued, looking up at her brother, "if we were back in the old days you would get it all anyway."

"But we are not back in the old days, and Mum always stressed we would be given an equal share."

"But circumstances have changed."

Martin smiled at his kid sister and winked. "Thank you, it is a wonderful . . ." He searched for the right words. " . . . caring gesture." They weren't quite right, but they had to do. "But it still hasn't really changed anything. It all still hangs on the trial."

The possibility that he could own and run Downlands Farm swept through his mind. It would be a dream come true, returning to the family farm and regaining his roots. He still knew a number of people in the area, the old stagers that had not moved, and remembered Martin as that lanky teenager of the past and not just the upright Royal Marine officer of today. He could settle down, maybe even keep hold of a girlfriend for longer than six months without having to fly off to some distant corner of the globe and putting the relationship under stress. Then again that might have been an excuse to allow him to keep his independence.

"Of course it changes things. It means we don't, or should I say you, Mum and Dad, don't have to sell up everything. Maybe a field, if that."

"Have you told them?"

"Not yet, I've only just told you. Do you think it is the right time to tell them?"

"Dad is pretty worried about the cost, I think Mum is too. It might help them, then again it might sound like you have reached this decision because of the charges Dad's facing."

"I know, but I think I will raise it some time when you are not here, maybe pretend that you don't know."

"That's fine by me. Thank you Ann. I really can't say how much this means."

Ann smiled and leaned back from the dog. Martin checked the time and finished off his drink.

"I'm going to go around the barns, are you going to be up when I get back?"

"No, I'm off to bed in a minute."

"Well, I will say goodnight and goodbye. I'll keep in touch." He walked over and kissed his sister on top of the head, it was an affectionate gesture, not lost on Ann, as the last time he had done so was on her Wedding Day four years ago. "Thank you again, and Richard. If you change your mind . . . "

"Have a good drive down," she interrupted, "and don't worry too much, we will look after Mum and Dad."

Martin nodded, called Bracken to follow him, she could have her night walk as he checked the barns, he left Ann sitting on the sofa staring at the dying embers in the wood burner.

After a time Ann stood up and checked to see if anybody had left any cups or glasses in the room that needed to be tided away, and noted that Martin had left his tumbler on the side table and tutted to herself. She crossed the room to pick it up. The sound of the telephone ringing shattered the calm of the house and made Ann jump. She put the glass down and made her way to the telephone in the hallway. The incessant telephone calls from newspaper reporters, radio stations and television networks had died away halfway through the week. Double-killings, even in the backwaters of Hampshire, can't keep an audience for ever. They had used an answer-phone to screen the calls for the first part of the week, but lately the answering of the telephone had got a lot easier.

The light was off in the hallway, but enough shone from the main room to allow her to see her way to the telephone. As she walked towards the ringing she shivered to herself. Was it her or was the house colder since that fateful morning? In the gloom of the long corridor she answered the ringing.

"Hello." There was silence on the other end of the line. "Hello?"

A low vicious growl emerged from the earpiece.

"I know where you live you murdering bastards, and I'm going to make you pay."

The evening session was drawing to a close at the *Pig and Whistle*, the pub had filled and emptied as the farmers had discussed the events of the week. Peter Squires was clearing tables in the two restaurant rooms, letting the farmers find their own time to leave.

"Off to check on your sheep George?" Tom's son asked.

"Yep, the main flock has just started to lamb."

"You want to get out of those bloody woolly things George. That's what got Harry into this trouble in the first place," Tom observed.

"You got broken into for your pick-up Tom, you can't blame that on sheep, you haven't got any."

"Every time you look at one of those woolly things you have to do something to them. Either shearing, or worming, or lambing, or moving the bloody things. And then they go and die on you for no reason." Tom Whitworth's hatred of sheep was well known, but the reason for it was lost in the past (although he had just mentioned a few).

"I would be happy to see them go if I was a wheat baron like yourself Tom, but us poor grass farmers have to rely on something."

"Get some cattle beasts, you don't have to tuck them into bed each night."

"They are a bit too big for me, I like things I can handle without fearing for my life," George smiled.

The conversation had returned to its normal good-natured banter between friends, the last of the beer was being drunk, pipes emptied, cigarettes snubbed out. Arrangements for the coming week discussed. Who was doing what on the farm, their social engagements, and of course the trial, never very far from any conversation.

"If anybody wants a lift to the trial, me and the boy will be going. I'll have space for one more at least, Mary's coming too."

"Family day-out Tom?" George suggested.

"We want to show our support, if you want to stay away you carry on. Don't mock me for wanting to help a friend."

"I wasn't mocking you, I'll be there if I can. We have told Betty we are available for any help if she wants it. It's just not as easy for us to get there."

"You two shouldn't fall out over this," David Longstaff intervened. "We are all concerned for Harry and Betty, we all have offered support, and we all know we will do all we can."

"Who's falling out?" Tom asked, looking suitably admonished. "I'm just offering a lift to anybody."

"Well, I'll take you up on it if I can," George replied. "Thank you."

The appointed drivers waited for the last dregs to be drained, glasses put down, cheerios called to Peter Squires, and another "Church Service" for the local farmers had finished. They sidled out of the pub, into the freezing night air, and went their separate ways, down the country lanes and home. The world had been put to rights for another week.

Mark Robson placed the receiver back on it's mount, pulled the collar of his donkey-jacket up, stuffed his hands into his pockets and shouldered open the door of the public telephone booth. He headed across the deserted road, street lamps illuminating his path, away from the *Red Lion Inn*, back to his flat. He had spent most of the afternoon, and all the evening, in the pub, folding and unfolding the scrap of paper that held the telephone number of his brother's killer, thinking of ways to avenge his death.

"That's just the start Seanie, I promise," he whispered to himself as he trudged back to the relative warmth of his flat. "That's just the start."

Martin returned around eleven to find Ann on her own in the sitting room, the lights off, her legs tucked under her on the sofa, chewing her nails and looking frightened. The fire in the wood burner had died, the television providing the only light. She looked up at Martin as he walked in.

"Are you alright Ann?" The emptiness of his question was not lost on Martin, but he couldn't think of anything else to say. Ann had been coping well, the conversation before he left for the barns had lifted her spirits, but it didn't surprise him that she may have been bottling things up and had finally succumbed to the situation. "Can I get you anything?"

A shake of the head. Martin moved towards his sister and sat down next to her in the shadow of the room.

"Do you want to talk about it?"

Ann turned and looked at him. Where to start she thought, all the fears surrounding the trial, and now the fears of a faceless, nameless man, bent on revenge. What would he do, where would he stop?

"I'm scared," she blurted.

"I know Ann, so am I."

"No you don't realise, I'm scared . . . for all of us. We, I got a 'phone call . . ." she started to sob.

Martin looked puzzled, but allowed Ann to continue at her own pace, not forcing her to tell. Ann rubbed her nose with the back of her hand, and sniffed. She didn't like to show any weakness in front of her older brother, she had always looked up to him, boasted of him to her school friends, always proud of him. She didn't want to look weak before him now. She straightened her back and ran a shaking hand through her hair in a gesture of strength.

"We had a 'phone call. He said 'I know where you live'."

"A 'phone call?"

"He . . . he . . . said he knew where we lived. He said we were murderers."

Martin put his arm around her shoulder and drew her close.

"He . . . he, said he was going to make us pay."

"It's alright Ann. It's alright."

"No it's not Martin, it's not alright, it's a nightmare. It's a horrible nightmare."

"Shush now. Its alright. It will be OK." But he also knew it was a nightmare far from over.

The soft words did little to comfort Ann, she still knew that things were far from alright. She wanted to be with her husband, she wanted to turn back time and have her happy life again. Just one week ago she had everything, an honest, hard-working husband, two beautiful children, their own farm, and her parents just down the road, a perfect future. Now the stress of the situation was showing. She was short with her husband and children, she flitted from one home to the other, never enough time at either. She felt she was carrying the whole world on her shoulders. She felt tired, hemmed in, unkempt. She had no time to herself. She felt unloved and ugly, everyone had more time for the twins, ignoring her. She let all her emotions flood out, sobbing on her brother's shoulders.

Martin didn't understand that this was a culmination of feeling, but thought he understood the emotions she was going through. All he could do was hold her softly and stay with her until she had cried it all out. He thought of the threatening 'phone call and how to handle it. He was meant to be back in Devon by seven the next morning, he wouldn't have time to wait for the police and he didn't want them coming over tonight, perhaps waking up his parents, tipping them off to what had just happened. If he could spare his parents from further worries he would. He decided to ring 1471 and record the number, then drive into town and report it straight to the police there, hopefully someone would be manning the desk even in the early hours of a Monday morning. As he cradled his sister in his arms he wondered why anyone would ring up their intended victims and tip-off their hand. The answer came to him instantly, to scare them first.

Ann sniffed and raised her head from his shoulders, she wiped her eyes and said sorry.

"Don't be silly. Look if it makes you feel any better, I'm going to go into Annavale and report this now. I'll drive down to Devon and see my C.O. and see if I can extend my leave. I would rather do it face to face than over the 'phone."

"But then Mum and Dad will know something's wrong. The call was probably just a crank trying to scare us," Ann said, trying to convince herself as much as her brother.

"I can't leave them here alone, and you need to get back to Richard. This bloke might call again, get Mum. She would be petrified."

"You can't stay here for the next three months," she sniffed. "I think we should tell them, warn them that this has happened, then it wouldn't be such a fright. Tell them the police know and are looking into it. The telephone companies can trace calls now, convict the person doing it."

Martin desperately wanted to stay for longer, but he had to be on parade the next morning. He saw the logic in his sister's opinion and decided to follow it.

"OK, I'll go in to the police station in a minute, when you are alright."

"Go now, I'm alright."

After Martin made sure Ann had recovered her composure he dialled 1471 and noted the number. He then drove into town, rang the night-bell at the station and reported the threatening call. The duty officer, knowing the situation at Downlands Farm, noted the incident and said that someone would be around in the morning to run through the event with his parents. The policeman added that it was probably a sick prank that wouldn't come to much, but they would look into it all the same. Martin then returned to the farmhouse and slept for three hours before he headed back down the dual carriageway towards Dartmouth, leaving Ann to explain the appearance of the police in the morning.

The week following Martin's departure went smoothly. Harry and Betty were left on their own in the evenings. To begin with Ann popped over every day, along with the twins, but that soon stretched to every other day as things began to settle down.

To the relief of all, there had been no follow-up threatening telephone calls. The telephone company had managed to trace the call back to a public telephone booth on the east side of Southampton, but further inquiries by the police revealed no local connection with the deaths of William Stevens or Sean Robson, both from the other side of the city. The police could not associate the man known to them as Spencer Marks, a suspected drugs dealer yet to be caught and charged, to one Mark Robson, elder brother to the deceased Sean Robson.

Mike and Sarah Cairns kept a close eye on things, inviting the Sintons over for lunch or tea, asking if they needed or wanted anything. Betty and Harry were grateful for their friendship. Martin rang his parents every second day and his sister the other; he felt cut off in Devon and had started inquiring about coming out of the Marines early.

Gerald Evans organised the Defence team. He wanted follow-up reports and extra information concerning the background of the raiders, especially the boy Allen who he considered held the key to the

Defence. Discredit him, and the jury would be half won. The team studied all the relative police reports, and researched any related Court case that may help their cause. They had frequent meetings with Harry and Betty, to keep them up to date with their progress.

Paul Allen had still not ventured back to his work experience placement, preferring to watch television and slouch around the streets, constantly aware that one day Mark Robson would be tapping him on the shoulder. He had had his Summons through the post to go in front of the Magistrate's court on charges of attempted burglary. This did not worry Paul unduly; he expected another slap on the wrists, maybe some Community Service this time, but nothing he couldn't handle. He was more worried about the debt he owed Mark Robson.

Wendy Stevens, still constantly drunk, had settled in to her new home, and had even tidied up a bit. For the first three nights Bob slept on the sofa, but on the fourth, after he and Wendy had got a lift back to the flat, Bob to pick up the BMW, Wendy to recover the hidden stash of bank notes, they had both drunk in a private wake to Billy. In the morning Bob found himself naked in his bed next to a semi-naked Wendy. He couldn't remember how he got there, if they had gone separately or together. He didn't know whether to stay and let Wendy wake up next to him to see what direction the situation took, or to get up and try and stay sober the next night, so he could remember who led who in the morning. Wendy was still unconscious, and he decided to get up and wait. He had dreamt of having women in his bed for years, he could wait a little longer he told himself. He had only to wait for that evening to become Wendy's lover. Wendy had found her latest saviour.

The Robsons continued to shut themselves off from the world. They had buried their youngest, and as far as they were concerned only son, and were now inquiring about properties in Dorset. They had spent their holidays there before their two boys came along. They thought they could start afresh there. Mr. Robson sounded out his foreman on the possibility of selling the business to him, and found he was keen, although not wanting to be seen as taking advantage of the circumstances. Mrs. Robson had ventured back into the office, but still in a state of shock, she couldn't concentrate and had left after two days. They would have sold up and moved before Harry Sinton's trial began.

Harry Sinton had managed to venture back into the farmyard. He and Betty had waited for George, Ken and Andy to finish their work one afternoon, then, hand-in-hand, accompanied by Bracken, they walked the path from the farmhouse to the buildings. Harry had managed to get to the entrance of the concrete yard before, but had always turned back. Now with Betty at his side, and Bracken ahead, he managed to enter the main barn.

In the fading daylight the barn seemed different to what he had remembered that fateful Monday morning. It was lighter, more open. The transit van that had seemed so large was no longer there, and the quad bike was locked away in the workshop. The sheep were lying down contented, their lambs by their side, mostly asleep. Betty kept asking if he was alright, and Harry kept nodding his head, not trusting his voice.

As they walked past the pens, Harry averted his eyes from the area where the two bodies had lain, towards the warm boxes where he was pleased to see Tiny still alive. Tiny, having heard voices and sounds outside the confines of his box, had stood up and started to bleat in his small, shaky voice.

"You wouldn't believe it has only just been fed, would you love?" Harry asked his wife.

"His belly looks full enough."

Harry Sinton bent down, patted the pet lamb's head and offered his little finger for the lamb to suck. The lamb, ever hungry, latched on to the finger and greedily sucked with all its might, shaking its tail in delight. Betty smiled to herself; she hoped she was seeing the first signs of her husband's recovery.

They walked back towards the entrance and passed, for the second time, the place where William Stevens and Sean Robson fell. Harry Sinton never looked across at those places, he kept staring ahead towards the lambing barns. He didn't realise he was walking faster or that he was squeezing Betty's hand harder, but she didn't mind; her husband was facing his fears and she was happy for him.

They slowly walked around the lambing barns, penning up three that had lambed since Andy had left that afternoon. Harry enjoyed being back in the middle of the lambing. The next morning, to the surprise of all, he met his workforce in the barn, and that night he offered to do the early morning shift again.

He was apprehensive as he walked out into the cold morning air, but after the first morning he settled back into the routine. All concerned were delighted to hear that Harry had overcome his fears. It was the twenty-fifth of March, eighteen days after the killings.

CHAPTER FIVE

HAMPSHIRE BACKWATERS

A dank, cold mist hampered Mark Robson's final approach to the farmyard, the cold snap in March had been replaced by heavy rains in April. Mark had driven up from Southampton after the pub had finally closed, using the cover of darkness for his work. He had limited himself to five pints all night, and only enough heroin to keep himself sane: he wanted his wits about him. He had an address, and a road map, but little clue as to the difficulty of finding remote farms in the backwaters of Hampshire. It was almost comical, his attempts to find his intended victim's home.

He would drive to a junction, stop, find the relative villages on the map, make a decision which way, and then continue. Sometimes the signposts told of a village not on the map, while at other times a village on the map was omitted from the signpost. If someone had been so inclined, and had sat waiting at any number of these intersections, they would have seen Robson return about twenty minutes later, coming from a different direction, stop, turn on the interior light of the car, read his map again, then head off on another route. He had done this on more than one occasion, and it was doing little to alleviate his nerves or anger.

The mist allowed Robson to drive slowly, and peer at the signs in relative anonymity. On a clear night his borrowed, battered Ford Sierra Saloon would surely be seen and remembered for its suspicious movements. He had managed to persuade Iain MacDonald, his tablet supplier, to lend him the car with the promise of more business. MacDonald would swear the car had been stolen if anything went wrong. The fact that MacDonald had no Vehicle Tax, MOT or insurance mattered little to Robson; he just needed the ability to get to his destination. It was the first time Robson had driven since he had killed the little girl, not due to any remorse or guilt, but mainly due to lack of funds, and little need to go anywhere that public transport couldn't take him.

As he passed the sign stating he was entering the village of Ilton(Please Drive Carefully), and approached the same farm gates that his brother had approached three weeks earlier, his excitement grew. At last he was going to hit back at the people who had taken away his one true and trusted friend. These people had deprived him of his brother, killed him in cold blood. Now they were going to pay. Robson didn't believe in the justice system, and he had first-hand knowledge of it, he would argue. It protected its own and kept the likes of him down. He believed in his own brand of justice, and tonight was to be the first instalment.

He didn't know what to expect as he drove towards the farm entrance, his only forward planning was to purchase twenty-five litres of petrol and make sure he had his lighter on him. He wanted to scare his victims, to damage them in some way. He had called them only once, just enough to frighten them. He had then decided to let things cool down for a while, let these people fall into a false sense of security.

He drove past the gates, which were now shut and chained every night ('stable door and horse bolted', was muttered more than once by friends of the Sintons) and continued on down a hill until it levelled out into a small valley, he then pulled over onto the grass verge. Only now did Mark Robson start to think of how he was going to carry out his act of vengeance. He wanted to pour the petrol through the letter-box of the house and throw in the lighter, he had given no thought of the approach and withdrawal. He had imagined the house being on the road, and all he would have to do was stop the car, pour the petrol over and through the door, put a light to it, and drive away. It was all going to be so simple. Now he had seen the sign he knew he was at the right place, but he couldn't see the house. He realised he couldn't leave the car in the valley and walk to the house, he would probably get lost in the mist and be caught, dying of pneumonia, in the morning.

He had passed no other cars on the road since he had turned off from the major route, and believed himself to be totally alone on these small country lanes on this dank dark night. He drove on, looking for a place to turn around. He was getting more anxious by the second, he wanted to get it done and get out. He drove to a T-junction and swung around. He decided to park the car by the gates, leave the engine running, creep through the farmyard and on to the house he hoped would be close, do the job and get out. The bright digital clock on the dashboard told him it was three-thirty in the morning.

He drove back to the farm entrance and left the car pointing at the gates, the headlights struggling to penetrate the mist. He retrieved the petrol from the boot, closed his door and the boot softly and proceeded to shatter the night's peace by slamming the metal can into the gate as he tried to climb over it. He kept looking around nervously as he scurried along the track parallel to the main barn. He wondered if Sean had used the same track, seen the same sights, had the same cold mist seeping into his bones.

He got to the entrance of the concrete yard and really noticed the barns for the first time, they seemed to loom out of the mist, illuminated by the floodlights inside and outside the buildings. He remembered the story of his brother's murder, how he was killed in a barn. The reality suddenly hit him. This was where Sean had died, one of these barns was covered in his brother's blood. He had not thought about it before; the fact that his brother had been killed in a barn had been secondary to him, the fact that he had been shot was the main issue. But now, looking at the scene of his death, the actuality of the events stopped him in his tracks. It became clear to him: he would set alight the barn where his brother had been killed, murdered. He would burn the bastard thing down, wipe it off the face of the earth. It would cleanse the place where Sean had been murdered, and still inflict pain on the murderer.

He walked towards the main barn, trepidation in his steps as he neared the entrance. Did he want to see the place where his brother had been killed? Would there be someone inside? Which barn did it happen in? What would he find? He saw the entrances to the two lambing sheds were closed off by metal gates, and sheep lying down in the straw. What would Sean have been doing in those barns? He discounted them and continued to the main barn. The barn was exactly the same as when his brother saw it three weeks earlier, except the quad bike was in the workshop under lock and key. The trailer was in place, loaded up with the morning's rations. Lambing had peaked and was now coming to an end, but the barn was still full of ewes in their pens, with their lambs, waiting to be turned out to pasture.

Mark Robson stood at the mouth of the barn for what seemed an age, looking around the inside of the barn. How could his brother have died here? This was a nothing place, a dirty, smelly waste of space. The sheep didn't stir, some looked at him in their nonchalant way and continued to chew their cud, while others completely ignored his presence.

Robson then noticed the stack of straw and hay bales in the right-hand corner of the barn, six bales high, eight long, and four deep. The stack had just been replenished the day before from the main straw and hay barns. He crossed over towards the stack and placed the petrol can down on the concrete floor. Some of the sheep now rose to their feet, more interested in the movements of this person, and one or two gave an inquiring bleat. Robson ignored them; he had more pressing things on his mind. He got to the stack, and saw the difference in the hay and straw bales but didn't know the reason, and didn't care; he knew they would burn. He reached up to the top level and pulled a couple of the bales down. More sheep were taking interest now, they knew that activity by the stack usually meant another round of food.

Robson wanted to cut the bailer twine around the bales he had just dislodged but couldn't find anything sharp to cut them with. He looked around wildly, hoping something would spring out at him, but nothing did. He started to grab at the straw, pulling little bits of stalk out. He wanted a starting point for his fire, some kindling, but time was pressing, he wanted to be done. He clutched at the twine and tried to break it with shear force, the twine held, cutting into his fingers. Again he stared wildly around, his actions getting more and more feverish, he was getting desperate. He then saw a half-used bale at the end of one of the rows of pens. He rushed over and swept it up in his arms, carried it back to the stack and dropped it on the loose bales on the floor. The sheep by now were starting to find their voices, bleating and baaing away, hoping for some unexpected food.

Robson opened the top of the Jerry-can and started to splash the petrol over the heap of straw and dislodged bales. The image of fire and flames sweeping over the stack excited him. He didn't care about the splash-back over his clothes and hands, he continued to spread the flammable liquid as he shuffled back towards the middle of the barn. He was enjoying himself, and all in the name of his brother.

Back in the middle of the barn he stopped and looked around, he still had about a quarter of the liquid in the can. In the opposite corner was a table covered in aerosol cans to spray-mark the sheep, empty wine bottles to feed the pet lambs, sacks of powdered milk and an assortment of medicines and paraphernalia for the lambing season. Robson emptied the last of the petrol over the table and threw the can away, not caring about the noise: the sheep themselves were making enough to wake the dead. Parallel to the table were the pet lamb warming-boxes. Robson bent over and grabbed a handful of straw, waking up two lambs that were slumbering under the lamp. The third, Tiny, was already up on his feet, tail shaking, hoping for some extra milk.

Holding the straw in one hand, he reached into his pocket and produced his lighter, he span the flint with his thumb, causing the sparks, and lit the gas. The flame shone bright and straight, it greedily accepted the offered straw. The straw flared, the flame orange, and Robson watched for a time, fascinated by the power and appetite of the fire. He then threw the bouquet of flames at the table and stepped back towards the middle of the barn. The petrol fumes caught the flame in a whoosh, lighting the barn with its brilliant yellow flash. Robson felt the heat on his face, turned and grabbed for a second handful of straw from an empty pen. He hurried with his lighter, failing to get a flame on the first two turns of the flint, but producing a light on the third, setting the handful of straw alight. He didn't waste time watching this burning bundle of straw, he threw it towards the stack of straw and hay, failing to send it half way, but the petrol he had splashed on the ground readily caught hold of the flames and hurried them towards the soaked stack.

Robson was oblivious to the surrounding noises of the barn, the sheep bleating at the sight of one of their primeval fears, fire. All he could hear was the rush of the flames, the popping and crackling of the burning straw. He watched in glee as the stack caught alight, as thick pale smoke billowed from the hay. He was destroying his brother's place of death, purging it with flames. His eyes were wide with excitement, his face covered by a wide, wild smile.

"Burn you bastard, burn!" he roared in triumph.

An aerosol can exploded, bringing him back to his senses. He looked around the barn and realised it was time to escape. He ducked through the passageway, turned to his left and saw the lights of his car shining through the mist and metal gates. He ran to the vehicle, clambered over the gates and got in, slamming the door and crunching the gears into reverse. He pointed the car in the direction he had first come into the village and took a look back at the barn. He couldn't see any flames through the drizzle and darkness. Had the straw caught the barn alight? Had he used enough petrol? Doubt crept into his mind.

He slammed the car into reverse and raced back towards the gates. As he approached he made out the faint glow of orange coming from the fog-clad barn. The sight eased his fears of failure, he knew his job had been done, the flames were doing their work.

Forcing the gear stick back into first he sped away through the village, only to be lost in the labyrinth of village roads and the all-consuming mist. It would have taken him half as long to reach a main road if he knew where he was going, but at the time all he cared about was to get away from the fire, as fast as he could.

He had done it, he had struck his first blow against the murderer that took away his beloved brother. He couldn't control his elation, his relief. He was laughing out loud, screaming inside the car, defying anything and anyone to mess with him.

Harry Sinton woke with a start, and sat up in bed. Betty stirred, reached out with one hand to pat her husband reassuringly and mumbled something about it being alright. Harry wondered why he was so awake. He had found it steadily easier, if still fitfully, to sleep since the fateful morning as the weeks passed, but he was still plagued by nightmares. The images of Stevens and Sean Robson falling back, lying dead on the floor, kept running through his subconscious. When he woke to escape those scenes, he had always been drowsy, and always remembered the reason for waking. This time he could not recollect the dream and he was wide awake. Something else had woken him, a change in the normal surroundings of the night. The sounds in the dark were different, no longer the soft sounds of a restful farmyard, now there were cries of fear and anguish coming from the barns. The more he noticed the noise, the more he realised the enormity of the sounds. Something was horribly wrong in the barns, the sheep were creating merry hell.

Harry eased out of bed and rushed to the window as fast as his old frame could take him. Betty was now sitting up in bed.

"What is it dear?"

Harry pulled the curtains back and looked out towards the farm buildings. On a clear night he could make out the shape of the sheds, and even see into the main barn. Tonight the mist enveloped the surroundings to such an extent that he would have struggled to see the weak white glow of the flood lights. Tonight there was a different glow to the night, more orange in colour, and not as stable. It seemed to be constantly moving in the night sky, growing stronger, then fading, then growing again.

"What is it dear?" Betty repeated.

"I . . . I think the barn's on fire."

Betty scrambled out of bed and joined her husband by the window.

"Oh my dear Lord! I'll call the fire brigade."

Harry was already putting on his work clothes, not bothering to take off his pyjamas first. "It may only be small, I'll go and see if I can put it out first. We don't want to call them out for nothing."

"Don't be silly Harry, look at it!" she exclaimed. "If we can see it from here on a night like this, it's got to be big", and with that she headed down the stairs for the telephone in the hallway and rang for the emergency services.

Harry had pulled on all his clothes and followed Betty down the stairs, fastening his belt as he went. His first thought was for the sheep in the barns. He would have to get them out, let them roam free in the yard, as long as they were away from the flames. He also knew in his heart that the fire had caught and the fire brigade was needed. Maybe it was hope that made him think he could handle it, maybe he was trying to protect Betty from further torment. He certainly didn't connect the two occurrences in the barn. He wondered what could have caused it as he hauled on his wellington boots and waxed jacket. Maybe the warming-lamps in the pet lamb boxes had fallen onto the straw bedding. Maybe the electrics in the barn had shorted, causing some sparks. The barn walls were covered in dust and dirt, layer on layer from years of harvests and lambing. The thought frightened him.

"Call George!" he shouted from the back kitchen, realising he would need all the help he could get. He waited for a confirmation that Betty had heard. When he repeated the request, Betty answered him with a "Yes yes" and he left the house for the barn. He had forgotten his torch and he had to turn back, unable to find his way in the misty night without it.

Harry Sinton hurried to the barns, the orange glow coming brighter with every step. "Oh no, oh no," he kept saying to himself. He could now hear the sound of the flames, mixed in with the cries from the sheep. He could hear the sound of wood splitting under the pressure of the fire, the noise of aerosol cans exploding, metal creaking. He rounded the corner and carried on straight to the main barn. He saw that the flames were concentrated at the far end of the barn by the drier and intake pits. He knew there was layer upon layer of dust and chaff at the bottom of those pits, all his good intentions of clearing them out were always lost as more important jobs were found.

The smoke was billowing out through the roof. The straw and haystack were a black heap in the corner of the barn, the medical table had collapsed and flames were spreading through the individual pens. The sheep were in a state of panic, chasing around in their pens, smashing into the hurdles that held them captive as the flames and heat steadily approached. Lambs looked on in bewilderment as their mothers knocked them over in their panic. Already the first two rows of pens had caught alight, wool melting onto skin, skin blistering away from the body. Some sheep had collapsed, only wisps of smoke rising from their blackened skin where thick protective wool once stood, slight movements betraying the signs of life in the sorry mass. Lambs lay dead, charred and mangled. The wooden warm-boxes had disintegrated, nothing could have survived the destruction.

Harry reached the first row of pens, dropped the torch, and started to fumble with the bailer twine to open the pen. He could feel the heat from the blaze on his back. The twine was taking too long to undo, he needed his knife, but he kept it on the medicine table. It was Harry's turn to look around wildly; he patted his pockets in a vain hope he had left a knife in one of them. He remembered the tractor, there was always a blade of some sort left in the tractor. He raced back into the open yard and to the tractor parked by the breeze-block wall of the lambing shed. His sudden appearance from the main barn startled the restful sheep lying at the entrance to the lambing shed. They stood and scattered from the gate, but Harry had no time to calm them. He lifted the tool-box lid and scrambled about through the assortment of bolts, nuts, nails and spanners until he felt the rusty serrated edges of an old combine header knife. Retrieving it from the toolbox, he hurried back to the barn.

The scene before him made his eyes fill up with tears, the pain and suffering of the ewes and lambs in the barn was unbearable. He thought about Tiny, trapped as the flames engulfed the high-sided warm box. He forced himself back into the barn, ignored the first pens by the entrance, and approached those nearest to the flames as he could bear. He started to cut away the bailer twine and open the gates, forcing the sheep out into the middle of the barn. Some ewes didn't flee, they kept turning around looking for their lambs. Harry had to block out the images of the dead and dying sheep in the rows before him, he could not reach the ones closest to the flames, the heat beating him back. He had to concentrate on the ewes and lambs he could get to. The whole barn was in a state of panic and confusion. Ewes and lambs were everywhere, bleating their distress, aerosol cans were exploding, wooden floors collapsing, smoke billowing as the flames kept advancing through the barn.

George Stone ran into the barn and saw what Harry Sinton was doing. He pulled his knife from his back pocket and started the same action on the opposite side of the barn, in front of the blackened stack of straw and hay. Both men worked without saying a word to each other. More and more ewes and lambs were milling around in the centre passage of the barn. Some had found their way out into the concrete yard, being followed by their lambs into the safety of the night, others kept racing from one startled lamb to another, looking for their offspring. When George had finished his first row he pushed the ewes out into the centre passage, shouting and hollering, waving his arms in an attempt to move them to safety, pushing any lingering lamb along with his feet. It was slow work under the heat of the fire.

Harry Sinton looked up at the sound of George moving the ewes and lambs, but didn't break from his efforts on the other side of the barn. Betty turned up in her wellington boots, a dressing-gown over her night dress, a duffle coat wrapped around her dressing gown. She stood in horror at the scene before her. Metal girders creaked, the roof started to collapse, bringing down slabs of asbestos smashing to the floor, adding to the calamity of noise inside the barn. Betty hurried over to her husband and started to force the sheep away to safety. They were beating the advancing flames, saving the majority of sheep.

An explosion rocked the yards, ripping slabs of asbestos off the roof, collapsing the wall at the end of the barn, littering the ground with rubble, showering George with debris and dust. Harry Sinton looked up in shock as he watched George slip and fall to the ground under the bombardment of flying rubble.

"Get out!" he ordered Betty.

Betty carried on pushing the sheep to safety as she walked towards the yard. Harry made his way over to George, and to his relief saw him haul himself up and stumble towards the entrance of the barn. When Harry reached him he put his arm around George and led him out of the barn.

"It must have been the petrol tank . . . I never thought . . . " George stuttered.

"Are you alright?"

"It must have been the petrol tank," he repeated.

The petrol tank was housed underground, built by Harry Sinton's father just after the war, when petrol rationing was still being enforced. It was situated at the side of the barn, and was only used for the Sinton's private vehicles, the rest of the farm machinery running on diesel. At the time of the fire it was only a third full but when the fire had found its way to the tank, caught the pool of ever-present spilt petrol at the bottom of the pump alight, the greedy flames had managed to set the whole tank ablaze, causing the explosion that had ripped through the barn, showering the surrounding area with concrete, metal and soil. Harry left George with Betty and started to go back to the barn. Betty grabbed his arm, pulling him back.

"Where do you think you're going?"

"There's still some ewes in the pens."

"Don't be so silly Harry!" she screamed. "You're not going back in there."

"I've got to do something."

"You've got to do nothing, there is nothing more you can do. We have to stay here. The fire engines will be here soon. I'm not losing you to that damn barn."

Harry looked back longingly at the ewes and lambs still held in their pens. He couldn't tear his gaze away at their plight as the flames continued to eat up the straw, tirelessly advancing towards the pens. Betty turned her attentions towards George, brushing away at the dust on his coat, asking him if he was alright. George's head thumped, his senses were spinning, but he couldn't tear his eyes away from the burning barn. George's wife arrived and replaced Betty at George's side, taking over the fussing. All four stood in the yard, feeling the heat of the flames, helpless as the fire engulfed the barn.

The two fire engines arrived at the farm gates within twenty-five minutes of the call-out; it would have been sooner but the mist hampered their response. The entrance gates were still chained and padlocked (George and Sandy having scrambled over in their hurry to get to the barn), so the firemen lifted them off their hinges and threw them to one side. They then proceeded to deploy their equipment and dowse the flames with water from their hoses. Sheep were milling around the yard as the firemen explored the buildings. They found the four onlookers standing in the middle of the concrete yard, staring at the scene of desolation in front of them. They looked a strange sight huddled together, illuminated through the mist by the glow of the flames, Betty with her dressing-gown and duffle-coat, George covered in dust and debris, Sandy fussing over him, and Harry with tears in his eyes. The firemen ushered them back from the blaze and asked if anybody, or if anything dangerous, was inside. Harry told them of the diesel tank that was connected to the grain drier.

The firemen explained that there was little they could do. They would contain the flames to the one barn, let the fire burn itself out, and then make the area safe. Sandy insisted she take George to the casualty department in Annavale Hospital, but George assured everyone he was fit and healthy and didn't need to go. Sandy won the argument and drove him in herself. Harry stayed and watched the slow destruction of his barn. Betty returned to the farmhouse and made up a number of flasks of coffee for the firemen.

The mist still hung in the air as the dawn pushed the night away. The light revealed the desolation of the barn, its contorted, twisted girders, and shattered roof loomed out of the smog. The blackened remains of the drier stood desolate at the end of the barn. Firemen, cloaked in their heavy safety gear, poked and prodded, pulled and pushed at the remaining walls and roof. A number stood around the hole left from the exploding petrol tank, shaking their heads. Smouldering straw, blackened sheep carcasses, bits of breeze-blocks and shards of asbestos littering the floor.

Harry Sinton had watched as the barn disintegrated, and numerous thoughts filled his head. What had he done to deserve this? Had it been an accident? Perhaps, he thought, he hoped, it would be for the best. Perhaps, some time in the future, it would be easier to forget without the barn there to remind him.

He returned to the house to retrieve his .22 rifle. He was going to despatch the ewes that had been caught in the flames but had not died of their burns. The gap in the gun cabinet where his shotgun used to stand was glaringly obvious to him: the police still held the shotgun as evidence. It was then that reality dawned on Harry Sinton. He would never forget the recent events, things would constantly remind him of it, whether he stayed at Downlands Farm or not. What had happened had happened, and he could never change the fact. It was at this moment he decided what he would do at his trial; he would tell his family when the time was right, but he had made up his mind.

The television cameras, photographers and reporters had once again assembled at the entrance to Downlands farmyard. Speculation was rife concerning the likely cause of the fire. It seemed a terrible coincidence that three weeks after the fateful shooting of two burglars, the same farmyard had now been the site of a major fire. The leading fire-fighter had told the reporters that arson was not ruled out and a full investigation was now under way. The police had returned to the scene, and having consulted with the firemen, noted the incident and placed it, along with the threatening telephone call, as an ongoing investigation.

Harry and Betty Sinton took the information that arson was suspected with solemn faces. Harry had resigned himself to the fact that he was now a target for someone's vengeance. Betty wondered how anybody could be so cruel to their sheep.

News once again swept through the local community. The same friends hurried around to offer comfort and help, telephones rang as the story was relayed from one person to another. The continuing saga of Harry and Betty Sinton had taken another turn. The Sunday evening farmers' "Church Service" had another topic to discuss.

Mark Robson stayed in his flat and impatiently watched every possible news bulletin until he saw what he was waiting for. By mid-morning the images of the burnt-out barn were played on the television screen. It brought a smile to his face. It had worked, he had destroyed the place of his brother's murder, and had hit back at the man who had murdered him.

He had stripped off his dirty, petrol-and-smoke smelling clothes on returning to the flat, throwing them in the corner, and had a shower. Now, dressed in relatively clean clothes, he headed out of the flat, on his way to a celebratory drink at the *Red Lion*.

"That will do for the time being Seanie," he muttered. "We don't want to overdo it now do we. Perhaps something closer to the trial."

Mark Robson had started to talk to his brother more and more, believing him to be by his side at all times. Eddie the barman winked at Mark as he entered the bar, he too had seen the news reports and had connected the two together. Mark smiled back but didn't say a word as he lifted his pint, taking a long slow drink. This arson business was thirsty work.

The commotion the fire caused slowly died down. The fire brigade's follow-up examination confirmed it was arson. The police had little to go on when they investigated the fire, even when they linked it with the threatening telephone call. As the weeks passed no other threats, or acts, were committed. The insurance company agreed to pay for a new barn; thankfully for Harry Sinton, arson was covered in the policy.

As the weeks passed, lambing ended and Andy went back to college, leaving Ken, George and Harry on the farm. Ann and the twins continued their pilgrimage to her parents, now twice a week, and Martin returned home at every possible opportunity. He said he had inquired about Premature Voluntary Release (PVR) from the services, but had to wait for a response. Harry and Betty tried to carry on with their lives, Harry resigned to his fate, Betty blocking out all thoughts of the future. Betty had resumed going to the Sunday night church service and Harry had ventured down to the pub for the farmers' so-called "Church Service" on a couple of occasions. The usual crew were there, all happy at his return. All, including Tom Whitworth, careful not to mention the impending trial. Harry Sinton had enjoyed the evenings, but had kept very quiet, rarely joining in the conversation. The others didn't mind, they knew it would take time, especially with the Court case looming; they were just pleased to see him.

Gerald Evans was in constant contact with the family, although he had little to say. He reported on Paul Allen's Court appearance, and kept his friends up to date with the Defence. They were still gathering facts, obtaining statements, researching similar past cases, but still he knew it all boiled down to the jury on the day.

Paul Allen, in his appearance in front of the Magistrates, pleaded not guilty to the charges of burglary for the theft of George Hollis's quad bike, and attempted burglary at Harry Sinton's farm due to duress. The Magistrates listened but still found him guilty on both counts, sentencing him to one hundred and twenty hours of community service and a two-year suspended sentence. His mother was in Court to offer support, his father stayed away.

The farm continued its seasonal performance, April had been wet, but May was beautiful. It brought the countryside to life out of the clutches of winter. Trees burst into leaf, grass seemed to rise overnight, barley-heads appeared swaying in the breeze, buttercups littered the green grass fields with their bright yellow petals. The staff were kept busy fertilising, spraying, sorting lambs and shearing sheep. June arrived too soon.

Southampton police had lost all trace of Wendy Stevens, she was nowhere to be found, her flat had been left open, the door kicked in by local youths who had had a field day ransacking the rooms and spray-painting the walls. Eventually the local authority boarded up the property and put into motion the process of its cleaning and return to a rented accommodation. Billy Stevens' body still went unclaimed, again it was left to the local authority to deal with. They buried William Stevens' body, with little ceremony, in a small plot in a new cemetery on the outskirts of the city.

With one week to go, the trial once again attracted the attention of the media, reporters were summoned, cameras organised. Mark Robson also renewed his interest in Harry Sinton.

CHAPTER SIX

ENGLISH COUNTRYSIDE IN JUNE

Martin arrived home on the Sunday, one day before the trial. He had been back before, at weekends that never seemed long enough, but this time he had arranged a fortnight's leave. He brought with him encouraging news concerning his early release. His C.O. had been good to Martin, understanding his position and offering advice. Martin had fifteen months left to serve from a twelve-year term. he advised against Premature Voluntary Release now, as he would have to give seven months' notice and would lose his pension. For the sake of five months he suggested Martin stayed in the regiment, but he would try and find a posting closer to his family for him. There were plenty of options, Salisbury Plain was only a short drive away and London was within commuting distance, both of which brought a variety of choices. The C.O. was sure he could find some way for Martin to complete his time, which would also enable him to live at Downlands farmhouse.

Martin entered the farmyard and was pleased to see the remains of the old main barn being dismantled, ready for the replacement barn to be erected in time for this year's harvest. The new building would not be putting further strain on the finances; the farm insurance covered arson, and the insurance company, although never eager to pay out on a claim, made sure everybody knew they were happy to settle on this occasion. They had a number of farmers on their books, and a show of co-operation would do their image no harm.

All donations were gratefully accepted, thought Martin as he drove past and on to the house.

Ann had told her parents of her and Richard's wish to let Martin inherit the farm, and they had received the news with restrained happiness. Richard had managed to tear himself away from the farm and accompany Ann to her parents when they announced their news. Harry and Betty kept a worried expression on their faces as they asked Ann and Richard if they were sure, had they thought this through, thanking them for their enormously kind gesture. All the time they were overjoyed: it meant that Martin could return and take over the family farm.

As the weeks passed and the trial edged closer, Betty had become very protective of her husband, fussing over him even more than usual. Harry was irritated by this. He had his own thoughts to contend with, but he would never complain, he knew it was only because she loved him.

Martin arrived at the house just in time to help set up the table for a family lunch in the garden. Ann was already there, keeping an eye on her children whilst helping her mother with the preparation. Richard was once again absent. He had a village cricket game to play, and being one of the stalwarts of the team he always arrived early to make sure of the pitch preparations. Harry would be back shortly from inspecting the recently mowed hayfield. The harsh winter and wet April had depleted his stock of hay, he needed to mow and bale extra fields to compensate. He wanted to see if the cut grass needed turning again before they baled it. The trial looked as if it would come slap bang in the middle of haymaking.

Mike Cairns had offered some of his staff to help Harry out at this busy time. Mike himself cut grass for silage to feed his dairy cows, and had therefore already got his first cut in and could afford to lend his friend some labour. Other friends had also offered help, but Mike had a big enough operation that he could lend two men, and various tractors, trailers and implements, and still be able to attend the trial himself. Harry, although ever proud, knew when he needed help and had accepted. The Cairns were pleased to be of assistance.

Mike Cairns had also offered, or suggested, a scheme that could help the Sintons if they were in financial difficulties, if the legal costs associated with the trial were putting a strain on the farm's accounts. He didn't know the Sintons' financial situation, but he could guess at it; he also knew Defence Barristers, Lawyers and solicitors were not cheap to hire. He only mentioned the proposal in passing, hoping not to cause offence. He hadn't, and Harry said he would think about it, not dismissing it out of hand as he would have done had it been suggested by anyone else.

As they sat eating their salad lunch, Martin told them his news. It was greeted by a general air of delight, all they needed now was the trial to end and Harry to be free, and they could try and get this harrowing business behind them. Harry, Betty and Ann still looked fragile, pale and thin. For a time, when the fire in the barn had passed, when no more threatening telephone calls came, when no more acts of violence occurred, and when the trial seemed a long way off, they all appeared to grow stronger, to recover from the initial shock and worry of the situation. But as the trial edged ever closer they began to wilt again. That afternoon, on the eve of the trial, everyone's nerves were on edge.

When they had finished their meal, Harry Sinton decided to tell his family of his wishes at the trial. He had been building up this speech since the night of the fire. He had discussed them with Betty on many an occasion. She knew better than to try and persuade her husband to change his mind when he had made it up. He was as stubborn as they come once he had reached a decision, even if it did take a long time to get there. He had also expressed his feelings to his friend Gerald Evans at one of their many meetings, and had received a cautious reply.

"If that is your wish Harry, than we can only comply, but I would strenuously suggest you wait until after the trial and we can scrutinise the proceedings."

Harry Sinton would not budge, and now with Martin back and Ann over for lunch, he decided to tell his children. He waited until they had eaten their light salad lunch. They were sitting in the garden under the shade of an old burgeoning oak tree. June had carried on the beautiful weather of May, and brought with it nervous laughter at references to droughts after the deluge in April. (The farm "service" favourite topic was the fickleness of the weather.) Now with hay making under way they knew it was bound to rain.

The Sintons sat in garden chairs with an assortment of cold drinks, enjoying the sights, smells, and sounds of the English countryside in late June. Ann kept a wary eye on her two children confined in a play pen (four hurdles fixed together in a square), who were now trying to stand up on their own and were becoming more mobile by the day. Martin leaned back, rested his head against the back of the chair, closed his eyes and let the warmth of the day wipe away the long drive from his stiff body. Bracken reclined in the shade by the back door.

"Your mother and I have discussed this trial," Harry began in his slow Hampshire drawl.

Martin looked up from his reclining position, and Ann looked over to him. They didn't like the sound of their father's voice. The trial had been discussed before, but usually in vague conversations, on the end of other discussions, never so blatantly.

"I, we, have come to terms with what happened here in March. Everyone has been very kind, but it really boils down to me. I did the . . . " He still could not bring himself to say murders or killings. "I caused this situation."

Ann and Martin would normally have told their father that it wasn't his fault, not to blame himself, but the weight of his voice made them sit in silence and listen. Harry reached over to Betty and held onto her hand for comfort and strength.

"I . . . I took the life of two men. I didn't want to, I would give anything to change what has happened but I can't. I have brought grief and torment to three families. I have never met the families of the two men I . . . well I wouldn't expect any sympathy. I have reached a decision on the trial, and your mother has backed me up."

He paused and stared at his grandchildren playing in the confines of the pen. Betty squeezed his hand.

"I will not appeal on whatever sentence I am given. I have committed a crime and I should pay for it."

"Dad, you're sounding like you've lost the case already, the jury may find you innocent," Martin pointed out.

"Then that will be fine, but if they find me guilty I will accept that too."

"Oh Dad," Ann sighed. She tried to find the right words. "It's not . . . it's not a matter of honour. It's, I don't know, playing the system. If you can . . . " she didn't want to say "get away with it".

". . . If you can avoid prison, I think you should use all means necessary."

"I have to live with what I've done Ann, nobody else. Yes, you have to live with the consequences of my actions, but I have to live with the . . . fact."

"Do you agree with this, Mum?" Martin asked.

Betty had taken out a handkerchief from her sleeve and wiped her nose, she sniffed and then nodded. Martin looked at Ann, who returned his stare. They also knew not to argue with their father, and could see his reasoning to a certain extent. But the conversation seemed to say that he would be found guilty, and they had refrained from thinking along those lines.

"Have you discussed this with Uncle Gerald? What does he think?"

"He respects my wishes."

"What if the trial is a sham, if . . . if the Judge misleads, misdirects?"

"I have to live with this Martin. Everywhere I go, things I do, constantly remind me of it. When I go into town I think people are staring at me. They might not be, but I think they are. If two or more people are talking, I think it is about me. I'm paranoid I know, but that's how I feel."

"It wasn't your fault Dad!" Ann said, exasperated at the number of times she had said this.

"That's not the point. Don't you see Ann I have to, I don't know, I have to stand trial, go before my peers. I brought this on the family and I need to face up to it."

Betty had kept quiet all through the conversation. She knew her husband had made up his mind, and in a small way she understood his reasoning, but she felt scared at the thought of being alone. She wanted Harry to swallow his pride and think of himself for once. He had always been so honest, so conscientious. She wished he would put his own family first, but would never mention it. She realised it was something he had to do to purge the guilt he felt, rightly or wrongly, for bringing all this trouble onto the family.

"But if they find you innocent you will accept that verdict?" Martin asked.

"Yes."

"Lets pray they find you innocent then Dad," Ann said.

"Amen," Martin whispered under his breath.

All four were now concentrating on the toddlers, they were an easy release from the heavy conversation. They watched as the twins played with their latest toys, or tried to stand in the makeshift play-pen, only to totter, sway and then fall back on their nappy-padded bottoms.

"Not long now," Betty said, referring to the much-awaited walking of the twins, breaking the silence that had descended after Harry's announcement.

The conversation turned to the children: who they expected to walk first, how long it had taken for Ann and Martin to stand and to walk, anything to return to the relaxed atmosphere they had before Harry Sinton's announcement. For all their efforts it was never the same; the moment had been broken, and the trial was now foremost in their minds. It was agreed they should all go for a walk: it was a beautiful day, Harry was not going to turn the grass that afternoon and they all wanted to take advantage of the family being together.

The walk was refreshing, especially for Martin who had started to look at the fields and woodland in a different way since he was told of Ann and Richard's decision. The enthusiasm he had at the thought of being able to run the farm was tainted by the thought of his father's situation. Martin had tried to come to terms with these conflicting emotions, but still felt guilty at his feelings of joy whilst his father faced such a terrible future. He tried to blocked those thoughts out for the time being. You never know, the jury might let him walk free, he tried to convince himself.

As they walked through the endless shades of green that sweep through the Hampshire countryside in late June, they talked of past events that happened on the farm. Of when Martin, at the tender age of thirteen, had crashed the Land Rover into the only tree in a thirty acre field, when Ann's parents had caught her kissing a boyfriend in a clearing of the wood. Betty and Harry held hands, Ann and Martin carried a twin each. Martin was subjected to constant 'suits you' remarks throughout the walk, as he entertained his nephew. Bracken lolloped along in front. The walk reminded them of earlier times, when they had often walked as a family through the fields of Downlands Farm. It struck home that occasions such as these might now be a thing of the past. They were determined to enjoy it.

Mark Robson had memorised the trial date, and now with one day left to go he embarked on his second act of vengeance. He had been pleased with the restraint he had shown in getting back at his brother's killer. He had told himself it would be a long-term thing, maybe for the rest of his life, just a little something every now and again, to remind them of their guilt, never letting them settle, keeping them on their toes. He had scant regard for the legal system and relied on his own form of justice. He believed Harry Sinton would be set free.

He stood in front of his bathroom sink and carefully dropped his morning efforts into the air-bubble padded envelope he had bought from a post office earlier that week and addressed the day before. He let the excrement slide down to the bottom of the bag, took off the protective cover from the glue on the flap; he had decided against an envelope that you had to lick to seal down and stuck the flap down.

"Shit for shit," he told himself in the mirror.

He then took the bag, holding it at arm's length between his finger and thumb, and placed it by the door. He would post it later, on his way to meet up with his tablet supplier; first he wanted a shower. He hoped the stamps he had stuck on would ensure the bag would arrive within two days, in the middle of the trial. He did not know the exact cost of postage, the thought of taking the bag into a post office to have it weighed made him laugh out loud. As long as it got there, he thought to himself.

The trial was set for Monday the twenty-eighth. On that Sunday evening, knowing that the Defence team were meeting in his Godfather's office for a final session before the start of the trial the following day, Martin took himself off to see Gerald Evans and the Barrister Patrick Parker. Harry declined from accompanying his son; he had been in enough meetings with his Defence team, he would rather spend the rest of the day, on the eve of his trial, with his wife, daughter, and grandchildren.

As Martin sat in front of his Godfather, the Barrister by his side, the junior solicitor behind him, the proposed Defence was explained. They told him they could not use the defence of provocation as that was only available to murder charges; Harry already knew this from an earlier meeting. They believed self-defence would be the best way to proceed, stating the relative facts, the threatening actions of the two assailants, and discredit the Defence's only eye witness. They knew Paul Allen had already been found guilty of burglary in conjunction with this case, and had dragged up some other relative information concerning his statement.

Patrick Parker reiterated that it was Harry Sinton's word against Paul Allen's, and it would be up to the jury to decide. He said the best weapon they had in the Defence was Harry Sinton himself, an old man, a pensioner, who happened to stumble upon a gang of raiders and had to protect himself from their threatening advances. He said the general public was getting tired of criminals targeting the elderly and believed the jury's sympathy would already be on their side and half won-over before the trial began.

"Even if they didn't know about the case before they arrived, which in all legal terms they shouldn't but the media does have a way of pre-empting the story, I'll get your father to stand up in the witness box and show the jury this frail old salt-of-the-earth farmer who had no other option but to defend himself."

Patrick Parker's only concern was the Prosecution bringing up the issue of necessary force. He reassured them he could argue around the accusation of excessive force and believed he could sway any jury into a lenient view of Harry Sinton's action on that morning almost four months ago.

Martin thought Patrick Parker seemed confident, almost arrogant, that he could argue his father's case well. He also realised that he had given no firm declaration of his ability to get his father to walk free. They all seemed tense and nervous, except for the Barrister, but Martin realised it would not be him sent to prison if the Defence failed. To Patrick Parker it would be a case chalked down to experience, and then he would be on to the next appointment.

When the Barrister excused himself, shaking Martin's hand and saying he would see him in Court, the junior solicitor also left the office, allowing Martin to express his concerns.

"He doesn't give any guarantees."

"It is a very foolish man who does, Martin. You just don't know what a jury will find. If your Father is to walk free, then Patrick is the man I would back to see that happen. Juries are known to be more lenient, especially in these sort of self-defence cases when an honest man is forced to commit an unlawful act against a dishonest aggressor."

"So what has he told you? What does he think the chances are?" Martin asked.

Gerald Evans took off his glasses and cleaned them on his tie. Martin knew this to be a delaying tactic rather than a necessary act of cleaning the bi-focals. He waited patiently as his Godfather replaced his spectacles and arranged his tie to his satisfaction.

"He has told me," Gerald Evans paused, "he quotes a fifty-fifty chance."

"And you?"

"I would like to think of a more sixty-forty. The facts are unquestionable, your father did take the lives of two men, it is the circumstances that have to be detailed. I am sorry I cannot offer you more encouragement, but I believe you would rather hear the truth. Sixty-forty is better than nothing."

"I am slightly concerned that the boy Allen says that the other youth was either giving himself up, and, or, trying to stop Stevens from advancing when your father shot him. All the same, Patrick Parker seems confident he can discredit this chap's statement." Gerald Evans then started on a speech he had been mulling over in his own mind for some time.

"Your father is lucky he is not like our friend Mr. Whitworth. If Tom had to take the stand, charged with the same offence, one look at him, one blatant right-wing view and the jury would have no choice but to find him guilty. Tom would probably stand up and say he was pleased he did it and would do it again next time. Patrick Parker is quite correct when he said the biggest thing in your father's favour is your father. He is meek, mild-mannered, and one of the nicest men I have ever met. One look at him and the jury cannot help but to see those virtues."

"I also think it is a bloody shame this thing has happened to the most genuine person I know and who I am proud to call my friend," Gerald Evans added in a rare show of emotion. He then regained his composure and continued.

"The other thing that is in your father's favour is the fact he had his shotgun on him for a different purpose, not with the intention of protecting his property, although some may argue that hoping to shoot a fox is the same thing. If he had seen the burglars from the house, grabbed the gun and went out to confront them then he would be on the much more serious charge of murder.

"The police established it would have been a physical impossibility for your father to see the burglars, which he would have to have done from an upstairs window as the lambing barns blocked the view to the main barn from the ground floor. Charge downstairs, retrieve the keys and unlock the gun cabinet, take the shotgun, locking the cabinet after him (as this is how the police found it), and then race around to challenge these intruders before they had driven off again, means he could not have had malice aforethought and therefore could not be charged with murder."

"So why are we still talking about prison?"

"Because your father did take the lives of two human beings, one of whom was unarmed, the other only carrying a baseball bat. Some people may feel he took the law into his own hands and that cannot be allowed, that it would encourage more people, farmers, shop owners, anybody with property, to protect their interest by force."

"It's this force thing that it boils down to then isn't it? It will be up to the jury to decide if he used too much force in defending himself."

"It is up to Patrick Parker to persuade them that your father had no other option, and it is down to the prosecuting Barrister to persuade them that your father didn't need to kill the two men to defend himself. It comes down to who is the most persuasive Barrister."

"Do you know the prosecuting Barrister?"

"I have been told of him. His name is Maurice Brown, he is younger than Patrick, in his late forties I believe, and he is ambitious. He sees this work as a stepping-stone to greater things."

Martin stood up and crossed over to the window. He wanted the trial to be over, it all seemed such a lottery to him, the most persuasive Barrister, the jury, and then the Judge.

"And if Dad is found guilty, it is up to the Judge to sentence him?"

"Correct, it is up to the Judge's discretion, although he has guide lines to follow. He also sums up the case to the jury before they leave to consider their verdict. The judge that has been appointed is known to be quite a liberal fellow, not a 'hang 'em high chap'," the solicitor added in a vain attempt to lighten the conversation. "That will stand in our favour."

"So the Judge could still give Dad a suspended sentence or something?"

"He could Martin, but all this conjecture is getting us nowhere. There are still many variables. We have compiled the best Defence we believe possible. It is now up to Patrick Parker to put our case forward and direct the jury to acquit your father."

Martin turned away from the window, ran both his hands through his hair and then rubbed his eyes in a show of despondency. He knew there was nothing left to do, he knew he could only wait and pray. He crossed over to his Godfather and offered his hand to shake.

"Thank you Uncle."

Gerald Evans stood up from behind his desk and accepted Martin's outstretched hand.

"Go home and spend time with your father, Martin; he has resigned himself to this trial, you should do the same."

"That's another thing I wanted to ask you about, he says he doesn't want to appeal, whatever the outcome."

Gerald Evans sighed at this, and still holding onto Martin's hand replied: "I know, but we shall have to wait for the outcome of the trial, hopefully there will be nothing to appeal against."

Martin thanked him again and, not for the first time, took his Godfather's advice and made his way home to spend as much time with his father as he could.

"See you in Court," Gerald Evans whispered to himself as Martin closed the door. He sighed and sat back into his padded leather chair. He was giving serious consideration to retiring full-time once this trial was over; he didn't enjoy the cut and thrust any more, the pressures of the work. He would have to step aside for a younger man, or woman he corrected himself, one with an appetite for the challenge. He dreamt of his cherished garden and despaired at the state it was now in due to his lack of attention. This trial had taken up all of his time. No, he decided, he would no longer miss this work.

CHAPTER SEVEN

CROWN COURT

The atmosphere in the farmhouse on the morning of the trial was oppressive. No one had slept well, Harry, Betty and Martin all walked on egg-shells as they killed time before the drive to Winchester. Good Luck and *'Thinking of You'* cards lay unopened on the kitchen table, nobody wanted to open the post or read the newspapers. The television and radio were both switched off at the mains. No one could stomach breakfast, cups of coffee their only sustenance. Ann arrived at the house, minus her two children, with five minutes to spare. Tentative smiles and awkward kisses ensued.

It was a beautiful June morning; on any other morning everyone in the car would have commented on it, but not this morning. They all sat in silent dread, deep in their own thoughts on what the day might bring. Harry Sinton was dressed in the same outfit he had worn to his committal hearing. They were his best clothes, and he wore them to any important event, only adding a jumper for winter engagements. Martin wore a blazer, Chino trousers, a striped shirt and tie. He looked every inch an officer of Her Majesty's Armed Forces. Betty and Ann wore light floral patterned dresses; they wouldn't have looked smarter if they were meeting the Queen herself.

The drive to Winchester took twenty-five minutes. They found a parking space in the multi-storey car park at the top of the city, the Crown Court was only a short walk away. Winchester Crown Court was as impressive as the Magistrate's Court in Annavale was disappointing, even though they had both been built at roughly the same time. It sat at the top of the city overlooking a large, enclosed square. Next to the Court stood the Great Hall of Winchester

Castle, itself long associated with the administration of justice, the scene of many notable trials, including Sir Walter Raleigh's. Winchester had once been the capital of England and seat of King Alfred, of cake-burning fame.

To the right and at right angles to the Court, up another set of wide steps, stood the County Council offices. Built in the same style as the Great Hall, using columns of Purbeck Marble, and more local napped flints, they enhanced the square's splendour perfectly.

The Sintons had pushed past the waiting media that were held back from the square by sturdy metal railings, ignoring any questions fired at them. They walked across the stone square and ascended the steps to the Crown Court which loomed ominously over them.

Inside the building they were amazed at the grandeur of the open-plan entrance hall. The ceiling was two storeys high with modern chandeliers suspended in its centre. They felt tiny in the expanse of the marbled hall. Behind the security barrier, two broad marble staircases, one at either end, led up to a balcony.

The whole edifice gave credence to the fact that this was the second highest Court in the land, surpassed only by the famous 'Old Bailey'.

The Sintons were met by Gerald Evans who guided them through the security barrier and up the left-hand staircase to the balcony, where they joined Patrick Parker and the young junior solicitor.

"That's the bail money back," Gerald Evans whispered to Martin in an endeavour to lighten the situation. Martin gave a quick, strained smile in recognition of his Godfather's effort, but the tension was still obvious in all the family's features.

The balcony was designed in the same open style as the entrance hall. Groups of comfortable chairs and coffee tables were positioned along its length. It resembled a viewing concourse of an airport. The Sintons recognised faces of friends who were sitting down, enjoying a cup of coffee or tea, they gave forced smiles in recognition of their support.

After the initial greetings, Gerald Evans explained that they had been allocated Court four (there were eight in all), and pointed out the route to the public gallery for Martin to take his mother and sister. Before they parted, Harry and Betty hugged, both holding back their emotions as best they could, Martin said good luck and Ann kissed her father's cheek. Martin asked Betty if she wanted a cup of something; she declined, saying she wanted to get to the public gallery as soon as possible. They made their way to the lift that took them up two floors to their seats overlooking Court four.

Harry Sinton watched his family as they stepped into the lift, feeling totally alone. He was then shown, along with his Defence team, towards the Court room by the Court Usher. It was nine o'clock, the trial was due to start at ten-thirty.

Martin led the way to the public gallery. A space on the front row had been kept for them by Tom Whitworth who had arrived earlier and made his way, with his wife and son, straight to the front row and then proceeded to guard three seats for Betty, Ann and Martin. They all thanked Tom for his thoughtfulness and acknowledged other familiar faces that were already there with nods and more strained smiles. Mike and Sarah Cairns sat behind them, leaning over and giving words of encouragement every now and again. George Hollis could not attend the proceedings, his haymaking had kept him at home. He hoped to be finished before the end of what was anticipated to be a three-day trial. All the other devotees of the Sunday night farmers' "Church Service" planned to be there.

Martin wondered how many friends of the deceased would be here, watching and waiting for justice to be done. He would not recognise any, but Sean Robson's grandparents would be arriving later, along with two of his aunties. Sean's parents were trying to settle into their new house in Dorset, ignoring the trial of their son's killer.

Slowly the public gallery and Court filled up, reporters took their seats, the clerk of the Court, two ushers and the Court stenographer took their designated positions.

The outlook from the public gallery reminded Martin of the upper circle in a theatre, his seat giving an unbroken view of the stage below. The wood-panelled back wall rose magnificently to the ceiling two storeys above. A Royal Shield, hanging directly above the Judge's chair, halfway up the wall, enhanced its dignity. Although the architecture of the room gave an open, spacious feel, the floor of the Court looked cluttered. Numerous files sat upon work surfaces, electronic equipment vied for space among books and documents.

As the onlookers waited, an air of reverence filled the room, as if the Court was akin to a place of worship. People talked in low whispers, even Tom Whitworth was restrained.

Harry Sinton was led in and took his seat with Patrick Parker, who was now sporting the famous white wig and black robe. The prosecuting Barrister sitting across from them wore the same. Behind them Gerald Evans sat with his junior solicitor by his side, he was leaning over and whispering something into his ear, the junior solicitor was nodding in response.

As the clock ticked towards ten-thirty the mood in the Court room tensed; the arrival of the Judge, Mr. Justice Thorn QC, was all that kept the proceedings from starting. The clerk of the Court re-entered the room and all the muffled chatter slowed. He asked the Court to rise, all present duly complied, and announced the Judge's arrival to the Court. The Judge entered, walked over to his position behind the bench, arranged his robe, and sat down. Harry was surprised to see the Judge didn't wear a full all-enveloping wig; he wore a similar small one comparable to the Barristers, but he still had an aloofness about him that men in power all seem to have.

The clerk called Harry Sinton's name. Harry made his way to the dock and confirmed his identity. The Court clerk then read the charges.

"Harold Charles Sinton, you are charged with the manslaughter of one William Stevens, and one Sean Robson, that on the seventh day of March this year, you did shoot and kill the aforementioned men. How do you plead?"

Harry Sinton tried to swallow before he answered the question, his throat was dry, all eyes were upon him, he hoped his voice would not betray his nervousness.

"Not guilty," was the quiet, shaky reply. A ripple of comments came from the public area, it wouldn't have surprised many of them if Harry had pleaded guilty, and accepted the sentencing.

They were all pleased he hadn't, you could take pride so far. A stern look from the Judge, peering up towards the public gallery, brought the Court back to order.

Betty's eyes started to fill up with tears, she was staring at her husband standing alone in the dock. He looked so vulnerable, bewildered. Ann held her hand, Martin put his arm around her shoulders, but she still started to shake. She could not tear her gaze away from her husband, standing forlorn, awaiting his future, their life together, to be decided by the twelve unknown men and women who were now entering the Court and being sworn in. She didn't know how much of this she could take, she wanted to leave the room and get back to the farm, but she knew she couldn't and wouldn't. She had to stay and show support for her husband, she would never desert him, especially now in his hour of need.

The Court watched as the jury, six men and six women, were shown to their seats. Even in the restrained atmosphere Martin had to chuckle to himself at the contrast in seating arrangements between and the Judge the jury. The Judge sat resplendent on his high-backed padded leather chair, behind a beautiful wooden bench that stretched the width of the Court. The twelve members of the jury, on the other hand, when squeezed into their seats in their appointed box, resembled a sardine tin.

The jury looked a perfect cross-section of the general public with ages ranging from twenty-two to sixty-one. Neither Barrister saw the need to challenge the make-up of this jury, they both believed they could argue their side of the case effectively to the twelve people present.

Once the jury was sworn in it was time for the prosecuting Barrister to make his opening speech. Mr. Brown rose slowly to his feet, picked up a number of sheets of paper he had before him and pretended to study them intensely. The right for the Prosecution to make the opening speech was priceless, and Mr. Maurice Brown knew this. He would never squander it, either by rushing or by giving the Defence any sort of assistance, any loop-hole they could use in a counter-attack. With a sigh of a world-weary man he dropped the notes onto the desk, took off his spectacles, and addressed the jury.

"Ladies and gentlemen of the jury, I have been given the task of prosecuting the man you see before you. He has been charged with the manslaughter of two men, one in his teens, more a boy really. In statements made to the police that same morning, the accused himself admitted to the taking of these two lives. An eye witness at the scene of the crime, himself scared for his life, backs up the chain of events.

"The evidence is irrefutable. Harry Sinton shot and killed two men with his twelve-bore shotgun. They died instantly as the shot ripped through their chests, removing part of their heart as well as a third of their lungs."

Maurice Brown refrained from mentioning that the men were in the process of stealing Harry Sinton's property, or that when they were shot, they were advancing threateningly towards Harry; he would slip that in later. He concentrated on the facts he wanted to put over to the jury. He wanted to conjure up a scene of imbalance, a baseball bat against a double-barrel shotgun.

"At the scene of the carnage, a single baseball bat was found. One baseball bat between two men, against a twelve-bore shotgun. The contrast in weapons could not be more distinct. The fact that there was only one between the two deceased points to the fact that one of them had to be unarmed. It is known that one was Sean Robson, a college student of seventeen, studying for his A-levels, hoping to go on to University, his whole life ahead of him. Mr. Sinton himself confessed that, and I quote . . . "

He reached for his notes in a show of authenticity. Maurice Brown knew the words off by heart, but a show of reciting them word for word backed up his speech. He replaced his spectacles and read from the notes.

" . . . the younger one wasn't carrying anything."

He was pleased to hear the ripple of whispered conversations in the public gallery, he could see by the looks on the faces of the jury that his theatrics had hit home. The Prosecution had decided to concentrate on the death, of Sean Robson. The fact he was only a teenager, with no prior convictions, and unarmed at the time of his death would have a greater impact on the jury than trying to defend a man of Stevens' reputation, armed with a baseball bat, advancing towards an old man with all the intent of causing him serious bodily harm.

Betty, Ann and Martin sat in despair; they had been warned by Gerald Evans that the opening speech by the Prosecution would be hurtful. He had told them that it was the time when the Prosecution would have the biggest impact on the jury. At the end of the trial, when the Barristers embarked on their closing speech, it is the council for the Defence that has the last word. Those words would be fresh in the minds of the jury when they went to consider their verdict, as long as they are not undone by the Judge's summing-up. But now the stage was clear for the Prosecution to lay the foundations for their case and Maurice Brown made full use of it as he continued with his opening speech.

"Mr. Sinton, in his signed statement, admits pulling the trigger. Ladies and gentlemen of the jury, it is the duty of the Prosecution to prove Mr. Sinton's guilt, but when the accused himself, in a written and signed statement, confesses that his actions killed the two deceased it, it . . . " Maurice Brown pretended to stumble over the words, " . . . well it just makes the case for the Prosecution so much simpler."

Tom Whitworth was beside himself with anger, this man had not even mentioned the fact that his friend had acted in self-defence. The picture that was being painted was damning to the extreme. He clenched and unclenched his hands, his face turned red, he shifted his position on the seat. It was all he could do to refrain from shouting out, denouncing the prejudice he was hearing.

"Ladies and gentlemen of the jury, I will lead you through the chain of events that led to the unlawful killing of the two deceased. I will produce expert witnesses on ballistics and pathology, produce pictures taken at the scene, call on the policeman who was first on the scene and the officer who led the investigation, and I will present to you an eye witness that saw the lives of the two men being taken."

Maurice Brown then went on to summarise the case, explain the evidence he would be using, and detail what the witnesses would say. It was now that Maurice Brown had decided to tell the jury of circumstances leading up to the deaths.

"The chain of events leading up to the deaths of William Stevens and Sean Robson has been expertly investigated by the Hampshire Constabulary. On the morning of the seventh of March this year, Mr. Harold Sinton confronted three intruders he found in a van in his farmyard."

Patrick Parker listened with interest, he was wondering how his learned friend would portray why the gang of raiders were in the farmyard in the first place. He smiled to himself at the use of words the counsel for the Defence was using. Confronted, rather than stumbled upon, summed up a picture of intent. 'Intruders' rather than "gang of raiders" depicted a softer image of the burglars. Patrick Parker smiled to himself, he would have used the same tactics.

"Without any word of warning he fired his shotgun at the vehicle, causing excessive damage to the body, bonnet and radiator, rendering the vehicle useless. Then, when faced with two men, one an unarmed boy of seventeen remember, he callously reloaded his shotgun, took aim, and pulled the triggers, killing them both instantly."

Harry Sinton sat head bent down, listening to this damning version of the incidents. Was that how it happened? Could he have prevented the deaths in some way? He started to doubt his version of events, but he could still see the look of menace in Stevens' eyes as he walked towards him.

"All this was witnessed by a terrified boy, again only seventeen, who had very wisely stayed in the vehicle. He watched as his best friend was blown backwards from the force of the shot. Killed in front of his eyes."

Maurice Brown now leant one hand on the desk before him, tucked the other under his robe, just above his chest, and looked straight at the jury. This was his favourite stance when ending his opening speech. He believed it showed him in a light of strength and honesty. He had them in the palm of his hand, and was enjoying the moment.

"Ladies and gentlemen of the jury, the taking of a life is the most serious crime known to man. It not only deprives that person of their future, but it deprives a family of a son, a chance to enjoy grandchildren. It deprives a wife of a husband and leaves all concerned, family and friends, devastated.

"This is not a complicated case. You will hear hours upon hours of facts, details and statements, listen to hours upon hours of witness accounts, some from the Prosecution, some for the Defence. Whilst you are being bombarded with facts, detail, and accounts, you must ask yourself three questions. Could Mr. Sinton have prevented the deaths of William Stevens and Sean Robson in some way? Did Harry Sinton have to use such excessive force, as to kill William Stevens and Sean Robson? And what right did Mr. Sinton have to take the lives of the two men?"

"Ladies and gentlemen of the jury, what right did Harry Sinton have to be the Judge, the jury and the hangman?"

Patrick Parker was impressed, he could see no flaw in the Prosecution's opening speech. If he was on the opposition's side, he would have highlighted the same aspects, skirting around the same facets the Prosecution had. At the same time Patrick Parker looked totally disinterested. He made a show of not listening to the Prosecution, while all the time he was memorising every word. He hoped the jury would see his indifference as one of contempt at the accusations. He hoped they would believe this contempt would manifest itself into a superb defence of his client and all things just. It was an old tactic, used by both sides, but one he never tired of.

Betty started to break down and cry. She had listened to a complete stranger inform twelve other strangers, who had her husband's future in their hands, describe her husband as a cold, calculating killer. This was not the man she knew. She wanted to stand up, tell the jury of her loving husband, the caring father, anything to discredit the prosecuting Barrister. Martin offered to take her outside for a while but she refused, she would not leave the Court room. Sarah Cairns reached over and laid a hand on Betty's shoulder.

The same feelings were going through the minds of the many friends of the Sintons who had appeared to show their support. Tom Whitworth was seething with anger. He turned to his wife, and controlling his fury to a spitting whisper told her, "If this is British justice, then British justice is bullshit."

Judge Thorn had been keeping his own notes as the prosecuting counsel laid the foundations of their case. He too was impressed by Maurice Browns opening speech, but he was also waiting to hear from the Defence counsel, pondering their likely tactics.

Maurice Brown was now ready to call his first witness, and called the police ballistics expert. He asked questions relating to the type of shotgun that was on show as a piece of evidence, informing the jury that this was the actual weapon that Harry Sinton used to kill William Stevens and Sean Robson. Maurice Brown would always refer to the two dead men by their full names, he believed this made them more real, more human than referring to them as 'the deceased', or 'the two men'. He continued with questions relating to force of shot and size of spread. The ballistics expert, with the use of diagrams and video footage played to the Court on the two big television screens that sat on the bench, either side of the judge, answered the questions frankly. At the end of the questioning, Maurice Brown had successfully informed the jury of the power possessed by a twelve-bore shotgun, loaded with six-shot cartridges, and its destructive capabilities when fired at a target not ten feet away.

The Defence counsel had no questions for the ballistics expert.

The time ticked away slowly in the Court room, the low baritone voice of Maurice Brown commanding the arena. The lunch recess was taken, a civilised affair of an hour and a half. In that time the Defence counsel tried to reassure Harry and Betty that all was not as bleak as it looked, and that they would have their time soon. When the hour and a half was up they all trooped back into the Court, Maurice Brown ready for his afternoon performance.

The next witness called to the stand was the police pathologist who had carried out the autopsies on the two bodies. Again the witness answered fairly and frankly. Neither of the expert witnesses had any axe to grind, they were only interested in the science, the facts. Using diagrams to put his explanations across, he told that the cause of death, in his professional opinion, was severe cardiac arrest. The pathologist, using graphic language, told of how, on inspection of the two bodies, the wounds were remarkablysimilar. They had both been shot in the chest, just above the sternum, the result of which was to tear a hole the size of a fist through the rib cage, shattering the bone, adding to the internal injuries. The shot continued to rip away roughly one-third of the lung, and rupture the heart. The shot was so powerful, he added with scientific glee, that it passed right through the body, causing extensive damage as it went, puncturing the trachea, fragmenting part of the spinal column and shattering the left scapula as it exited the victim's body.

Maurice Brown brought this down to layman's terms, explaining that the force of the shot, that ripped out roughly one third of the lung and half the heart, had caused William Stevens and Sean Robson to have a massive coronary seizure, a heart attack. The pathologist added that the shock and loss of blood would also have been contributing factors.

Again the Defence counsel had no questions. Nothing would be gained by keeping the witnesses at the stand.

Members of the jury looked quite pale after listening to the pathologist's vivid account. They could be seen looking over towards Harry Sinton, faces aghast. Could this old man, sitting so meekly in his chair, have done such a terrible thing? He had admitted to it in a signed police statement. It was incredulous.

Maurice Brown's opening speech, and his first two witnesses, along with the swearing-in of the jury, had taken the first day of the trial up to four-thirty. When he had finished with the police pathologist, and the Defence counsel waived their right to cross examine, the Judge called an adjournment to the day's proceedings, stating they would resume tomorrow morning, again at ten-thirty.

Maurice Brown was pleased with himself. Not only had he laid the foundations for the Prosecution, building up a picture of the defendant's guilt. He had also successfully monopolised the Court for the whole day, not giving the Defence counsel any chance of putting their case across, that would have to wait for tomorrow. Maurice Brown knew that the jury would only have one side of the argument to mull over for the rest of the day, that night, and most of tomorrow morning. The graphic account of the wounds sustained by the two dead men was a perfect way to end, leaving the images fresh in the minds of the jury. All in all, Maurice Brown concluded, it had been a good day's work.

The public gallery emptied, heading down towards the balcony. Some used the lift, others descended the stairs. Betty was in shock, she could think of nothing to console herself with. Martin tried to tell her that it would be different tomorrow, that their Defence would have a chance of speaking, putting their side of the events across. This helped little. Tom Whitworth repeated his damming verdict of British justice to Martin and stormed out, his wife and son trailing behind. Other friends tried to give encouraging smiles as they shuffled out of the Court building. Mike and Sarah Cairns hung around in case they could be of some use.

Martin, Ann and Betty waited for Harry to join them. He was accompanied by his Defence Ccounsel, Patrick Parker and Gerald Evans who reiterated Martin's words, telling all concerned that the worst was over, that tomorrow they would have their say. Harry said nothing, he took Betty's hand and held on tight. He had never felt so alone, so vulnerable and exposed, as when he had stood in the box. He wanted to go home.

The Sintons walked back to their waiting car, shielding their eyes from the cameras and microphones that were jabbed in front of their faces, ignoring the questions hurled at them from expectant reporters, as they passed through the waiting media.

Patrick Parker, Gerald Evans and the junior solicitor, standing on the steps of the Court house, watched in dismay as the media scrum formed and jostled around their client and his family.

"What do they expect to get from them, a blurted confession or something?" the junior solicitor groaned, unable to hide his contempt.

Gerald Evans ignored his young assistant and turned to Patrick Parker.

"What do you think?" he asked referring to the day's proceedings.

"Much as expected. He was very good, but we shall have our time, starting tomorrow."

Gerald Evans nodded his agreement, and all three moved off towards their relative vehicles, Patrick Parker in one, and the two solicitors in another. They wanted to get away before the media could turn their attentions towards them.

The drive back to Downlands Farm was depressing, no one spoke in the car. Unlike the return journey from the committal hearing, nobody could find anything positive to say. Once again Betty and Harry sat in the back seats, holding hands.

At the farmhouse, Ann gave her apologies and headed back to her husband and children. She felt guilty for leaving her parents, but she desperately wanted to see her children after the stress of the Court proceedings. They said they understood, told her not to worry, and that they would see her in the morning. Ann tried to think of a way to bring the twins over, to have something to distract her parents from the insufferable pressures of the day's events. Maybe tomorrow her mother-in-law could wait with the twins for their return. She would suggest it to Richard and his mother, see what they thought.

Martin sat his parents down, Bracken at their feet, and went to make them all a pot of tea. Whilst he waited for the kettle to boil he leafed through the greetings cards that had been left unopened in the morning. He studied the postmarks, amazed at the places some of the cards had come from. They had been receiving cards for a week running up to the trial. They came from friends, family, associates and strangers, all wanting to show support, provide some strength, to prove that they were not alone at this 'dark time'.

Martin had given himself the task of opening these cards when his parents were out of the room. He still remembered the sight of Ann after the threatening 'phone call, sitting alone and afraid on the sofa. If he could intercept any malicious letters he would, although none had arrived as yet.

When the pot of tea was ready, Martin placed it on a tray, along with the cups and saucer, milk, sugar, tea spoons, a variety of biscuits and the good luck cards. They sat in silence as they drank their tea, each deep in their own thoughts. No one touched the biscuits.

Mark Robson watched the summary of the first day of the trial on the early evening news on the television, that was placed out of reach, in the corner of the lounge bar of the *Red Lion*. The report didn't tell him anything he didn't already know, so he just continued to nurse his pint of lager, trying to ignore the two people at the other end of the bar.

When he had walked into the pub he had been taken aback to find his ex-girlfriend getting very intimate with Eddie the barman. Eddie had smiled at Mark, his ex had ignored him. When Eddie sauntered over with Mark's pint he asked if he minded.

"Couldn't give a toss Eddie, help yourself."

Eddie then returned to his new love, and gave her his undivided attention. Mark watched on with a twinge of jealousy, but told himself there was plenty where that came from. He returned his thoughts to his brother's murderer. He contemplated 'phoning them again, asking if they had got his present. He then decided against it, he would wait until the trial was over, when they thought they had escaped the torment. Then he would attack.

Martin offered to make the evening meal, and to his surprise Betty agreed. It was a measure of how badly she had taken the day's proceedings when she couldn't bring herself to cook for her family. Martin could not remember the last time his mother had not cooked the evening meal, maybe never. Martin would never profess to be a good cook, he preferred quantity, not quality. He realised both of those traits would have to be sacrificed, nobody had an appetite that evening.

He made a spaghetti bolognese, which his parents chased around their plates, eating little. He washed up as Harry and Betty, walking like ghosts through the quiet, cheerless house, returned to the sitting room. He asked them if they wanted anything else, and they said no thank you. Then, calling Bracken, he left his parents sitting silently on the sofa, side by side. He wanted to give them time to themselves and he needed his own space, to think the day's events through. He took Bracken for a long walk in the fading evening sun.

The morning of the second day of the trial was identical to the first. It was a glorious day, not a cloud in the sky. Spiders' webs glistened in the morning light, the grass sparkled as the dew reflected the sun's rays. It was a morning that held promise of a stunning summer's day. It meant nothing to the Sintons as they trudged to their car, ready to take them once again to the Crown Court.

The run-up to the arrival of the Judge, Mr. Justice Thorn, was identical to the day before. The same amount of media filmed, photographed, and reported their arrival, Harry was led away with his Defence counsel, Betty, Ann and Martin made their way to the public gallery. Tom Whitworth had once again arrived early and saved the three seats beside him. Mike and Sarah Cairns retained their seats behind Betty. An expectant buzz filled the room as the jury shuffled in and took their seats. The Court room was once again full.

The clerk of the Court once again asked for all present to rise, and announced the arrival of Judge Thorn, who, right on cue, entered the room and took his seat. The clerk then pronounced the Court in session. Maurice Brown stood and addressed the Court.

"I would like to call Sergeant Alex Phillips of the Hampshire Constabulary to the stand."

The Court Usher duly called Sergeant Phillips from his position in the witness waiting room outside the Court room. The policeman had been waiting patiently all afternoon the previous day, and was pleased he could get his part in the trial over with and return to his favoured work, chasing criminals. Alex Phillips had been in Court on numerous occasions, but still felt nervous when he took the stand. He took the oath, and with notebook in hand, waited for Maurice Brown's questions.

Sergeant Alex Phillips answered questions concerning his first observations when he was called to the scene. He spoke of the two dead bodies, one spread-eagled on the floor, the other crumpled inside a pen, of how he could find no vital signs of life when he inspected the bodies. He told of the baseball bat by the feet of William Stevens, and the shotgun discarded not ten feet from the victims.

Maurice Brown was building up the scene inside the barn. He

produced pictures for the jury to see. They showed the two bodies, gaping holes in their chests, blood soaking the surrounding floor. The graphic detail of the photographs made the jury shudder, some took a quick glance, others seemed to be transfixed by the images. They stared at the pale faces, at the unseeing lifeless eyes staring into the camera. It was the reaction Maurice Brown wanted.

He continued questioning the officer, building up the picture of that morning's events. The statements from the shocked farm workers, telling him that Harry Sinton was in his house. How he had found the Sintons in their kitchen.

"Did Mr. Sinton express any regret?"

"He said sorry to his wife," Sergeant Phillips read from his notes, "I'm sorry Betty."

"He didn't speak of any concern for the two men lying dead in his barn."

"No sir."

"Did he know they were dead."

"I wouldn't know sir."

"You don't know if he tried to help them."

"No sir."

"Thank you officer. No further questions."

Maurice Brown sat down. He believed he had laid the foundations of guilt in the minds of the jury. He now hoped the Defence counsel wouldn't undo too much of what he had built up.

Patrick Parker rose for the first time since the proceedings started. He had sat patiently as the prosecuting counsel made their case, feigning indifference. But now it was his turn to make his mark. He asked questions, expanding on the first statement Harry Sinton had given leading up to the confrontation in the barn.

"Officer Phillips, how would you describe Mr. Sinton's state when you found him."

"Distressed."

"Distressed," he repeated " . . . and in this state he apologised to his wife?"

"Yes sir."

"A very caring man, wouldn't you say. Apologising to his wife after he had been through the trauma of being threatened by a gang of raiders on his own property."

"It would seem so, yes sir." Sergeant Phillips had his view of the case, and anything he could say to help the defendant, he would.

"And you say the shotgun was left in the barn."

"Yes sir."

"Not the actions of a cold, calculating killer as the Prosecution would have us believe. Leaving his weapon, discarding it?"

"No sir."

This was more like it, thought Tom Whitworth. He liked the sound of this Barrister. Betty herself seemed to relax a little, their side of the case was being shown.

"He stated that the van was being driven at him, that he accidentally fired the first shot."

"Yes sir. Small skid marks on the concrete floor backed up his statement. "

Patrick Parker turned his attentions from the police officer, and towards the jury. He had set the scene for his first defence of his client.

"It must have been a terrifying experience, a one-ton vehicle being driven towards you. I expect it would scare almost anyone. Especially if you hadn't expected it to be there in the first place. And then when you have accidentally, in your fright and panic, fired off a shot that hit the van, you get confronted by two men."

Patrick Parker paused and shook his head slowly.

"Well, not a very pleasant experience first thing in the morning. Stumbling onto a gang of raiders, who had just stolen your property, and then being confronted by two men armed with a baseball bat, advancing with, what must have seemed at the time, the intent to do you physical harm.

"A sixty-five-year-old man, an old aged pensioner, who for the last forty years has been doing this same morning ritual, finding himself threatened by two men half his age."

This was the imbalance the Defence counsel wanted to portray. He let the words hang in the air.

"Did Mr. Sinton, in his distressed state, show any sign of anger towards the raiders?"

"No sir. He was more upset at his own actions. He kept

repeating," the policeman studied his notes, "they wouldn't stop, they just kept coming."

"He showed no anger towards the two raiders even after they had threatened him, forcing him to defend himself?" Patrick Parker, for the first time in a day and a half of proceedings, mentioned the words "defend himself ".

"No sir."

"Bear with me please, Officer Phillips, I am just trying to imagine the scene," Patrick Parker said, more for the jury to imagine than himself. "Mr. Sinton had stumbled upon the gang of raiders in his barn. They had already placed a piece of Mr. Sinton's property, a quad bike, in the back of their van, without Mr. Sinton's consent. The van was then driven towards Mr. Sinton in what seemed like an aggressive manner, this is backed up by the skid marks found on the barn floor. In a state of fright and panic Mr. Sinton accidentally fired off a shot that hit the front of the van, causing it to stop. Two men then jumped out of the van, one armed with a baseball bat, the other following close behind, and advanced threateningly towards Mr. Sinton."

Patrick Parker once again paused, letting the image of the two men advancing towards the old man in the barn, sink into the minds of the jury.

"What a terrifying thought, two men half your age, armed with a baseball bat, intent on what seemed like causing you serious harm. And you, a man of over sixty-five, not as strong as you once were, having to defend yourself."

Patrick Parker shook his head in apparent disbelief.

"And after all this, the sight of a van trying to run him over, the threats by two men, the confusion he felt from the shock of the morning's events; after all that, Harry Sinton's only thoughts were to apologise to his wife, for actions he was forced to do, to defend himself."

"Yes sir," came the simple reply from the officer.

"Thank you Officer Phillips, I have no further questions."

Patrick Parker sat down as P.C. Phillips left the stand and made his way out of the Court, avoiding eye contact with anybody in the room. Patrick Parker had succeeded in portraying Harry Sinton as the caring husband who had been forced into actions he didn't want to commit in order to defend himself. Harry Sinton's side of the story had finally been heard by the jury. Perhaps this case wasn't as clear-cut as they were led to believe the day before.

The Prosecution's next witness was Chief Inspector Anthony Kemp. He took the stand and swore the oath in his strong, forceful manner. He had been in the witness stand many times, it held no fears for him.

Maurice Brown wanted to expand on the initial statements and inquiries. He asked the Chief Inspector questions relating to his first interview with Harry Sinton. Prising away information he wanted the jury to hear, skirting around anything that may help the Defence case, all the time developing his argument that Harry Sinton had used excessive force when confronting the two men.

"In Mr. Sinton's statement, he said he did not recognise William Stevens or Sean Robson."

"That is correct."

"He had not seen them before."

"Correct."

"And in his statement he said that he wanted them to leave."

"Correct."

"Did he ask them to leave? Did he express in any way that he wanted them to leave?"

"In his statement, he did not say whether he asked them to leave or not, what he . . . " Maurice Brown cut the officer's answer short. He turned and addressed the jury.

"How could William Stevens and Sean Robson have known that Mr. Sinton wanted them to leave. He had just stopped them doing just that, by very forceful means, by firing his shotgun at their vehicle. If Mr. Sinton had wanted them to leave, why hadn't he simply stepped out of the way and let the vehicle pass? He then could have then noted the number plate and rung the police. He could have let the proper authorities deal with the situation. There was no need for this confrontation in the first place, no need for William Stevens and Sean Robson to lose their lives over a piece of farm machinery.

"Harry Sinton took it into his own hands to confront William

Stevens and Sean Robson. That fatal decision resulted in a wife losing her husband and a family losing a son and grandson."

Maurice Brown continued his questions, building up the picture of the inquiry. At one point he asked the Chief Inspector to tell the Court the police results from the skid marks the van tyres had made and what that had equated to in terms of speed.

"The results showed the speed of the van at being no more than seven miles an hour."

"Seven miles an hour," the prosecuting Barrister repeated. "Not particularly fast. It should have been easy enough to step out of the way I would have thought." He refrained from asking the Chief Inspector if he agreed. He didn't know how the officer would answer, and rather than letting the policeman shatter his line of questioning by giving an unhelpful reply, he allowed himself to ponder the question.

The Chief Inspector continued to answer the questions put to him by the prosecuting Counsel. The questioning was expertly done, it only allowed Chief Inspector Anthony Kemp to state what Maurice Brown wanted the jury to hear. He would have to wait for the Defence counsel to convey the other side of the story.

When Maurice Brown finished, he sat and let Patrick Parker have his turn.

"Chief Inspector, would you say that Mr. Sinton was co-operative when you were questioning him?"

"He was very co-operative."

"Answering all your questions?"

"Correct."

"How would you describe his manner at the police station?"

"He was in shock. He seemed bewildered, frightened."

"And in his statement, what did he say about the two men who got out of the van?"

"He said they kept coming at him, shouting threats."

"Shouting threats. Did he say what threats?"

"No, he was not specific on the threats the two were shouting. What he did say was that the threats were so strong that he feared for his life."

Bingo! thought Patrick Parker, that was what he wanted to hear, and he wanted to make sure the jury did as well.

"Feared for his life," he repeated slowly. "Mr. Sinton, in a state of shock, bewilderment and fright, believed his life was in danger. Mr. Sinton was suddenly confronted by two men half his age, two men who kept advancing towards him, threatening him. One armed with a baseball bat, the second backing up the first. No wonder he was scared for his life. An old-aged pensioner, alone, against a gang of raiders."

Patrick Parker didn't pause, he kept up his questioning, he switched his line of attack to discredit the prosecuting counsel's earlier statement that his client could have stepped aside.

"Earlier, Chief Inspector, you stated that the speed of the vehicle the raiders were driving was seven miles an hour."

"Correct."

"That seven miles an hour was achieved over what distance?"

"Ten feet." He answered without needing his notes.

"Seven miles an hour over ten feet by a . . . " It was Patrick Parker's turn to pick up some paper in front of him, and make a show of checking his facts. " . . . A one ton vehicle, powered by a two litre petrol engine. Not the fastest of vehicles ever built I would think. Would you say that the driver must have been accelerating hard to reach such speed over such a short distance in such a heavy vehicle, that had two quad bikes and three men inside it?"

"The analysis of the skid would support that assumption, yes."

"Ladies and gentlemen of the jury, my learned friend suggests that Mr. Sinton should have stepped aside, allowed the raiders to go. Maybe in the cold light of day, when you are not faced by a gang of raiders, accelerating hard towards you in a one ton vehicle, with your property you worked hard to pay for inside the van, maybe that would be your first thought as well. Maybe he should have. Maybe the question should be whether he *could* have, instead of *should* have. How could Mr. Sinton, sixty-five remember, have jumped aside: *jumped* aside I think would be a better description of the actions needed than *stepped* aside. How could Mr. Sinton have jumped aside when he didn't' know if the van was going to follow him? He didn't know if the driver was going to swerve towards him or not. It is unknown, unknown then and unknown now, and certainly unknown to Mr. Sinton when the van was bearing down on him."

Patrick Parker now paused, he let the image of the vehicle bearing down on Harry Sinton sink into the jury. After a suitable period of time he resumed his questioning of the Chief Inspector.

"I mentioned two quad bikes. The police report stated that there was a second quad bike already in the van, along with Mr. Sinton's. Where had that bike come from?"

"The second quad bike found in the van had been reported stolen by the time I arrived at the scene. It had been stolen from a farm about eight miles away that same morning."

Patrick Parker then carefully extracted the information he wanted the jury to hear. How the gang had already broken into one farm and stolen a quad bike, how they were thwarted at the second, and then disturbed at the third. Patrick Parker desperately wanted to convey the fact that William Stevens had a long history of violent crime, but such information was inadmissible in Court. Instead he concentrated on the evidence he could show, pointing to the fact that this was not just a one-off raid, that it was a professional operation.

"Chief Inspector, in your report you state that the number plate on the vehicle used by the gang was illegally taken from a similar vehicle nearly ninety miles away in Reading. And that on inspecting the vehicle itself it was found to be reported stolen two years ago."

"Correct."

"Why would the raiders go to such lengths to cover up the identity of their van?"

"The stolen number plate related to a van of the same make and similar age. If for any reason the police stopped and ran a check on the van the gang was using, the number plate being shown would relate to the van in Reading that had not been stolen and therefore the van would come back as a legal vehicle and the police would have no reason to impound it."

"The fact that the van was stolen, that the number plates on the van were illegal and that there was already another quad bike in the van, would seem to point to a professional, almost ruthless, gang of raiders?"

"We believe so."

"Thank you Chief Inspector, no further questions."

The jury were now uncertain of their thoughts. It was not as clear-cut as the prosecuting counsel would have them believe. They looked over to Harry Sinton and tried to imagine this meek, tired-looking old man having a one tonne van accelerate towards at him and then being confronted by two raiders. The thought appalled them.

The questioning of the two policemen had taken the proceedings up to one o'clock. The Judge called for the lunch recess, and the Court erupted with the sounds of people standing and heading towards the door which led down to the cafeteria on the second floor. Some needed the toilet, some needed to feed their nicotine habit, all wanting to stand and get the circulation back into their bodies. Other sounds rose from the public gallery, the sound of various voices expressing their opinion on the latest twist in the case.

"A bit more like it," Tom Whitworth muttered as he pushed past Martin, on his way to get some fresh air, and not-so-fresh pipe smoke, into his lungs.

Martin, Betty and Ann all stood and stretched their legs. The Cairns smiled and backed up Tom Whitworth's statement. They followed the crowd down towards the second floor. Betty seemed more relaxed, pleased that her husband's side of the story was being heard at last. They met on the balcony, joined the queue for some food, bought little and ate even less. They were just pleased to be close.

Patrick Parker, Gerald Evans and the junior solicitor were deep in conversation, as were their counterparts. The Prosecution had three more witnesses to call. Again Maurice Brown hoped the timing would be on his side. He wanted to play it so as to leave his penultimate witness enough time for his questions only, leaving the cross-examination for tomorrow. His penultimate witness was Paul Allen, already sitting scared, next to his mother, along with the other two witnesses, in the witness waiting room. None of them wanted to stray onto the concourse while the lunch recess was on.

When the Court reconvened, Maurice Brown called Mr. Henry Robson to the witness box. In his opening questions Mr. Maurice Brown established that Henry Robson was Sean Robson's grandfather. Through careful questioning he was able to tell the jury that the parents of Sean were too distraught to appear in Court, and for their sake the prosecuting counsel, wanting to appear kind and considerate, declined from forcing them to attend, not wanting to add to their grief.

The thought of asking Wendy Stevens to attend the proceedings, on behalf of the Prosecution, to show the distraught, grieving wife, was soon dismissed. She would be a liability, likely to do more harm to their cause than good. She would have to answer the question of why had she left her husband's body, which she claimed she loved beyond all things, lying in the morgue for the local authority to bury. The idea of the Defence counsel calling her, as the distraught wife of one of the victims, was just as foolish. In the end, the chance to subpoena Wendy would not have been realised as no one knew where she was, she had vanished, disappeared overnight. A missing persons report had been compiled, but the police hadn't followed it up too closely, they had better ways to spend their time. If she turned up, all well and good, but they were not going to lose any sleep over her.

Maurice Brown's questions allowed Henry Robson to tell of his son's and daughter in law's grief at the loss of their son. How they had sold their business, built up over a number of years, which they hoped Sean, if he wanted to, would one day take over. He told the jury that they had left their home city, their family and friends, to try to put this harrowing experience behind them. How the death of their son had crushed their very being.

Henry Robson did not mention Mark in his questions. Both the Prosecution and Defence counsels knew of a brother and his past exploits, they also knew his contribution would have a detrimental effect on their arguments. For the Prosecution the mention of Mark Robson and his past would show a history of criminal activity in the Robson family. For the Defence the mention of Mark and his past, would put a sense of greater loss for Sean. Mark Robson's existence was never revealed, and that pleased all parties concerned.

Henry Robson managed to portray his grandson as a carefree, fun-loving, football supporting seventeen year old. A hard-working, bright young man, who was the centre of his parents' world, and who had numerous friends who all shared in the grief at his loss. When Henry Robson admitted being biased, as all good grandfathers are, the jury admired his honesty and strength. They liked his openness, he answered the questions frankly, and with dignity.

When the prosecuting Barrister had finished, it was Patrick Parker's turn to cross-examine the witness. He saw how the jury had taken to this frank, thoughtful old man, and he knew he had to be wary of his questions. Too blatant an attack on what Henry Robson had already said would damage the Defence more than it would undermine the Prosecution. With this in mind, Patrick Parker started his questioning.

"Mr. Robson, I have not had the good fortune to become a grandfather as yet, but I am a father, and I would like to think I am a good father, that I know my children well. But now and again they surprise me, and I have to reassess their characters. It is usually when they have reached a certain watershed in their lives. The first time they come home late for instance, the first time they swear, or the first time you catch them out, and you know they have lied to you. I am not saying my children are bad in any way, I am merely suggesting it is what children all over the world do, as part of growing up. Would you agree?"

"That is the way of children, yes." Henry Robson was not aggressive towards this man many of the jury believed would represent the enemy to him. He answered the questions coolly and calmly, it continued to enamour him to the jury.

"What I am suggesting is that as a father, I might not know my children as well as I would like to think, and therefore, being a grandfather, and one more link away as it were, then you might not have known your grandson as well as you would have liked to think you did."

"I knew Sean well enough to know he was a good boy."

"As you say. Did you know he went on these farm raids often?"

"I believe he was bullied into going."

This was an unexpected answer, Patrick Parker had expected a denial of some sort. This answer led him onto a new course of questioning, which he pursued immediately.

"Bullied into going? Bullied by whom?"

"Billy Stevens."

"Bullied into going by William Stevens once, or more than once?"

"I wouldn't know."

Patrick Parker was now back to his original line of inquiries, but he had established that William Stevens was a bully of seventeen-year-old youths. Whether this was true or false, it could only help his case.

"Exactly, how could you know? That is what I am trying to put across, just how well do we know our children, our grandchildren for that matter? I am not challenging you in your belief that your grandson was good to you, or to others of his family or friends. I am suggesting that when it comes down to intimate knowledge of children, especially teenagers who want to grow up so fast these days, then there will always be secrets. Would you agree Mr. Robson?"

"I knew Sean well enough to know he was a good lad," Henry Robson repeated.

"Yes, so you have said. What I am asking is, do you believe teenagers have to, or even need to, keep secrets from their parents, their grandparents? It is part of what makes a teenager."

Henry Robson was now getting irritated by this line of questioning, and the tone of this Barrister's voice.

"There is a difference between keeping secrets, and getting bullied into going on a, on a . . . "

"On a morning raid, to steal someone's property? Well yes I agree with that, but what I am saying is that teenagers like to keep secrets from their parents, and grandparents. Would you agree with that, Mr. Robson?"

"I suppose."

"And those secrets could include things like, well, early morning raids on farmyards for instance."

"He was bullied into going."

"Yes so you repeated, but bullied how often? Once, twice, half a dozen times?"

"I don't know."

"Exactly, you couldn't have known, your son couldn't have known. It was a secret your grandson kept to himself."

"Because he was scared."

"Well, we will look into that later," Patrick Parker said dismissively. "For the time being, would you agree with me that your teenage grandson kept his parents, and his grandparents, in the dark about his early morning activities?"

"So would you, if you were threatened if you talked."

"Please answer the question Mr. Robson, we will come to the reasons later. Do you agree that your grandson kept secrets from his parents?"

"Yes."

"Thank you Mr. Robson, and do you know what he said to cover for his early morning jaunts?"

"He told his father he was looking for a motor cross bike."

"Which he had done before?"

"You know he had."

"Yes or no, Mr. Robson."

"Yes, Sean had been looking for a motor cross bike before, that isn't a . . . "

"He had said he had been looking for a motor cross bike, when he had been breaking into Mr. Sinton's farmyard. Now, how do you know all the other times he said he was out looking for this motor bike, he wasn't breaking into other places? We have established that he kept secrets from you and his parents, that he lied as to his whereabouts that Monday morning."

Patrick Parker was pleased with his cross-examination of the grandfather, it was certainly easier to pressurise him than it would have been Sean's mother or father. The jury saw the grandfather, although grieving, as slightly detached from the immediate loss. All Patrick Parker's work in discrediting Sean Robson as an innocent, caught up in the morning's events through no fault of his own, came crashing down. Henry Robson, furious at being trapped into speaking out against his grandson, pointed at Harry Sinton and shouted, "That doesn't give that bastard the right to kill him!"

Voices in the crowded gallery started to flare, a sense of unrest rippled through the Court house. The audience had been stifling their feelings for too long, they wanted to speak up. The Judge rapped his gavel on the wooden anvil on top of the bench.

"Silence in Court."

"Have you got grandchildren?" Henry Robson shouted across to Harry Sinton. "Are you going to watch them grow up?"

Harry Sinton reeled from the sudden verbal attack. He stared in horror at Henry Robson, shocked by the words of venom he was screaming, the anger in his face.

"Silence in Court!"

Tom Whitworth was on his feet, pointing and shouting obscenities down towards the man in the witness box.

"Why was he there in the first place? Bloody little criminals!"

"Or is some bastard going to take them away from you?" Henry Robson continued.

"Silence in Court!" the Judge shouted, rapping his gavel repeatedly. He would not tolerate this sort of behaviour in his Court. The bustle of noise died down. "Any further outbursts from the public gallery and that person will be forcibly removed. And you Mr. Robson will restrict your responses to the questions asked, and to language befitting a Court of law, or you will be charged with contempt. Do I make myself clear?"

"Yes your Honour," Henry Robson replied, still staring at Harry Sinton, the hatred still apparent in his features. He had made his statement, he was pleased to leave it at that.

"Mr. Parker, you may continue," Judge Peter Thorn bid the Barrister.

"Thank you, your Honour." Patrick Parker had to start from scratch, but instead of looking irritated, he continued as if the outburst never happened. He now wanted to concentrate on the relationship Sean had with Stevens, and perhaps convey to the jury what sort of man Stevens was.

"Mr. Robson, you say your grandson was bullied into going with Mr. Stevens on these early morning raids."

"That's what I said."

"Was your grandson easily intimidated?"

"Not that I know of."

"So William Stevens must have been an aggressive man to be able to bully your grandson into doing something he didn't want to do?"

Maurice Brown was about to raise an objection to the question the Defence counsel had asked his witness. He saw the insinuation that Stevens "must have been an aggressive man" as leading the witness on. Henry Robson could also see where this line of questioning was going, and decided to give nothing away.

"I didn't know the man myself."

Maurice Brown decided against objecting and allowed Patrick Parker to continue unhindered.

"But you knew your grandson, you said yourself, he was a good lad. Therefore Billy Stevens must have been able to scare your grandson in such a way, that he accompanied Stevens on this trip, if not others. Did Sean go on other early morning farm raids with Stevens?"

"I wouldn't know, and I don't know Stevens." He had heard of Stevens' reputation only after Sean's funeral. Whispered conversations at the wake he had helped to organise, confidential talks he had with friends in his local pub. Henry Robson was damned if he was going to help this Barrister by answering his questions too truthfully.

Patrick Parker considered bringing up some new information the Defence team had unearthed in the police report, but decided the moment was lost, that Henry Robson would be of little use any more, and that the new information would be better used on the next witness. Patrick Parker said he had no further questions, and Henry Robson left the witness stand. As he walked out of the Court he continued to stare at Harry Sinton in the dock, hoping to catch his eye, hoping he could convey the hurt, the anger, the loss the farmer had brought upon his family. Harry Sinton never looked up.

The next witness was called, Paul Allen entered the Court room. A buzz of whispered conversation filled the air. For the first time since the fateful shootings at Downlands Farm, Paul Allen saw the man who had killed his best friend. As he took the oath in the witness stand, he stared across at the farmer; he looked different to how Paul remembered, smaller, paler, almost withered. He certainly didn't look frightening, more pathetic, Paul thought to himself.

The judge rapped the gavel for good measure, the muffled noise died, and Maurice Brown rose from his seat. If he wanted to finish the day with his questioning of Paul Allen, again allowing the jury to retire for the night with the words he wanted them to hear, and not the Defence's, he would have to pad out his questions. Otherwise there would still be time for the defending Counsel to cross-examine.

Maurice Brown started his questioning slowly, letting Paul explain his friendship with Sean, how they had grown up together since school and went on to college together. Paul had been coached in the art of answering questions in the witness stand. He was told never to elaborate, just to answer the questions as truthfully as he could, and where the Defence was concerned, imparting as little information as possible.

Paul told of a friendship that was strong, their plans for the future, anything to show the jury his loss. Paul stood hunched in the stand, looking as nervous as he felt. He wore a white shirt, buttoned up to his neck, a sombre tie, and smart trousers, the same clothes he had worn at his own trial, all bought by his mother. His hair was cut short at the sides, with gel used on the top to keep the style fixed. For all his and his mother's efforts, he still looked scruffy, ill at ease in his crisp new clothes.

Maurice Brown, after establishing the relationship Paul had with Sean, moved on to the events on the morning of the seventh of March. The Barrister ran through questions that allowed Paul to explain that he and Sean had been bullied into going with Stevens, how they had already broken into one farm, before going on to what he now knew to be Downlands Farm. Paul never mentioned the bad mood Stevens was in; he had not been asked, therefore he didn't need to say. Maurice Brown led Paul expertly to the scene of the confrontation.

"After you had secured the quad bike as William Stevens had ordered you to do, what happened then?"

"We got into the front of the van."

"And then?"

"Then that man came out of nowhere and shot at us," Paul said, pointing at Harry Sinton sitting in the defendant's box. Harry Sinton was staring at Paul. Was he the same age as the boy he had shot? He looked so young. Harry's heart sunk at the thought.

"You saw Mr. Sinton shoot at you?"

"Yea, he came from nowhere, and with no warning he shot at us, hitting the van."

"Were you stationary in the van when Mr. Sinton opened fire?"

"No, no. We were driving out. We were just about to leave. We weren't going very fast. Another minute and we would have been out of there and Sean would still be alive."

"What sort of damage did Mr. Sinton's shot do to the vehicle?"

"It was knackered, I . . . I mean it was bad. We couldn't carry on in it."

"Ladies and gentlemen of the jury, we have already established, through the police evidence, that Mr. Sinton's first shot rendered the vehicle inoperative. The radiator was punctured, which would have made the engine overheat in a short space of time. What Paul is saying backs up this evidence."

Paul Allen liked that, his story and the police's evidence matched, therefore he believed the rest of his account would be accepted as true.

"Paul, please tell the Court what happened next."

"Well, Billy got out to have a word. You know, this bloke had just shot at us, smashed the front of Billy's van. Billy wanted to talk to this bloke."

"Talk, he didn't threaten Mr. Sinton in any way?"

"Not that I heard. Yea, he took a baseball bat with him, but you would want something if that bloke had just shot at you, he still had his gun."

"Quite. It must have been very frightening."

"Yea, yea. It was. Sean got out too, just to see what was going on, I don't know. I stayed in the van, I didn't have time to get out."

"You didn't have time?"

"No, before I could think of moving that bastard shot them."

"You will refrain from using such language Mr. Allen," the Judge told Paul politely. Judge Thorn could see the distress Paul was in, continually fidgeting while standing in the box, his eyes darting from pillar to post, across to Harry Sinton, then the jury, up to the public gallery and then back to the jury.

This was the crux of the case, Maurice Brown knew it, Patrick Parker knew it, and so did the Judge. All the other witnesses were just peripheral, their evidence building to this scene. The case came down to Paul Allen's word against Harry Sinton's. Maurice Brown took his time, it was still touch and go whether the Defence would have time to cross-examine that day.

"You say you had no time to move?"

"Yea."

"Did Mr. Sinton say anything?"

"No, I didn't hear nothing. I tell you he just shot them. First Stevens, and then he just turned on Sean and killed him too. Sean wasn't doing nothing, he had just got out, he didn't threaten him or nothing, he was giving himself up."

"Paul, I realise this is distressful for you, but please bear with me. You say that after Mr. Sinton had shot at the vehicle, William Stevens got out to talk with his attacker, and Sean also left the front of the van."

"Yea."

"But before they could say anything, Mr. Sinton, with no warning, raised his shotgun, aimed, and pulled the trigger. Killing William Stevens first, and then turning, taking aim a second time, and once again pulling the trigger, this time killing Sean who was making no threats, who was even trying to give himself up."

"Yea. Sean was standing still, trying to give himself up."

"Sean was standing still, almost surrendering?" Maurice Brown laboured over this point. It showed that Sean at the least was not posing a threat towards Harry Sinton at the time of his death.

"Yea, he was stood still."

"It must have been a horrifying sight."

"Yea it was. Sean was blown backwards, he . . . he ended up in a sheep pen. I could see his legs in the air. I was scared, scared shi . . . . for my life."

"I am not surprised. What happened next?"

"Nothing. I didn't do nothing, just sat there. I couldn't believe it.

I couldn't move. I didn't want to show myself to him, he would have shot me too. I didn't know what to do."

"What did Mr. Sinton do?"

"He just sat down. He just sat down and watched. Looked at what he had done."

"He didn't try and see if Sean was still alive, or if William Stevens needed medical help?"

"No, he just sat down and looked at what he had done."

"And then what happened Paul?"

"I waited till he turned away, and then I ran for it, I had to get out."

"You didn't try to give yourself up?"

"No way. He had just killed Sean for no reason, I wasn't going to let him do the same to me. I got out of there."

"And then what?"

"Then I got to some town, rang a friend. He came and picked me up. I was so scared, I didn't know if he had followed me or what."

"Where did you go when you were picked up by your friend?"

"We went straight to the police. We reported it straight away."

"You didn't go home first?"

"No, we went straight to the police, told them everything."

"You told the police everything, even though it implicated you in a break-in?"

"Yea, that bloke had killed Sean, I had to tell them, tell them what happened."

"So instead of going back to the warmth, comfort, and safety of your home, you went straight to the police and reported the event."

"Yea."

"Even though you might have got away with it. Who else knew you were there?"

"No one, we didn't tell no one."

"And you still decided to go to the police?"

"Yea, I had to tell them. I had to tell them what happened. I didn't know what that man would say, how he would say what happened. I had to tell them the truth, how it really happened."

Maurice Brown was coming to the end of his questions; he hoped, with a little luck, the Judge would call an early end to the day's proceedings, perhaps let Paul Allen have some time to recover from the experience of recounting the morning's events before he had to suffer the Defence counsel's cross-examination. To help the Judge come to this decision, Maurice Brown started on a new tact.

"Thank you Paul for being so brave, I realise this couldn't have been easy for you. It must bring back some awful memories that will haunt you for the rest of your life. I see from the case notes that you are seeking medical help to overcome these emotional problems. Is that correct?"

"Yea."

"Have you been able to go back to college?"

"No, no not yet. I, I can't seem to concentrate."

"Paul, thank you for your help in what must be a very difficult time for you. No further question your Honour."

As Maurice Brown retook his seat, Judge Thorn looked over and spoke softly to Paul.

"Paul, the Defence now has the right to cross-examine you, do you understand?"

"Yea."

"It is up to you Paul, I don't want to put you under too much pressure. You can either carry on today and get it over with, or we can call a halt to the proceedings now and you can go home to recover, finish off the questioning tomorrow."

To Maurice Brown's dismay, Paul said he wanted to get it over with. He was irritated, the junior solicitor he was using should have briefed Paul, got him to understand the importance of leaving the jury with their side of the case to mull over for the evening, night and next morning.

The packed public gallery was now hushed, looking down on the stage below, waiting to hear how the Defence would handle Paul Allen. Patrick Parker rose, and got straight to the point. He showed little sympathy, almost disdain, for the Prosecution's star witness.

"You say you didn't hear Harry Sinton say anything as these two men bore down on him?"

"He didn't say nothing."

Patrick Parker refrained from correcting Paul's grammar and continued with the cross-examination.

"You were still in the front of the van as your two partners advanced towards Mr. Sinton."

"Yea."

"So you are saying you didn't hear anything, or you couldn't hear anything?"

Paul look vaguely at his questioner. Patrick Parker acted impatient.

"Did you mean to say you didn't hear anything, or couldn't hear anything Paul? From your position in the front of the van, could you actually hear if anything was said?" Patrick Parker didn't wait for an answer. "I have been in my car when two people were talking in front of me, and even with the windows down I couldn't hear what they were saying. Did you not hear anything at all Paul?"

"I didn't hear nothing."

"Now then, there is the difference. Now you say you didn't hear anything, whereas before you said Mr. Sinton didn't say anything. This is a very important distinction Paul. Harry Sinton may have said something, but in your position in the front of the van, over twelve feet away from Mr. Sinton, you may not have heard him."

"He didn't say nothing, I could see it."

"So you were watching Mr. Sinton all the time?"

"Yea, and his mouth didn't move."

"So you could see his mouth?"

"Yea, and it didn't move. He didn't say nothing. He didn't tell them to stop. He didn't tell them sorry. He didn't tell them nothing."

"So you could see his mouth Paul?"

"Yea."

"So the gun couldn't have been up to his chin?"

Again Paul looked puzzled, just when he had thought he had answered the question well, telling the Court the farmer didn't speak a word, he was now being trapped into something else.

"You said you could see Mr. Sinton's face, his mouth, his chin. Now if Mr. Sinton had been taking proper aim," Patrick Parker imitated the stance of a man leaning into a shotgun, "he would have had his head down, and the gun up, looking down the barrel, completely masking his face from view. What you are saying Paul, is that Mr. Sinton couldn't have been aiming at the two men bearing down on him."

"He was aiming."

"You must have excellent eyesight Paul, either that or excellent imagination."

"He had his head up . . . "

"So he wasn't aiming. Thank you Paul for clearing that up. Now if you were watching Mr. Sinton, and William Stevens was walking away from you, I would think that even you couldn't see if his mouth was moving or not. How do you know he didn't say something to Mr. Sinton?"

"Because I didn't hear nothing, I keep telling you."

"Yes you do, but surely there were other noises in the barn. Were the sheep making any noise? Was the engine still running? I would expect there to be a whole range of noises, how could you be sure William Stevens didn't say anything when he had his back to you?"

"I didn't hear nothing I tell you."

"Didn't or couldn't?"

Again Paul was lost for words. He felt trapped, he felt that the Defence Barrister was twisting his words. All his plans, all his lies, all his stories he wanted to tell were being dismantled. He turned to the Judge, seeking help.

"I want a break, I can't go on."

The Judge apologised to Paul, but told him it was his decision to carry on.

Patrick Parker continued his attack.

"I put it to you Paul that in the confusion and noise in the barn, with William Stevens walking away from you, with you still in the van, you would not have heard William Stevens' threatening remarks towards Mr. Sinton."

Paul was silent, averting his gaze from his interrogator.

"Let us start at the beginning, Paul. You said that William Stevens bullied you and Sean into going on this farm raid, and that this was the first time for both of you."

"Yea," Paul replied sullenly.

"So you don't argue with William Stevens?"

"No you bloody don't!"

"Mr. Allen," The Judge said in exasperation. "I have asked you once, please refrain from using such language in my Court."

"So if William Stevens asked you to do something, you would do that, even if it was illegal?"

"Billy didn't ask, he *told* you."

"How did he coerce you Paul?"

Paul stared back blankly.

"How did William Stevens bully you into going with him that morning? What method did he use?"

"He threatened us."

"What with. Was he going to tell your parents you had helped him before?"

"No, no because we never been out with him before." Paul was pleased he wasn't caught out by that question. He had been ready for it.

"So what method did he use, Paul?" Patrick Parker desperately wanted Paul to admit to Stevens' reputation as a violent man, but he was careful not to lead the witness on, and give the Defence anything to break his line of questioning. "You have already said you don't argue with William Stevens, why was that?"

"Because he would kick shi . . . He would beat you up."

Hallelujah, Patrick Parker thought, it had taken a time for Paul Allen to admit to it, but at last he had something to go on. Maurice Brown sighed to himself. He had known Paul Allen would be a risk to put on the stand, but the Prosecution had no one else to call.

"Was he a violent man, this William Stevens?"

"You didn't mess with him, if that's what you mean."

"No wonder you had to go. William Stevens threatening you with violence like that." Now Patrick Parker had shown the jury the nature of this man Stevens, he continued to press the point home.

"It must have been very hard for you both, caught between two men like that. William Stevens threatening violence to get you there, and then being confronted by Mr. Sinton. Paul, do you think Sean got out of the van and followed William Stevens because he was more frightened of what Stevens would do to him if he didn't?"

"I don't know," he replied honestly. "He just got out."

"Paul, we have written and signed statements from the police, by some of Sean's friends, saying he had gone on these raids before."

"They're no friends of Sean."

"Why is that, because they told the police the truth?"

"I didn't know he had gone before."

"Your best friend hadn't told you. He told others, boasting about it apparently, showing-off the cash he received from Stevens for going, and he didn't tell you. We have these statements in black and white."

Patrick Parker held up a couple of sheets of paper, no one could see what was on them, but nobody challenged their authenticity. This was the evidence Patrick Parker nearly used on Henry Robson, but as he told Paul of these revelations, and saw the interest in the jury's eyes, some making notes on the pads of paper before them, he was pleased he had kept it until now.

"I never went before."

"But Sean could have done."

"He never told me," Paul lied.

"If Sean had been before, boasting about it, showing-off some money, it doesn't sound as if William Stevens had to bully him. Why pay Sean if he was going to do it out of fright anyway?"

"He bullied me into going."

"Paul I would like to believe you, but it just doesn't add up. Your best friend had been out on these trips before, boasting and waving about the cash he got from going, and you didn't know about it. And then your best friend let this man Stevens, who you have already told us had a reputation as a violent man, bully you into going. As I said, it just doesn't seem to add up."

When the police had interviewed Paul Allen at the station, they had also found this hard to believe, but Paul had refused to change his statement.

"I never went before."

"That I am not contesting. What I think happened, Paul, was you saw Sean flashing the money he received from Stevens for these farm raids, and you wanted a part of it."

"No."

"So you persuaded Sean and William Stevens to take you along."

"No, it was not like that." Paul cried, looking over to the jury.

Patrick Parker ignored Paul's denials, he had put across two of the main points he wanted to convey to the jury. One, that William

Stevens was a violent man with a reputation, and two, that Paul Allen's story of being bullied into going was flawed. Patrick Parker now changed tact, and went for the kill.

"You say that after being picked up by your friend," the Barrister studied his notes, "Mr. Andrew Goodman, you headed straight for the police station in Southampton."

"Yea, I wanted to tell them what happened, that a mad farmer had . . ."

"You passed at least two other police stations on the way, one in Annavale, and one here in Winchester. Why didn't you go to them, report it faster, it may have saved your friend's life. If you had told the police the situation, they would have certainly brought an ambulance along."

"Sean was fucking dead! I could see he was dead!"

"Mr. Allen, one more outburst and I will charge you with contempt, is that clear?" Judge Thorn said, starting to lose his patience with the young witness.

"He's making these things up, that's not how it happened!" Paul cried in desperation. "We didn't know where the other police stations were, we knew where the one in Southampton was, so we went there."

"But you could have called the police from the cafe you say you were in when you were waiting for your friend Mr. Goodman. Everybody knows the 999 number. Paul, you said yourself that you waited over an hour for your friend to pick you up, and then it took you another hour to get back to Southampton. Over two hours before you told anyone, that your best friend was lying dying in a farmer's barn. Over two hours."

"Dead, Sean was already dead. The farmer had already killed him."

"But you couldn't have known that at the time. I put it to you that you used those two hours to make up your story, to fabricate a tale that showed you and your friend in the best light, and put William Stevens, a known violent man, as the man who bullied you into going, and Harry Sinton as an unprovoked killer. I put to you that it is all lies, to cover your own guilt in going, and then not helping your friend.

"It is only your words that tell of Sean Robson standing still, giving himself up. One minute you are saying the farmer gave no time for your accomplices to say or do anything, the next you are saying Sean was giving himself up. Mr. Allen, if you have the gall to lie to this Court, would you please do us the honour of making it believable."

"I'm not . . . "

"No further questions your Honour," Patrick Parker cut Paul off dismissively.

"You are free to go, Mr. Allen," the Judge told Paul.

Paul sat still, he couldn't believe it was over. One minute he was being bombarded with questions, being tied up into saying things he didn't mean, the next it was all over. He wanted to continue to talk, tell the Judge, the jury, the people in the public gallery the way it had happened, or at least the way he had told the police, his friends, and even Mark Robson, how he wanted it to have happened.

"You may go," Judge Thorn repeated.

Paul stood, looking disorientated. Both Barristers ignored his looks, the jury watched him leave, Harry Sinton followed his progress out of the Court. An uneasy silence hung over the Court room as Paul walked down the passageway towards the doors that would allow him to escape the confines of the Court. He felt as if the whole Court was watching him leave. It reminded him of the cafe where he had waited for Andrew Goodman to rescue him almost four months ago. As he pushed through the doors, onto the corridor outside the Court room, he was met by the open arms of his mother, given a loving hug, and then taken away with the promise of his favourite meal once again.

Judge Thorn decided the time was right to adjourn the proceedings for another day, and told the Court as much. Maurice Brown had one more witness to call, and then it would be the turn of the Defence counsel to state their case.

Once again the Court emptied, once again Gerald Evans and Patrick Parker chatted about the day's proceedings, both being rather pleased that they had finally put their case across. And once again the Sintons battled to their car before driving home, this time surrounded by a more relaxed atmosphere. Martin and Ann said how pleased they were with Patrick Parker's cross-examination, how pleased they were that he had discredited Paul Allen. Harry and Betty sat in the back of the car in silence.

On arriving home they saw Ann's mother-in-law's car in the drive, and were greeted in the garden by her and the twins. Betty and Harry were soon lost in their grandchildren. Ann brought her mother-in-law up to date with the trial, whilst Martin changed into his farm clothes, ready to help George Stone and Andy Falks in the hayfields where he also brought them up to date with the trial.

George Stone was to attend the Court the next day, as a witness to the Defence, and was already nervous, especially at the thought of being cross-examined by the prosecuting Barrister. He especially didn't want to say anything that would harm his employer. Martin tried to calm his fears, telling him to stick to answering the questions as truthfully as he could, and all would be fine.

That evening the mood in the farmhouse was easier, the knowledge that the jury had finally heard Harry's side of the story, and that the Prosecution had nearly finished their case, meant that things were more relaxed. There were more good luck cards, and Martin once again screened them for any malicious content; there were none.

Ann's mother-in-law was asked to stay for dinner, and she accepted, Betty did the cooking, and Harry busied himself with entertaining his grandchildren. Even with the twins to distract him, he could still see the accusing finger of Henry Robson being pointed towards him, his words of blame and accusation ringing in his ears. He also knew that tomorrow he would be standing in the witness box, and the thought sent a shiver down his spine.

The third morning of the trial only differed from the first two by the slightly easier feeling in the house. Today their side of the case would be heard, but the thought of the prosecuting Barrister cross-examining Harry kept an edge to the mood. An early morning mist had dampened the ground, giving a slight respite before the heat of flaming June baked the earth. As they drove to Winchester, they noticed the colours of the countryside, the endless shades of green now interspersed with sweeps of bright yellow from the oil seed rape, pockets of lavender from the linseed. Numerous fields of barley were light brown, their heads bent, soon to be harvested.

In Court they took their seats, again saved for them by Tom Whitworth, who looked upon guarding the three seats in the front row, ready for the arrival of the Sintons, as his duty of the day and he was proud he could be of help. Once again they waited for the Court to fill and the clock to tick towards ten-thirty.

At exactly ten-thirty, Judge Thorn entered the Court and took his seat. The Court Usher then pronounced the proceedings were under way. Maurice Brown rose and called Andrew Goodman to the witness stand. The prosecuting Counsel knew that Andrew Goodman would shed little light on the morning's events, but he could back up some of Paul Allen's statements. To this end Maurice Brown ran through the questions. He allowed Andrew to tell of his early morning mercy-dash, the terrified state he found Paul in, the reason for heading straight to Southampton police station rather than finding one closer.

Andrew said that by the time Paul had told him all the story, including telling Andrew the two in the barn were dead, he wanted to get to a police station he knew, one close to home so his and Paul's family wouldn't be too far away. Andrew Goodman stated that it was his belief that Paul Allen had been genuinely scared for his life, he could see it in his manner, and in what Paul had told him in the front of his car.

When Patrick Parker cross-examined Andrew Goodman, he managed to get him to repeat Paul Allen's declaration that William Stevens was a violent man, and somebody you didn't 'mess with'. He also got him to state that he had known Sean to go on these trips with Stevens before. Andrew knew some of his friends had told the police as much, and saw no point in lying to the Court when the Defence could call upon evidence to show he was lying. Andrew had been irritated by Sean showing-off his cash, and bragging about his early morning raids with Stevens, and he wasn't going to lie for the sake of Sean's memory.

Patrick Parker then tried to hint that Andrew and Paul spent the time travelling to the police station in Southampton to fabricate a story showing Sean and Paul in a better light. Andrew stood his ground defiantly, repeating that by the time Paul had told him all the story it was easier to go straight to their local station.

When Patrick Parker had finished his cross-examination, Andrew Goodman was dismissed and he left the Court, the prosecuting counsel had finished his case. It was now the turn of the Defence counsel to call their witnesses. Muffled conversations broke the silence of the Court as people in the public gallery grew excited at the prospect of the Defence counsel putting their story across. Another stern look from the Judge, peering up at the gallery, brought the room to a respectful hush.

Patrick Parker rose from his seat and started the case for the Defence. He had few witnesses to call, the initial testimonies were there to give a glowing report of Harry Sinton to the jury. They spoke of a hard-working man, who loved his family and farm, who had never been in any trouble before. The prosecuting counsel's only attack on these witnesses was to make certain the jury knew them as Harry Sinton's friends, and were unlikely to say anything other than good things. The witnesses included George Stone, who told of his sights and actions on the morning of the seventh of March. Again the prosecuting Counsel had little to get their teeth into and George Stone found his worries about being cross-examined had little foundation.

Chris Holland was called to the stand, it was he who had given Paul a lift to Carlton on that frosty morning almost four months ago. Chris Holland told the jury that when he had heard of the killings at Downlands Farm, and that one of the raiders had run away, he had immediately reported his encounter with Paul to the police. He felt terrible that he had not taken Paul to a police station, he said that if he had known the circumstances he would never had dropped Paul off in the local village, but driven him straight to the police. He told of being new to the area and not knowing many people, therefore he didn't take too much notice when he didn't recognise Paul as a local. He told of Paul's obvious fright and how he lied about the reason for being there.

Under cross-examination by Maurice Brown, Chris Holland repeated to the Court Paul's state of distress, and how he couldn't blame Paul for lying, he was obviously frightened, and didn't trust anyone in that area.

The first witnesses for the Defence took the proceedings up to the lunch recess, the next witness was the Defence's last, their main, and their client. As Harry Sinton took the oath, he looked just as Patrick Parker wanted him to look: old, tired, meek and mild. The jury studied him intensely as he stood, ready to answer questions from his Barrister.

Patrick Parker led Harry through the events of that morning, getting him to tell of his reason for being up so early, and for having the shotgun on him at the time. The Defence Barrister was slightly concerned with the references to shooting a fox. He knew the hunting and killing of these animals could be an emotive subject, and some of the jury may take great offence that his client had taken his shotgun out that morning with the express purpose of killing a fox. He also knew he had to show that his client wasn't in the habit of taking his gun out each morning in case he happened to stumble upon a gang of raiders. That would show intent and open up a whole new can of worms. Instead he concentrated on conveying to the jury the need to control fox numbers on a farm, especially at lambing. Patrick Parker stressed that his client had already lost five lambs to this predator, and some form of action had to be taken.

Carefully he guided his client to the confrontation with the raiders. Harry Sinton answered in his slow, soft Hampshire drawl, Betty watched her husband with a mixture of pride and fear. Pride at the strength he was showing in the witness box, fear for the questions he would soon be having to answer from the prosecuting counsel.

"Mr. Sinton, please tell the Court what you saw as you rounded the entrance to your barn."

"I saw this blue van in the middle of the barn, and just past it I could see that my quad bike was missing."

"And then what happened?"

"The van drove towards me. The engine was roaring like he was in some kind of hurry."

"The prosecuting counsel said you should have stepped aside, let these thieves through."

"I didn't have the time, they were racing at me. I just, I just protected myself. I didn't mean any harm but they were driving towards me. The gun just went off, it was a shock to me, it must have been a reaction or something."

"Could you see the gang inside the vehicle?"

"No, the light was reflecting off the windscreen."

"So you didn't know how many men were inside the van?"

"No."

"Then what happened?"

"The van stopped and two men got out. One was holding a bat or something, he was shouting and swearing at me. The other one was next to him, slightly behind him. He looked like he was backing the older one up."

"Did you say anything to these two men?"

"I asked them to stop, I wanted them to leave, I told them sorry."

"You told them sorry?"

"I was sorry, sorry I stopped them, sorry I shot their van, but I couldn't help it, I couldn't have done anything else," Harry Sinton's voice started to tremble. "They kept coming at me, threatening me. What could I do?"

The jury listened captivated as Harry Sinton told his story, the public gallery was silent, the reporters scribbled in their note pads, all were enthralled by this quietly spoken man telling his chilling story. He told it honestly, as honestly as he remembered.

"I wanted them to stop, to go away, leave me, but they kept coming. I had to protect myself."

"You say these two men threatened you. Did they say what they were planning to do to you?"

"Only the first one, the older man threatened me. He said he was going to teach me a lesson. The other one was backing him up, saying nothing. They kept coming at me, the older one had a horrible look on his face, angry, vicious. He wouldn't stop. I was scared for my life."

"You believed your life was in danger?"

"Yes."

Patrick Parker turned to the jury. "This man is sixty five years old, and through no fault of his own, found himself confronted by two men half his age, threatening, he believed, his life."

Patrick Parker then asked Harry Sinton to continue telling the Court the morning events as he remembered them. Harry Sinton told his story how he remembered it, telling of feeling faint, dropping the gun and sitting down on a bale of straw. He told of the noise of someone fleeing, and then the appearance of George Stone. How he was taken back to his house, the arrival of the police and the statement he gave.

The closer Harry Sinton got to finishing his story, the more his voice gave way. He stammered and stuttered his last answers, constantly clearing his throat, taking sips from the glass of water provided for him. He realised that as soon as Patrick Parker had finished his questions, it would be the turn of the prosecuting counsel. The thought filled his heart with dread.

When Patrick Parker repeated the morning events as stated by his client to the jury, stressing that Harry Sinton feared for his life, that he had no option but to defend himself, he declared he had no further questions for his witness, and sat down. It was now Maurice Brown's turn to discredit the Defence counsel's star witness.

Maurice Brown took his time, he shuffled some papers in front of him on the desk, cleared his throat, and stood up.

"Mr. Sinton, I am at a bit of a loss when you say that the shotgun you were holding accidentally went off." He paused to give a puzzled frown at the defendant.

Harry Sinton stared blankly back at the Barrister. Harry Sinton didn't know if he should say something or not, had it been a question or a statement? Maurice Brown knew that one of the greatest weapons a Barrister had in Court was the fear of the witness, get them scared and they don't know what they are saying. After what seemed like a lifetime to Harry Sinton, Maurice Brown continued.

"You say the shotgun accidentally went off."

"Yes."

"Mr. Sinton, I have been taught the correct way of holding a shotgun when walking, or even waiting, the safe way."

Again Maurice Brown paused, and again Harry Sinton didn't know whether to say something or not.

"Are you telling me that a man of the soil, born and bred on the land, wasn't taught the safe way of carrying a shotgun?"

"I was, my father showed me when I was young." At last Harry Sinton could answer a question.

"Could you describe to the jury the safe way."

Harry Sinton nervously told the jury the recommended way of carrying a shotgun when loaded, broken at the chambers, in the crook of the arm.

"Well Mr. Sinton, that was the way I was taught as well. What I don't understand is, why was the gun loaded in the first place?" Maurice Brown stopped and waited for the answer, he knew what it would be, but he didn't want the answer to get in the way of his next question.

"You never know when you will see a fox, you always have to be ready."

Maurice Brown liked any reference to the defendant's desire to kill a fox, he hoped that some of the jury, at the very least, looked upon a fox as a soft cuddly animal, and hoped some saw it as an innocent, smeared and persecuted by farmers to allow them to justify their own barbaric blood sport. Anything to sway the jury towards his argument.

"If you say so, Mr. Sinton. Now my second question is how, one moment, you could have the shotgun broken in the crook of your arm, and at the next have it snapped together and ready to shoot, by accident."

"I, I don't know."

"And then there is the safety catch. I take it your gun had a safety catch, Mr. Sinton?"

"Yes," Harry Sinton almost whispered his reply.

"So let me get this straight. You were walking with the gun broken in the crook of your arm one minute, and then the next, when you see a van being driven in your direction, you snap the gun together, take off the safety catch, lift the gun, point towards the vehicle, and pull the trigger, all of which, four separate actions before you even pull the trigger, you say was an accident?" As Maurice Brown was talking, he was showing the jury, with elaborate movements, the procedure necessary to make a shotgun ready to fire.

Harry Sinton nodded in his seat.

"That is a serious accident. You are saying you had time to do all that?" Maurice Brown repeated his performance, pretending to take the gun out of the crook of his arm, snapping it together, pushing the safety catch off, and raising the weapon. "As an accident, a reaction, but you didn't have time to step out of the way, move to one side?"

The jury watched and listened intently.

"I was confused."

"Not as confused as I am now Mr. Sinton."

"I didn't know what was happening, they were driving towards me."

"This is what you keep saying, but where else were they supposed to drive, you were blocking the only exit when you shot the van. Mr. Sinton, say that at a long stretch of the imagination we believe your explanation for shooting the van, would you not agree the driver had a right to step out and see what you wanted?"

"He wanted to hurt me."

"He wanted to talk to you, see why you shot his vehicle. Mr. Sinton, you had a shotgun, you showed that you were prepared to use it. I would seriously doubt that any sane man would want to threaten you, armed only with a baseball bat, let alone young Sean Robson who wasn't armed at all." Maurice Brown shook his head in apparent disbelief.

"This brings me onto the next point which I find confusing. You say that you accidentally shot the first cartridge, but the gun is only double barrelled, you would have had to reload the shotgun with a new live cartridge to be able to kill both these men. Are you trying to tell the Court you accidentally broke the shotgun, extracted the spent cartridge, loaded a live one, snapped the gun together, and aimed at William Stevens, all by accident, again?"

"No, I meant to load up, I needed to . . . "

"You purposely loaded a live cartridge into your shotgun?" Maurice Brown exclaimed, pretending to be shocked by the answer.

"There were two of them, I needed both barrels to . . .

"Kill them both?"

" . . . defend against them both."

"Mr. Sinton, you say you asked both William Stevens and Sean Robson to stop, you say you said sorry, that you wanted them to leave, whereas an eye-witness before you said he didn't hear you say a thing, and that he didn't see your lips move. Could it be you want to believe you said those words, whereas in reality you didn't. In reality you didn't show them in any way that you were sorry, that you didn't want a confrontation. Did you try and move away from the advancing men, Mr. Sinton? Did you take a step backwards, show that you didn't want to oppose them, didn't want a fight?"

"I was scared."

"How do you expect Sean Robson felt, how William Stevens felt, suddenly confronted by an armed man who had already shown his willingness to use his shotgun, and had reloaded it ready so he could kill them both. Don't you think they would have been scared? Don't you think they had a right to ask you to stop, to ask you what you were doing?"

"They were threatening me."

"Were they, or were they just asking what you were doing? You said yourself you were confused, did you confuse a question with a threat?"

"No."

"Did Sean Robson say anything?"

"I, I . . . "

"Did he ask you a question that you thought was a threat?"

"I, I don't remember."

"Or didn't you give him time? Did you just turn and fire your gun without letting him do anything, letting him back-off. Surrender if you like? You had just shot and killed William Stevens, don't you think that would have been enough deterrent for young Sean Robson?"

"I, I . . . "

"What were they doing there in the first place!" Tom Whitworth could contain himself no longer, he was standing up, pointing down towards the prosecuting Barrister. He could not believe his friend was being subjected to such a harsh interrogation, how this man was twisting Harry Sinton's words.

"You will sit down and be quiet," Judge Thorn ordered from his seat, staring up at the gallery.

"You shouldn't be letting him interrogate Harry like that," Tom challenged the Judge.

"I will do in my Court, as I see fit and if that man in the front row disturbs my Court again, I will have him thrown out. Do you understand?"

Tom Whitworth sat down with a thud.

"Please continue Mr. Brown," Judge Thorn said, his annoyance obvious in his voice.

"Thank you your Honour. Mr. Sinton, before we were so rudely interrupted, I was putting to you that you had no reason to kill either man. William Stevens was approaching you, maybe to clarify the situation, calm it down so nobody would get hurt. Maybe you saw it as something else, some kind of threat. But wouldn't you agree that after Sean Robson had seen William Stevens blown in half by your shotgun, that any thought of attacking you, if he happened to have one in the first place, would have vanished?"

"They were threatening me, they kept advancing towards me."

"Are you saying that even after you shot and killed William Stevens, that Sean Robson kept coming towards you?"

"No, I. It all happened so fast."

"Was Sean Robson stationary when you shot him?"

"I can't remember, he might have been, it all happened so fast."

"He might have been. It all happened so fast," Maurice Brown repeated slowly. "Sean Robson might have been standing still. How could he have been threatening a man with a shotgun, when he was standing still, and unarmed? It all happened so fast. Perhaps you didn't give him time to surrender before you took his life, before you sent him crashing into your sheep pens, minus half his chest. It all happened so fast. Perhaps you didn't give either of them time to explain what they wanted."

Maurice Brown left his questions hanging in the air. Half the jury were watching him, the other half were studying Harry Sinton. Harry Sinton was shaking as he stood, he was even more pale than at the start of the cross-examination, tears were building up in his eyes. In the public gallery Betty, Ann and Martin wished they could take his place, somehow deflect the pain he was going through. They hated seeing him like this. The rest of his friends in the gallery felt ashamed at seeing this once proud and happy man sitting broken in his chair, at the mercy of the prosecuting Barrister. They felt they were invading on a private moment of grief. Some averted their eyes, other tried to show support by giving him half smiles. Harry never saw any of the smiles, he never looked up towards the public gallery.

"I didn't want to hurt them," came a whisper from the witness box, "they kept coming at me. It wasn't my fault they were there."

"Mr. Sinton, I find it hard to believe that a man who had already shot at a vehicle, reloaded his gun, pushed the safety catch off, aimed and deliberately pulled the trigger, not once, but twice – the second time on an unarmed, stationary youth . . . how a man can then say he didn't mean to do it."

Maurice Brown was pleased with his cross-examination, these meek witnesses were always the best, never getting riled, answering softly, or getting confused and floundering. He believed he could get witnesses like that to admit to anything, and he believed he just had.

"Your Honour, I have no further questions for the defendant."

"Thank you Mr. Brown. Mr. Sinton, you may step down and return to your seat. This Court will adjourn for the day, and reconvene tomorrow morning at ten-thirty. This should allow enough time for the two counsels to prepare their closing speeches." And with those words from the Judge, the third day of Harry Sinton's trial was over, all the witnesses had been called, all the evidence had been heard. Only the closing speeches and the Judge's summing-up remained before the jury would leave to consider their verdict, and announce Harry Sinton's future.

It seemed the public gallery took longer to empty, people looked almost stunned as they left their seats, and headed out of the door. There was certainly less talk than the day before. As Tom Whitworth passed Martin he gruffly muttered, "You should have backed me up."

Martin ignored his father's friend, concentrating more on his parents. He had watched as his father seemed to shrink in the witness box under the questioning of the prosecuting Barrister. It had been worse than the opening speeches. Martin knew for sure his father would be going to prison, and it struck him like a sledgehammer. He realised his mother and Ann would be thinking the same thing, he tried to think of something to say but his brain failed him. He was rescued by Mike Cairns.

"I wouldn't worry too much about that little episode Martin, the jury will only remember the closing speeches, and it is your Barrister that has the last words, which will be ringing in the jurors' ears."

Martin nodded his appreciation of the thought, but he didn't believe them one hundred per cent, still it was something he could repeat to his family. Sarah Cairns was standing with Betty and Ann, arm around Betty, speaking words of encouragement.

Once on the concourse of the balcony, Betty, Ann and Martin waited for Harry. When he emerged from the Court he made his way, in the midst of his Defence counsel, over to his family. On reaching the group he hugged his wife, the others looked on, unable to escape and allow these two people the time alone they wanted.

Gerald Evans took Martin to one side and suggested letting his parents have as much time alone together much as he could, and Martin agreed. Gerald Evans also backed up the words of Mike Cairns.

"Things may seem bad now Martin, but all is not lost. We will have the chance to remind the jury of the truth in our closing speech. Head-up, and have faith."

Once again the Sintons braved the waiting media, and escaped back to the security of their home. The sombre mood in the car was carried on into the farmhouse. Even with the twins their to take the minds off the situation, the atmosphere was once again oppressive. The whole scene, the beautiful June evening, Bracken giving a warm welcome, the twins vying for attention, all seemed to remind them of the frailty of the situation, of what Harry Sinton could lose if the verdict went against him.

After Ann, her mother-in-law, and the twins had left (dinner wasn't mentioned this evening) Martin followed his Godfather's advice and left his parents alone as often as possible, but he was never far away. He would forgo his walk, and the hay could wait for one day. He would see the staff in the morning.

He opened the post, but was unprepared for the contents of the brown padded parcel. He flinched from the odour and took the bag immediately out of the door, towards the dustbins standing at the side of the garage. Just before he was about to drop it into the bin, he stopped himself. He decided to keep it, and to show the police when he had the chance, which would now be after the trial. He hid the offending packet behind some old paint tins that were sitting on a shelf inside the garage.

Walking back to the house, Martin wondered if the telephone call, the fire, and the parcel were all related. If they were, then there was a single man (a male voice had threatened Ann) intent on causing harm to his parents, in a calculated, controlled manner. If they were not, then there was more than one person intent on vengeance. He didn't know which scenario was worse.

For the second night running, Mark Robson had steered clear of the *Red Lion*. He told himself it wasn't through any jealousy over seeing Eddie with his ex-girlfriend, he just wanted to watch any reports of the trial in peace. The brief reports, quick mentions of the day's events in Court on the local channels, meant little to him. He knew he had to return to the pub sooner or later, he still had important business to conduct from his self-styled office, but he argued he could wait for a couple of days, until the trial was over.

Mark Robson decided to get his frustrations out by planning the next series of attacks on his brother's killer. As he lay on his mattress, can of lager in one hand, an ever-present cigarette in the other, he mulled over various options. Further telephone calls, dead semi-decomposed animals in parcels. He would go on new trips to the countryside, help himself to some sheep, cut the farmer's wire, burn the crop in the field. The choices were endless, he chuckled to himself.

That night, as Betty and Harry lay in their bed together, neither could sleep. Both wondered if this would be their last night together before the jury returned a verdict, whether it would be their last night together for a very long time, or if they would finally put the worry of separation behind them. Neither mentioned their thoughts. They lay on their backs staring at he ceiling in the moonlit night, holding hands, on one side hoping for sleep, on the other wanting to keep this moment for ever.

Martin woke in time to meet George and Ken in the yard, he was pleased to see the majority of the hay barn full with fresh bales. George had returned straight from the Crown Court to continue with the haymaking. Martin thanked George for his words in the witness box, and asked after the day's work. George hoped the hay would be in by the afternoon, saying the help they were receiving from Mike Cairns' men was invaluable, he couldn't remember a hay making season going so well and so fast.

Both men asked after Martin's parents, and wished them luck at Court today. Martin thanked them and, with Bracken by his side, returned to the house. He wasn't concerned when his parents, who were habitual early risers, were not up and about, but after half an hour, when he hadn't heard any noise from upstairs, he started to worry. Fear suddenly gripped him, his stomach knotted at the thoughts racing through his mind. He tried to recall, had he heard any sound from their room all night? Any noise in the morning? What if the whole situation had got too much for them? What if they had decided they couldn't bear the thought of being forced apart, for what may be an eternity to them.

Reason calmed his fears, he told himself his parents were stronger than that, that they would see this thing out to the end, but still a nagging doubt remained, and he started to creep upstairs. At their bedroom door he stopped to listen, leaning an ear close to the door. He couldn't hear a thing. The door was slightly ajar, but not enough to be able to look in. He knocked softly on the door, calling his parents in a whisper.

"Mum, Dad, are you alright?" he asked, slowly pushing the door open.

What would he find? Did he really want to look? His mind raced as he opened the door and steeled himself to glance inside. He saw nothing, his parents had vanished, the bed was made and their clothes were gone; at the same time he heard Bracken bark from downstairs. He turned and made his way back towards the kitchen, all the time hearing familiar sounds of doors being shut, and boots being pulled off. He walked through the kitchen and looked into the scullery.

"We thought we would go for a quick walk," Betty explained to her relieved son, "are you alright dear, you look out of sorts?"

"I'm fine Mum, just fine," he told her, deciding against telling them of his earlier fears and antics.

Harry and Betty finished taking off their wellington boots and waxed jackets. The clothing was still necessary in late June, the mornings had a chill to them before the sun could warm the day.

Betty pushed past Martin and filled the kettle. Harry talked of the walk, how he had seen the hay fields nearly finished, how the crops looked good swaying in the breeze, the shorn sheep looking well, the lambs fit for market. He asked after the men, nodding his appreciation of their work. The mood had brightened. Maybe it was the new day, maybe the knowledge that all the witnesses had been called, the thought that they could do no more, or that the end was in sight. Whatever the reason, Martin welcomed the change, but he was still wary: the undercurrent of dread was still there.

Ann arrived, and they went through the routine of the morning, identical to the three other mornings. Driving to Winchester, parking, negotiating the Press, Harry Sinton being taken to one side, Tom Whitworth keeping their seats, and waiting for the hands of the clock to reach ten-thirty.

At ten-thirty, after the announcement of his imminent arrival, the Judge entered, prepared himself, and called on Maurice Brown, prosecuting Barrister, to begin his closing speech. Maurice Brown thanked Judge Thorn and began to remind the jury of all the information he had conveyed through the course of the last three days, the testimony of the ballistics expert and the pathologist, he reminded them of the graphic police photographs of the two dead men. He recalled a grandfather who was just one member of the family who had lost a relative for ever. Friends who had lost a companion for ever. He thanked them for their kind attention but just wanted to stress the more important points. He would stress the testimony of the two main witnesses, the two who were the only ones that really knew what had happened on that cold, bleak, pale grey morning, almost four months ago.

"Ladies and gentlemen of the jury, in my opening speech I told you this was not a difficult case; I still believe it is not a difficult case. You have heard all the surrounding arguments, the circumstances which have led you to be sitting here, in judgement of the man before you. In my opening speech I asked you to keep in mind three questions while you listened to the long hours of testimonies. They are still the most important questions.

"Even if you believe that the first shot Mr. Sinton fired was an accident. Even though he admitted it took four separate actions to bring the gun ready to fire. Four distinct procedures before he could accidentally pull the trigger. He has himself admitted he loaded the gun up again, with the intention of defending himself. He had the intention of using the gun again, not by accident, but with intent.

"Mr. Sinton stated that both William Stevens and Sean Robson were walking towards him, threatening him. William Stevens with a baseball bat, Sean Robson unarmed. Even if you believe Mr. Sinton's testimony that they kept advancing, he said himself he was confused. If you believe that they were threatening Mr. Sinton with violence, not inquiring why he had shot at them, and if you disregard the testimony of Paul Allen, who was there, and who saw his best friend blown backwards. Remember, Paul Allen stated that his friend was standing still, unarmed, not offering any threat. Mr. Sinton himself admitted he could not be sure if Sean Robson was advancing towards him or not.

"If you have taken all this as true, and believe me it is a very, very big 'IF', you must ask yourself those same three questions. Did Mr. Sinton try to prevent the confrontation? Did Mr. Sinton have to use such excessive force on William Stevens, and especially Sean Robson? And what right had Mr. Sinton to shoot and kill both of these men?"

"I would ask you to consider these points. If Mr. Sinton had the time to accidentally shoot the van, did he have time to step aside, take the number of the vehicle, and let the proper authorities deal with the situation? If Mr. Sinton had shown a willingness to let the men go, stepped back, would the two men have backed away as well? If Mr. Sinton had shot a warning shot, would this have been enough to stop the men from advancing? If Mr. Sinton had aimed to inflict a wound, would that have been enough force? And finally, after Mr. Sinton had shot and killed William Stevens, in front of Sean Robson, did he then have to go on to kill Sean Robson? Surely the sight of William Stevens collapsing onto the ground would have been enough deterrent for Sean Robson to give himself up. Did Mr. Sinton give young Sean Robson the time to give himself up, or were Mr. Sinton's actions outright aggression towards the two men he found on his property?

"Ladies and gentlemen of the jury, the decision is yours, you have the facts, you have a defendant who admits to the killings, you have the two dead bodies, and two shattered families, all I am looking for is justice for the dead men. Did they deserve to die at the hands of this man? What right did he have to sentence them to death for breaking into his farm?

"Ladies and gentlemen of the jury, I implore you, for the sake of the two dead men, for the sake of their shattered families, for the sake of true justice, not this uncontrollable vigilante justice, I implore you to reach a verdict of guilty for the two charges of manslaughter."

Maurice Brown sat, the Court room was silent, the atmosphere was charged. Patrick Parker rose, picked up the glass of water in front of him, took a long, slow sip, placed it back down on the bench, cleared his throat, then began his closing speech.

"My learned friend gave you a lot of 'IFS', which makes me believe this case is not as simple as he would have you think."

Patrick Parker then took the jury, once again, through the facts of the last three days. He put the information across, showing the defendant's side of the story. He stressed the points he wanted the jury to remember.

"Ladies and gentlemen of the jury, it is not up to me to prove my client's innocence, it is up to the prosecuting counsel to prove his guilt. I would like, if I may, to take you back to that morning of the seventh of March. Harry Sinton had woken up at five o'clock, to look around the sheep on his property, which were lambing at the time. He had decided to take his shotgun along with him, in the hope of seeing the fox that had been killing his new-born lambs. It had killed five in the past ten days.

"After he had checked the lambing ewes, and walked the fields the fox had been most active in, he walked back to the barns. He had nothing in particular on his mind, thoughts of the coming day's work, the memory of a night with friends at the local pub, when suddenly, in the space of five minutes, those thoughts, and his life, were shattered for ever.

"As he walked to the barn he was confronted by a transit van being driven towards him, accelerating with a great roar in the quiet morning air. He didn't have time to think, he didn't have time to step aside as my learned friend rather simply put it. His reaction was to defend himself against the immediate danger from the oncoming vehicle."

"My learned friend says there are four separate actions Harry Sinton had to do before he was ready to shoot the gun. I don't deny that. What I say is to a man who has used a shotgun all his life, who is an expert with it, those actions can be done in a split second. We have all seen television pictures of people shooting clay pigeons. They are able to raise their gun, push the safety switch off, aim and pull the trigger in one swift, almost automatic, action. In a split second. The idea that if Harry Sinton had time to do this split second reaction, then he would have had time to step aside, is absurd.

"It is nearly as absurd as trying to tell you that a man of William Stevens' reputation, which has been confirmed by two of the prosecuting Counsel's own witnesses, would have then stepped out to ask some questions. It is more likely to be true that he was aiming to run over Harry Sinton in the first place.

"It is true that the Prosecution states that Harry Sinton had never met William Stevens before, and therefore could not have known of his reputation as a violent man. In the same instance, Harry Sinton could not have known if he wasn't a violent man. All he saw, after he had nearly been run over, after his property had been stolen, was two men, half his age, bearing down on him, swearing and threatening him. One with a baseball bat, the second backing up the first."

"The Prosecution would have you believe that in this instance, in this moment of confusion and terror, where one minute you were carrying on with your work, peacefully making an honest living, the next being confronted by two men who were threatening you with physical harm: in that instance they would have you believe Harry Sinton should have given up his weapon and run away. A sixty-five-year-old man against two men with an average age less than half of his, outrun those two men? The concept amazes me.

"Harry Sinton stated he asked them to stop, asked them to go away. Then you have the testimony of one of the gang members saying he heard nothing, saw Harry Sinton say nothing. A member of the gang who had broken into the farm in the first place, who was hoping to profit from their illegal activities, who didn't ring the police straight away, but preferred to wait over two hours to tell the authorities.

"It was the staff at the farm who called the police first.

"Paul Allen had to think up a story that would show him and his friend out in the best light. So he invented that they were bullied into going, when we had witnesses and signed statements to say Sean Robson had boasted about his part in past raids. It proved Paul Allen lied under oath. When did he stop lying? That is, if he ever told the truth in the first place. If I had to decide between the two testimonies, I know whose I would choose.

"Harry Sinton tried to tell the truth, he didn't lie when asked if Sean Robson was still advancing towards him. It would have been easy to say yes, but Harry Sinton answered honestly, he said he couldn't remember. In the confusion, in the terror of being threatened, he could not recall the exact sequence of events. Harry Sinton believed his life was in danger, whether this belief was real or not, he truly feared for his life as these two men, swearing and threatening, bore down on him. The Prosecution suggests that at a time like that Harry Sinton should have given himself up and talked to these men. The idea is ridiculous.

"The Prosecution talks about shattered families, well here is one in front of you. Here is a hard-working, honest man, never been in trouble before in his life, suddenly confronted by a gang of thieves. The resulting effect left him destroyed. He couldn't face going onto his own property, his wife was too scared to leave the house, all because Harry Sinton defended himself against a gang of raiders who were about to attack him. He didn't invite them onto his property: let us not lose sight of who the criminals are in this case.

"Ladies and gentlemen of the jury, although this is a complicated case, there are some simple facts. The first is that Harry Sinton disturbed a gang of thieves who were in the process of stealing his property. Two, when they were disturbed they tried to run him down. Three, when they were stopped, they got out of the van and threatened Harry Sinton with physical harm. Four, Harry Sinton truly believed his life was in danger. And five, Harry Sinton acted in self-defence.

"My learned friend implores you to uphold the justice of this country. I ask you to do the same. The justice of this country must allow a honest man to protect his property, and his life, when threatened. It must not punish for a crime committed out of necessity to protect oneself: that would be a miscarriage of justice.

"Ladies and gentleman of the jury, I implore you not to punish a man whose actions were thrust upon him, not to punish a man who acted in the only way he saw possible, not to punish a man who has been punished enough, who will always live with the nightmare of events that happened, against his will, on that March morning.

"Harry Sinton is innocent of the charges laid before him, and he and his family have been punished enough for deeds he did not want to do, but found he had no option due to the activities of a ruthless, professional, gang of raiders he happened to disturb."

"Ladies and gentlemen of the jury, Harry Sinton is the victim in this case; please don't punish an innocent man for a crime he did not commit."

The Court room was still, the jurors entranced by Patrick Parker's heartfelt plea. As Patrick Parker sat down, they started to switch their attention from the Barrister to the defendant. Their minds were racing, one minute they were convinced of his guilt, the next certain of his innocence. They studied the old man in the defendant's box. He looked so frail, old and tired. He reminded some of the jurors of their own father, while others saw only a withered old man, sitting desolate and alone.

Mr. Justice Thorn QC cleared his throat, and told the Court that all that was left, before the jury filed out to consider their verdict, was his summing-up. He turned to the jury and started on his speech he had already prepared.

"Ladies and gentlemen of the jury, it is your responsibility to decide if the man before you is guilty of the manslaughter of one William Stevens, and of the same charge concerning one Sean Robson. You have heard both sides of the case, it is now my duty to direct you on the appropriate points of law, and remind you of the main evidence in the case.

"The first thing I must remind you is that it is up to the prosecuting counsel to prove guilt, it is not up to the Defence counsel to prove innocence. That is a fundamental principle of our law."

"The facts are clear, Mr. Sinton has admitted pulling the trigger, the bodies in the photographs are real. The Defence has entered a plea of self-defence. The theory of self-defence is one that is easily understood, it is a straight-forward concept, with only common sense needed for its understanding.

"It is both good sense and good law that a man who is attacked may defend himself. It is also good sense and good law that he may only do what is necessary, and that of course depends on the circumstances. It would not be common sense to permit some kind of reaction that is wholly out of proportion to the necessity of the situation. If an attack is so serious it puts someone in immediate peril, then immediate defensive action may be necessary. If the moment is one of crisis for someone in imminent danger, he may have to avert the danger by some instant reaction. By that I mean to say that the person would not have to wait to be attacked to defend himself.

"It must also be recognised that in the heat of the moment, a person defending himself cannot weigh to a nicety the exact measure of his necessary defensive action.

"If the attack is over, and no peril remains, then the employment of force may be in the way of revenge, punishment, or pure aggression. In that case there would no longer be a link with the necessity of defence. An important consideration must also be given to the opportunity to retreat. It is not necessary for the person being threatened to take to his heels and run, but what is necessary is that by his actions he must demonstrate his willingness not to fight. He must demonstrate he is prepared to temporise, or disengage and perhaps make some physical withdrawal.

"The defence of self-defence will fail only if the Prosecution can show beyond doubt that what the accused did was not in the way of self-defence If the Prosecution has shown that what the accused has done was not done in self-defence, then the issue will be eliminated from the case."

Mr. Justice Thorn QC then went on to highlight the main points of the case. The jury had been sitting, listening to the evidence for three days. This was a chance for them to listen to a summarised version, to be reminded of facts that they may have forgotten over that time, and which would be given by an impartial member of the Court. They all listened intently, some jotted down points that they regarded as important onto paper .

At the end of his summing-up, which the judge read mainly from his notes taken over the three days, he reminded the jury of their options.

"There are three options open to you. Firstly, you may come to the conclusion, which is a matter entirely for you, that the accused is innocent of any offences at all, in which case your verdict would be Not Guilty. Secondly, you might come to the conclusion that although there was a strong suspicion, there was a reasonable doubt in the case, then the defendant is entitled to be acquitted. The third possibility is that you are satisfied that you are sure an offence has been committed, then it is your duty in accordance with your oaths, to find the defendant Guilty. You must try to reach a unanimous decision.

"The Court will now adjourn while the jury considers its verdict."

The silence of the Court was broken by the mass rising of all in the room, the jury filed out ready to deliberate in their isolated room, the Judge left for his chambers, the Barristers chatted to their relative teams, the spectators shuffled out towards the concourse, and the reporters headed off to their relative positions to give the latest update. The Court room was empty.

George Hollis had arrived half-way through the morning, his haymaking finished, so too had George Stone and Andy Falks. They could not find a seat in the Court room and had therefore stayed on the concourse. When the spectators spilled out of the lift and stairway, they made their presence known to Betty, Ann and Martin: they all wanted to show their support.

It was a tense time as all waited for the verdict. They stood or sat in isolated groups, milling about on the balcony, some had bought a snack or coffee from the cafeteria, others were too nervous to eat or drink anything. The consensus of opinion at the start of the wait was that a speedy verdict would be a good sign for Harry Sinton, but as the time ticked away, the thoughts changed to the belief that the longer the jury deliberated, the better.

Minutes turned into hours as they waited, no one dared leave in case the Court Usher told them the jury had reached a decision and asked them all to return to their seats. The Sintons stayed together, along with Sarah Cairns and Gerald Evans. Others came up to them and offered words of encouragement, which they duly acknowledged.

Tom Whitworth strayed outside the main entrance doors, on to the steps in front of the Court, lit his pipe and studied the waiting media below him. He was joined by the main core of the farmers' "Church Service" along with Ken Falks, George Stone, and Mike Cairns. They talked about the haymaking season, the weather, grain and livestock prices, the coming harvest, anything to pass the time. Tom then gave his opinion on the verdict.

"They got to acquit him, it was obviously self-defence."

"I honestly don't know," admitted Mike Cairns. "I hope to God they do."

"We tried to listen to the Judge's summing-up, but couldn't from the corridor, so we don't really know," George Hollis offered.

They stood about, scuffed their feet, trying to think of something to say.

The time dragged on, one hour turned into two. Two hours ticked towards three. The waiting was insufferable. Even with the open plan of the entrance hall and concourse, backed up by air conditioning, the atmosphere was stifling. The initial buzz of conversation when they first emptied out of the Court and into the passageway fell away to an uncomfortable silence.

After over three hours of nervous waiting, the Court Usher appeared and announced the jury had reached a verdict and were ready to return to the Court. The relative Barristers were found and recalled, the Judge summoned from his chambers, the reporters ushered back to their positions.

Before Harry Sinton was taken to the dock he gave Betty a long hug. He was more nervous now than he had ever been during the trial. He knew the jury had reached a verdict, but he didn't know what it was. At that moment he doubted if he could go through with his wish not to appeal if found guilty. Could he take being apart from Betty, his children, the farm and friends? If he was found guilty this would be the last time he would be able to hold his wife for as long as the Judge cared to decide. His heart was pounding in his ears, all his senses felt numb. He hung onto Betty's hand for as long as he could as he was led away. Betty started to cry and was comforted by her children, Sarah Cairns called to the group outside the Court and everyone returned to their places. Inside, when all had regained their seats, the room was silent as the jury filed back in and the Judge entered the room.

Martin remembered reading somewhere that a jury would never look into the eyes of the accused if they were about to return a verdict of Guilty. He studied the twelve men and women as they filed towards their seats and sat down. Some looked over towards his father, others kept their eyes averted. Martin was still in the dark on the verdict.

The Court Usher stood and called upon the foreman of the jury.

"Will the foreman please stand. Will you please confine yourself to answering my first question, yes or no. Has the jury reached a verdict upon which you are all agreed?

"Yes."

"For the manslaughter of William Stevens, do you find the defendant guilty, or not guilty?"

"Not guilty."

A wave of relief and joy filled the room, hopes were raised, expectations of a full acquittal imminent. The babble in the Court room was as fast to recede as it was to erupt, all held their breath for the next verdict.

"For the manslaughter of Sean Robson, do you find the defendant guilty, or not guilty?"

"Guilty."

A defending silence filled the Court room, a stunned disbelief at the foreman's answer.

"Is that the verdict of you all?"

"It is."

"Thank you, you may sit."

Harry Sinton sat slumped in his chair, Betty grabbed hold of her children's hands and fought back the tears. People looked from one person to another, disbelief and shock showing in their faces. A clamour of noise begun to rise as friends of Harry Sinton realised the enormity of the verdict. Judge Thorn was quick to regain the silence of the Court, he hammered his gavel onto the bench and waited for the unrest to settle. He then began the process of sentencing.

Harry Sinton had no previous convictions to be taken into account, only his Defence counsel's plea for mitigation was to be heard before the Judge passed sentence.

Patrick Parker had compiled his heartfelt plea for mitigation before the trial, although he had not informed anyone. He believed in being prepared for the worst. He told of a loving husband, a hard-working farmer who was needed on the farm and a trusted and valuable member of the local community. He maintained that Harry Sinton was forced into his actions and did not pose any threat to society. When he had finished his speech, he sat down, his active role in the case at an end.

It was Mr. Justice Peter Thorn QC who had the last words of the Court case. He made a show of reading his notes, and then addressed Harry Sinton.

"Mr. Sinton, you have been found guilty of the manslaughter of Sean Robson. The counsel for the Defence has given a strong argument for leniency, but the fact remains that a young man has lost his life, and a jury has found you Guilty. I have no alternative but to sentence you to a term of imprisonment. The amount of time you will serve will reflect the charge, but also take into account the circumstances and your good character before this episode."

The Court room was hushed, all eyes were on the Judge.

"I sentence you to five years imprisonment."

A collective gasp swept around the room. Betty could not control her tears any longer, she crumpled onto Martin's chest, weeping. Ann, herself fighting back her tears, held onto her mother's hand, stroking her arm.

The trial was over, the jury filed out for the last time, the Judge left for his chambers. The Barristers tidied their notes and slid them into their briefcases. Later, when they met each other in their private room, set aside for Barristers and Lawyers on the top floor of the Court building, they agreed the result was a one-one draw. The spectators, some still in shock at the verdict and sentence, took their time in leaving the public gallery. Whispered conversations and shaking of heads accompanied them out of the door.

As Harry Sinton was taken from the dock, and led down towards the cells below the Court room, he lingered and looked over his shoulder, high into the public gallery, trying to find his wife. At the same time Betty dug deep into her resolve and managed to straighten, lean forward and look down onto the Court room below, searching the dock for a last glimpse of her husband before he was taken away. The exchange of looks was heart-wrenching. Harry Sinton mouthed "sorry" to his wife, Betty could think of no reply, and watched as her husband descended to the bowels of the Court House.

Betty, Ann and Martin remained in their seats as all around them left. Even with their friends giving words of comfort, promises of help, advice on appealing against the sentence, they felt utterly alone.

Patrick Parker shook hands with his Defence team, expressed his view that an appeal may well see a reduction in the sentence, asked Gerald Evans to extend his sympathies to the family, and left. Gerald Evans went to find his friends, the junior solicitor tagging on behind. He met up with them on the concourse. He told them a sentence of five years would mean an actual prison term of around three years, with a parole likely after one year. He told them that hopefully Harry would only spend two years or less away from them. He also said he would work to see him placed in an open prison.

Martin left his mother with Ann and took Gerald Evans to one side. He thanked his Godfather for all his hard work, but said they couldn't really comprehend the finer points of the proceedings at the moment. That they would be going home to recover from the ordeal and shock, and would he please come over later in the week when they could show their appreciation for his work.

Gerald Evans said he understood, told Martin not to hesitate to call him if they needed anything, and then left the depleted family, taking the junior solicitor with him. Slowly the balcony started to empty as everyone made their way home.

Henry Robson, his wife and two of Sean Robson's aunties left silently. They were pleased this man had been punished for the death of Sean. They cared little for the verdict on William Stevens.

Martin, asking his Mother if she was alright, Betty nodding her answer, took a deep breath and, supported by both children, left the building for the last time.

Once outside the Court, the media, having made their reports, filmed and photographed the departing family from a distance. There was no announcement from either party's solicitors for the cameras to record. Onlookers stopped and watched as they made their way back to the car. Betty steeling herself, ready to be driven back to a cheerless house and an empty bed.

Mark Robson was on a high as he entered the *Red Lion*. He had just watched the news of Harry Sinton's conviction, and even though he would have liked a longer sentence, he was pleased with the verdict. He was now going to celebrate. Even as he walked the short distance to the pub, he was considering his next campaign against the family of his brother's killer. He wasn't going to leave it alone now, just because the killer had been sent to prison, Mark was going to continue to make them suffer. He already planned to ring them up that night, laugh at them, remind them that he still had not forgotten them, would never forget them. He also considered finding out which prison Harry Sinton would be sent to and see if he had any friends there: friends that would provide some extra discomfort for the target of his hatred.

All these thoughts, all these visions of revenge, kept Mark Robson smiling as he strode to the bar. Eddie served him but gave no comment on Mark's joyous news. He seemed remote, detached, as Mark talked him through the verdict. The barman kept scanning the room as Mark confided his plans for the future of the Sinton family.

Mark was annoyed when Eddie excused himself halfway through his revelations, but decided that Eddie must have something on his mind. Probably that pain-in-the-arse bitch, he told himself. Mark then forgot his annoyance and concentrated on his lager; this was going to be a great celebration, and he wasn't going to let anyone or anything spoil it for him.

Martin sat in his father's chair, Bracken once more at his feet, a tumbler of whisky in his hand. The house was silent, Betty had retired to her bed, reassuring Martin that she was fine, but just wanted to lie down for a while. Ann had left earlier, along with her children, and mother-in-law, returning to her house and husband. The return home had been awkward, even the twins couldn't weave their usual magic, and left an even bigger feeling of emptiness when they had left.

Martin knew his family would work through this tragedy, they had no real choice. He was worried for the health of his mother, and despaired for his father, alone in a horrible new world of walls, fences and locked doors.

He still had a week of his Leave to go, he would spend it with his mother, visiting his father whenever possible, and arranging for his last months in the Marines to be spent at Downlands farmhouse, keeping his mother company, looking after the farm.

Martin knew this was the start of a new life for him; it saddened him that his hand was forced by the events of that morning on the seventh of March.

The telephone rang but he left it to the answering machine. It wouldn't be till later that he heard the drunken voice of Mark

Robson, slurring his glee of the verdict and his future intentions towards the Sinton family.

Harry Sinton lay on the bunk in the cold sterile cell. Images of Betty in their home ran through his mind, pictures of his children growing up, scenes of his farm throughout his life filled his thoughts. Anything to keep him from thinking about this cell, and the next five years of his life.

CHAPTER EIGHT

EPILOGUE

Martin Sinton managed to stay at Downlands Farm for the remainder of his time in the Royal Marines. He kept an eye on the farm but, more importantly, kept his mother company. On leaving the Services he put all his efforts into the farm. George Stone took him under his wing, passing on his vast knowledge whenever and wherever possible.

Betty visited her husband at every available opportunity. Gerald Evans had managed to persuade the authorities responsible for the placement of Harry Sinton, to send him to the closest prison to his home, which happened to be Winchester, making Betty's visits easier and less of a strain on her pocket, if not on her personally. She hated seeing him in the confines of the visiting room, but hated leaving him there even more.

Ann, the twins and Martin accompanied their mother as often as possible, and with the regular appearances from friends, Harry Sinton was never short of visitors. It eased his time there, but it still took its toll. He looked haggard, drawn and invariably tired. He was rarely bothered by other inmates, who saw him as a sad old man and no threat to their pecking order. He had to contend with some minor jibes concerning his age, rural accent and general appearance, but thankfully nothing too severe.

Harry Sinton served the first six months of his sentence in Winchester prison, but the remainder in an open prison, situated about one and a half hours up the A34. Any inconvenience his family felt towards travelling the extra distance was displaced by the easier regime Harry Sinton appreciated. Harry Sinton himself, once at the open prison, kept himself busy on the institution's farm. He found an ability to pass on his knowledge to some of the more attentive inmates, and not only the farm responded to his attentions.

All of these things eased his time of incarceration, but every night he dreamt of his wife, hoping she was safe and well, and praying for the day he could be with her again on the farm.

Mark Robson was arrested in the bar of the *Red Lion*, three weeks after Harry Sinton's trial. He had been caught selling a banned class A drug (Ecstasy tablets) to an undercover policeman. The police had been tipped off by the barman of the pub. Eddie, on listening to his new girlfriend, had decided to expand his marijuana business and enter the world of the 'E' tablets. She had told him of the money to be made, the suppliers and buyers she used to meet for Mark Robson. She had suggested, even urged Eddie, to expand but told him he had to get rid of the local supplier first, a certain Mark Robson.

When the officer tried to arrest him, Mark Robson, knowing the gravity of the situation, and the real possibility that the police may find out his true name and therefore his criminal history, tried to get away. He hit out at the officer while still holding his pint glass. The officer protected his face with his arm, but the glass smashed and ripped through his shirt, causing the officer to receive a wound to his forearm that needed thirteen stitches. With further cuts to his forehead and cheek, the total amount of stitches required increased to twenty-three. Mark Robson ran from the pub only to be caught by the back-up squads, where he continued to resist arrest, kicking out and injuring another officer before finally being overpowered and read his rights.

Eddie Blackmore had told the police Mark's real name, his past history and his suspicions of his revenge attacks on the Sinton Family. Mark Robson, alias Spencer Marks, was charged with possession of a class A drug, with intent to sell, resisting arrest, and causing actual bodily harm to two of the arresting police officers.

The police could not get any evidence of his terror campaign against the Sintons to stick. The first telephone call that Ann had received had not been recorded. They had no evidence against him for the fire at the farm. The obscene package was covered in fingerprints ranging from shop assistants who sold the jiffy bag, to various post office staff who handled its progress, to Martin Sinton's own. The police forensic experts could not lift any sort of incriminating fingerprint to show that Mark Robson had been in contact with that bag. The voice on the recorded message Martin listened to on the evening of the verdict was slurred, and could not be successfully connected to Mark Robson. All the evidence was circumstantial, and Eddie Blackmore refused to sign a statement telling of Mark Robson's boasts; he argued he had done enough, and that it was up to the police to do the rest.

Martin was informed of the arrest and the police explained the circumstances and probable dismissal of charges relating to Mark Robson's hate campaign against his family due to the insufficient evidence. With that in mind and the guarantee from the police that Mark Robson would be going to prison for a lengthy stay anyway, Martin allowed the matter to be dropped.

At his trial Mark Robson was found guilty on all three charges and he had the book thrown at him. He was sentenced to twelve years imprisonment, twice as many as he had received for running over the little girl. Eddie Blackmore and his new girlfriend were overjoyed at the sentence, Mr. and Mrs. Robson did not attend the hearing. The hate campaign against the Sintons stopped.

Mark Robson and Harry Sinton never encountered each other while they both stayed at Her Majesty's pleasure.

Wendy Stevens stayed in a state of semi-drunkenness and dedicated her time to her new-found protector and provider. Friends of Bob Richards noticed a difference in him. He didn't go out as much, he kept himself cleaner, and looked happier, the reason for which they only found out six months later when Wendy emerged to be seen with Bob for the first time. Nobody mentioned Billy Stevens, and nobody mentioned the trial.

Mr. and Mrs. Robson stayed together for three years before the cracks in their relationship grew too large. Neither could come to terms with their loss, both found it hard to talk about it, both believed the other didn't understand. They had been told of the outcome of the trial, but it gave them little comfort. Nothing could bring Sean back, and the memory of the good, "innocent" son, had been lost for ever.

After the divorce Mrs. Robson returned to Southampton, living with her parents, finding work at a department store. Mr. Robson stayed in Dorset, getting work wherever he could. There was no animosity in the split, they were both just dead inside.

Paul Allen left his work placement course, and embarked on a life of mediocrity, always blaming others for his own deficiencies, always having his mother to fall back on.

Harry Sinton spent a total of eighteen month behind bars. The time had taken its toll, he looked ten years older and he talked even less than before. On his release there was no large party to welcome him home, only his immediate family, and the Cairns, were there to greet him. Martin had been running the farm, with considerable help from George Stone, and his father would not interfere with the situation, only helping out in times of need. He concentrated his time on his wife, the grandchildren, long walks and a new-found interest in gardening.

Mike Cairns had bought an adjoining sixty-acre field from the Sintons, at a price of two thousand eight hundred pounds an acre, to help towards their legal bill. It was bought with the proviso that the Sintons, if they so wanted, could buy it back for the same amount within five years, after which the price would be reassessed and the interest on the cost would also be taken into account. It was a handshake deal between friends.

Martin had bought a bungalow on the outskirts of the village when he had left the Royal Marines, moving into it only after his father was released, therefore keeping his mother company through those long lonely months. After two years they swapped, Martin moved into the farmhouse, and Harry and Betty took over the smaller bungalow.

Harry and Betty enjoyed their semi-retirement, never discussing the events of that March morning or the consequences, but delighting in their time together. They continued their patronage of their relevant church services, but their participation was subdued.

Although he occasionally helped out on the farm, Harry Sinton never offered to do the early morning lambing shift again.